MW00893827

Shaggy Beast

Nancy T Whitesell

ISBN: 9798884875593

Thank you and credit to Betsy Bierbaum for the author's photo. Thanks to Mace and Trick too!

Dedication

This book is dedicated to my much loved parents:
Arthur DeVere Talkington,
who believed I could do anything and
made me believe it too, and
Margaret Rowland Talkington,
who was so proud I became a veterinarian, but
believed in her heart I was meant to write novels!

ACKNOWLEDGMENTS

One of the best parts of writing *Fuzzy Brown Dog* was that it provided me the opportunity to both reconnect with friends and make new reader connections! It was usually through my Fuzzy Brown Dog page on Facebook, although I also had some incredible in person encounters at book signings that were extra special as well. These extraordinary people comprise the fuzzy brown dog pack that has been my constant support and inspiration for *Shaggy Beast* and I thank them from the bottom of my heart.

My first reader, Lenore Perry BS, MS was excellent as usual, full of encouragement and suggestions during the extended writing process. She added critical proofreading for *Shaggy Beast* as well, with my great appreciation.

My profound thanks to my expert advisors and

initial readers: Jean Beaubien, BSN, RN; Janet Bernier, VST; Janelle Bloxson BA; Allison Clark, PhD.; ABPP; Brad Coolman, DVM, MS, Diplomate ACVS; Sharon Riek, Attorney at Law; Donna Roof MSEd.; Cindi Walter; and Collin Whitesell, Attorney at Law. Any mistakes that might have crept into the story are mine alone.

In the acknowledgments of my first novel, *Fuzzy Brown Dog*, I shamefully neglected to thank Pam Mahlie, BS, RVT for her excellent help with all topics dealing with pet behavior and training in the book. More importantly, she taught me important lessons about how to live a kind, committed, compassionate life, long before she encouraged me to embrace modern positive pet training philosophies, and is still such a blessing in my life.

Most of all, thank you to all the pets that I have known and loved, at work and at home. When faced with impossible situations and decisions, it really does help to wonder what your favorite dog or cat would do, starting with living in the moment.

CHAPTER ONE

"I need help!" I shrieked. "Where is everybody?" But I was yelling to absolutely nobody.

I awkwardly scooped Toby up and squeezed him tight to my chest. He frantically threw his head side to side as his mouth gaped wide open and his back nails dug into my waist in abject terror.

Certainly I must have made it clear that Tabitha couldn't waste any time tracking Dr. Drama down. If he was MIA, I needed her to come back to hold Toby so that I could draw the fluid out from around his heart. I'd never done the procedure by myself before, but as Toby went limp in my arms and his pale gums took on a purplish cast, I understood that I was the only savior that Toby was going to get today.

Tabitha ran around the corner as I positioned Toby on the treatment table and, cutting off her explanation before she could utter a single word, I ordered, "Hold him down."

I grabbed the catheter and syringe, made one pass with the clippers, and wiped the skin a couple times with alcohol. At the same time I was cranking my neck around looking for the crash cart, which held all the precious equipment and emergency drugs that I so desperately needed.

Tabitha, an extraordinary technician, struggled to find a pulse, repositioning her grip multiple times, then looking around nervously she loudly pleaded, "Dr. Kat needs help now!"

I stayed focused on finding my anatomical landmarks and, after only one false start, popped the catheter in, watching on the ultrasound as it slowly advanced into the pericardial sac. I hastily drew off the blood tinged fluid and, while I couldn't help thinking about all the things I could have done differently, I focused all my energy into holding everything perfectly still so that I didn't lacerate a great vessel or poke a hole in his heart.

With a relieved smile, Tabitha nodded down at her hand taking Toby's pulse, and his color miraculously changed before my eyes! Relieved of the restriction of the fluid filled sac, his heart was able to freely pump life-giving blood throughout his body and his white gums became a pale pink and finally a reassuring bright pink color. Which was awesome until Toby started vigorously thrashing, now aware enough and feeling sufficiently strong enough to struggle against every single thing that we were doing to save his life.

I heard footsteps coming up behind me. Dr. Drama, my main mentor and one of our board certified surgeons, leaned over my shoulder and, putting his face directly into mine, demanded, "What the hell?" but then turned away to snap out quick-fire orders to the additional help as it arrived. He elbowed me out of the way and instructed, "Hold him still."

As he worked on Toby silently, I relaxed, knowing my patient was in good hands. I assumed I had escaped my expected tongue lashing, but as soon as Toby was sedated and resting comfortably, Dr. Drama, living up to his nickname, exploded with an extended run on tirade, "What's with your drunken clip job and why didn't you use an extension set and worst of all without a stopcock how are you gonna empty the syringe without giving him a pneumothorax and when in the hell do we do a procedure without sedation?"

I remained mute as I gazed up at him respectfully, hoping his questions were simply rhetorical, but he made a come on motion with his hand about two inches from my nose so I softly replied, "We didn't have a pulse."

"Or the crash cart," Tabitha added.

Dr. Drama glared at me ferociously, but then looked around the treatment area, over into surgery and the ICU, repeatedly opening his mouth like a landed fish gasping on dry land. Obviously he wanted to continue his rant, but confusion and concern washed over his face as he visibly struggled to make sense of the situation. Then he bolted away from us, abruptly blowing through the door leading to the front. I longed to follow him, now that he made me realize that there had to be another emergency playing out elsewhere in the hospital. But Toby wasn't out of the woods yet so I didn't dare leave him, and slowly Tabitha and I found the supplies we needed to adjust our peculiar, but lifesaving, system while Toby rested comfortably between us.

A little while later, an assorted group of people, led by Dr. Drama, trudged back into the treatment area, hauling both a large stretcher with a blanket covered body and the missing crash cart.

"They lost him," Dr. Drama explained morosely. "One of our Dobermans with cardiomyopathy. They had to do CPR right there in reception."

"One of Maisy's Dobies?" I asked frowning. Maisy was one of our favorite clients and her kennel was just down the alley from the house that I lived in. She'd had a really rough year personally after her husband and son were arrested for drug dealing and other criminal activity, but I hadn't heard that any of her dogs were fighting major heart problems. It was one of the medical problems that she had diligently bred to control for all those years; plus she wasn't feeding a weird untested grain free diet.

"No, not one of Maisy's dogs," he replied. "But Champ was just one of the nicest dogs you'd ever want to meet."

"I'm sorry," I said patting his arm. "I'm moving Toby to ICU now."

"Good save," he said mildly, as he pawed around in his desk drawer. "But tomorrow at rounds give a brief tutorial on the proper technique for pericardiocentesis and," as he handed me a pack of big red sticky paper arrows, "put these around the treatment area and label the places, other than the crash cart, that we store the supplies you needed."

"I will," I agreed happily. "Thank you."

He looked at me suspiciously, then appeared to accept that I wasn't being sarcastic and shrugged as he walked away. I let out a partially held breath and tried to focus on my paperwork.

"I'll help with the arrows," Tabitha said with a grin. "When the crash cart wasn't there and his pulse quit under my fingertips, I just couldn't remember where the duplicate supplies were kept."

"I know what you mean," I said. "And weirdly I kept hearing Dag say that 'you'll do in combat what you practice in training.' Proves we need to run more drills around here."

Tabitha nodded her agreement and asked, "Is Dag home yet?"

"No," I said pitifully, sticking my lower lip out. "It's been eight months. Not that I'm counting."

"Do you ever hear from him?" she asked.

"I've received a few random messages," I said. "And some really nice Christmas presents; in fact I'm wearing one of the shirts! But I'm sure his sister Issa bought them and put his name on them."

"I bet he'll be home soon!" Tabitha said.

"I hope so," I said smiling at her, but silently willed myself to not to even consider the possibility. I was working very hard to keep my sometimes volatile emotions under tight control.

Felicity, not one of my favorite techs except on a day like today when I wanted to get out on time, asked, "Are you ready to see the next emergency?"

"Give me five minutes to get Toby situated and I'll be there," I promised.

"It's a small wound on a poodle's neck," she explained. "Do you want me to clip it up for you?"

"Sure," I answered reflexively. Then I had an anxious feeling, although it was probably just left over adrenaline from my close call with Toby, and I changed my mind. "No, on second thought, I'll be there in a minute. I want to do my exam and make a plan first."

Felicity narrowed her eyes, trying to decide if I was somehow disrespecting her, but then she turned without speaking and left me to finish up with Toby. She was an excellent technician, but she was very difficult for me to deal with since every single exchange with her had to be a battle of wills. But appointments and emergencies certainly moved forward predictably with her in charge.

Sitting at a desk in the doctor ready area to work on Toby's chart, I popped an oatmeal raisin energy bite into my mouth. Ethan, my housemate and dog sitter, had made them for me… actually he had made them for everyone at the house, but I had the distinct feeling that my housemates did things for the group that would very specifically help me the most. I could be wrong, but it seemed like there was elaborate plotting going on to not only help me, but to disguise the fact that I was the object of their pity. For months I had tried to refuse their help, or to pay back every kind gesture with one of my own, but I was so short on time and money that I just couldn't keep it up. I still received an intern's salary, a pittance, therefore I promised myself I would try to catch up in the generosity department as soon as I transitioned to a real salary in a mere two weeks.

Felicity mean mugged me through the small window in the door so I reluctantly left my snack and took the new chart from her with a forced smile. As I opened the exam room door, the front office paged for a tech, and after seeing the tiny red poodle I decided I could handle her by myself and sent Felicity to answer the page.

"Hi, Mrs. Carson," I said with a more natural smile. "Rose was outside by herself, you heard a yelp and when you brought her in, there was blood on her neck, is that right?"

"Yes," the pleasant woman said calmly. "She seems okay, but I can't imagine what happened."

"Was she by herself?" I asked. "Do you have other pets?"

"No other pets," she replied. "There aren't even any pets next door, lots of kids but no dogs."

I scooped Rose up in my left arm and did a complete exam, leaving the tiny wound for last. When I reached for the beautiful curly red hair on her neck, Mrs. Carson said, "I'm going to go to the Ladies room while you do that. I have a shamefully weak stomach for blood."

"Sure," I agreed, grateful Mrs. Carson didn't try to tough it out and pass out instead, thus giving me two patients. Rose was being wonderful and didn't seem to mind as I teased the hair out from around and actually curling into the small round wound. I finally got a grip on a dense clump of crusty hair and pulled it. Suddenly there was blood gushing everywhere; the hair had been acting as a stopper in what could only be the large jugular vein. Rose began to throw herself around, and it took both hands to grip her tightly enough to contain her so I couldn't even grab gauzes or an instrument.

As I struggled to put pressure on the wound my index finger slipped into the hole and stemmed the pulsing tide of blood. I took a deep calming breath and Rose quieted in my arms. But now I truly had no hands free to open my door. I called out for help, which agitated Rose, so I attempted to wait patiently for the owner or my technician to return, but with the jugular involved I couldn't waste too much time.

I tried rapping on the door with my elbow, but that jarred Rose. I was afraid she would start to wiggle and dislodge my finger, which was functioning well as the new plug. I turned and donkey kicked the door to the hallway a couple times, which reverberated gratifyingly noisily and finally brought Felicity and Tabitha running. We ran straight into surgery and almost directly into Dr. Drama as I poured out my tale as professionally as I could with my heart pounding and my finger still lodged in Rose's neck. Dr. Drama lifted an eyebrow and started to speak, but then shifted into his quiet, efficient surgical demeanor as I clumsily rattled my explanation out.

I sent Felicity out to update Mrs. Carson while Tabitha wheeled a desk chair over so I could sit comfortably to hold Rose while surgery was set up. Action swirled around me, but there was truly nothing more important for me to accomplish other than keeping Rose calm as her pre-anesthetic sedative took effect. The minute Dr. Drama was ready for her, Tabitha held her for her anesthesia induction and only when Dr. Drama was holding his scalpel in the ready position did I catch his eye and remove my finger from her major vessel.

Surgery was quickly successful as he tied off the large vessel, thus stopping the bleeding, and popped out the pellet that was sitting right there. We took an intraoperative radiograph to make sure it was the only pellet and then declared the crisis over. I laughingly thought that the search into who shot the pellet might take longer than the surgery did, since Mrs. Carson was a Marion County Prosecutor and I had no doubt she'd be pursuing a vigorous investigation.

I sped through my paperwork to ensure that I'd be back at my apartment before everybody arrived for our last interns' pizza night. Notoriously at least one, if not all four, of the interns were late each week, but since we had our gatherings at my place it was extra awkward when I was the late one. I was glad we had been busy though. It kept us from spending time fixating on all the changes that were coming to our comfortable hospital routines.

CHAPTER TWO

I opened the door and, with a sweeping arm motion, ushered my cohorts into my living room. The three owners of our Hamilton County Veterinary Hospital complex: Dr. Vincent, better known by my nickname Dr. Drama if no clients were around, Dr. Blackwell, his best friend from veterinary school, and Dr. Tolliver, his wife and our radiologist, provided us with pizza, salad, and beer once a week. They only asked that we four interns research and then discuss a topic of their choice in payment for this generosity. But this week they let us off the topic hook since we'd already proven that all we could talk about were our plans for the upcoming year.

Stretch carried the pizza boxes in, Taren had the salad, and Melanie held the six pack of beer bottles and a pink box of pastries, which was ironic since she never used to partake of the alcohol or any treats. We never minded, especially about the beer, because the rest of us could each have two that way. Except tonight she had not only drunk a beer, she had started a second one on the way over so it already wasn't going to be our typical pattern. I had a stack of paper plates ready and had laid out the silverware, or more precisely carefully washed disposable plastic utensils, and we immediately piled our plates high. With money and time both so very tight this year, I walked around famished more often than not and these weekly meals, along with the dinners with my house family, had been my anchor for the entire year. At first we were quiet except for our ravenous munching, but once we started chatting we had trouble not talking over each other.

"I'll never get all my stuff packed and all my paperwork done,"

Taren said with a grimace, troublesome to observe because any expression that didn't feature Taren's beautiful deep dimples was chilling. "How could I collect so much stuff? I never had any time to go shopping."

"Don't you have two weeks off before you start your ophthalmology residency program in Chicago?" I asked.

"Yea," she admitted sheepishly. "I'm probably fixating on packing and paperwork because I don't want to think about what I'm really anxious about."

"Which is?" I prompted.

"The residency," she responded looking at me, and then cast her eyes down and continued, "leaving all of you," and then after a long pause, "leaving Lars."

Stretch smiled weak reassurance and patted her arm, "It'll work out. You'll do great. But how about me? You're the only one that still calls me Lars; I'll have some kind of identity crisis without you."

"Time will fly by because we're all going to be so busy," I said, giving Stretch a look to let him know that Taren needed more than lame jokes from him.

"Is that how it was for you this year after Dag left?" Taren asked with a challenging half smile and a single raised eyebrow.

"Sometimes," I admitted, "and sometimes I just wanted to leave all this behind and run after him. Of course not knowing where he was helped me resist that urge. But don't try to distract me, we're talking about you."

"I know," she replied. "I'm just being a baby. Four hours is not that long a drive."

Stretch had kicked back on my overstuffed turquoise chair while the three of us ladies sprawled on my big brown sectional. I put an arm around Taren on one side and around Melanie on the other, drew them to me and said, "In some ways it will be even easier to connect. We'll be at different hospitals, in different situations, it'll take away any competitive edge to our relationship. You know, all that sibling rivalry due to dysfunctional Daddy Drama!"

Melanie gave me a dirty look and sighed, but Stretch and Taren laughed out loud.

Stretch jumped up and said, "We're not that competitive," and then launched himself on top of the three of us and we slid into a pile on the floor. Max, my adorable rescue dog, woofed a protest and joined the pile, licking anyone where he could find exposed skin. He clumsily turned, bumping into my rickety hand-me-down TV table and accidentally flipped a pizza crust off someone's plate. He quickly grabbed it and ran to my bedroom with his prize.

I know I should've reacted to his bad behavior, but I joined in my friends' laughter instead as we continued to mock fight over our sofa seats. When we settled down I said, "I got double lessons in working alone today and I did not enjoy it one bit. I'd never really thought about it before, but I really prefer working as part of a group. I don't want other doctors to do my work for me; I just want them around to bounce ideas back and forth. Of course it's best when you really like and respect everyone, but I even prefer working with Quickcut versus having the hospital to myself."

"After Quickcut leaves for his new job in Texas and I'm the new surgical resident, are you going to give me a new nickname?" Stretch asked laughing.

"Nah," I said. "I'm looking forward to working with my pal Stretch."

One look at Melanie's worried face convinced me I had chosen a sore subject to explore. As I struggled to think of a topic that would make Melanie happier, recently an impossible mission, Stretch said, "Historically veterinarians have had extremely independent personalities, but I think our generation is different, a much more social group."

"How about you, Melanie?" I asked. "Will you be part of a group or working more by yourself at Consolidated Veterinary Associates? How will your schedule work?"

"I was shocked you chose that job," Stretch added placidly, but Melanie's instantaneous response was red hot.

"What an appalling thing to say," Melanie gasped out harshly. "I'm not lucky like you all are; I have over a hundred and fifty thousand dollars in student loans and nobody's helping ME! I can't afford to do a residency or take a job with enough time off to pursue my other interests. I have to make money to repay those loans and I have to do it now. I should never have done an internship. No matter how much I skimped and saved, I could barely cover the interest payments. I owe as much today as I started out with a year ago."

Stretch looked confused and tried to catch Taren's eye for direction. Melanie's face got redder and redder, and then she sprang up and said, "I'm out of here; I don't need this shit," and stomped toward my front door.

Stretch jumped up and tried to take her arm, but she dodged his touch and glared at him ferociously.

"For goodness sake, Mel," Stretch explained, "I just meant that you never had anything positive to say about any of the Consolidated hospitals, and then suddenly you announced that you're going to work for them."

Melanie stood with her hand on the door and sobbed, breaking my heart in commiseration. "I wanted to take a job in one of the underserved rural areas to get part of my loan forgiven, but I screwed that all up. I ran out of time to apply and didn't end up having a choice. Nothing ever works out for me."

I patted her arm gently and said, "It's only for a year," but she shrugged my hand away and still crying, slipped out the door.

Stretch, Taren, and I exchanged shocked looks, shaking our heads in confusion. We knew that she had been struggling, and we had all been concerned about her state of mind, but she had never shown blatant anger, at least not towards us. If I was the hospital queen of the silver lining, Melanie was the authority on the big black clouds of life and we interns were definitely her favorite audience. I thought we'd been our typical sympathetic selves, except maybe for Stretch's comment, but I have to admit that I was just as surprised as Stretch was when Melanie accepted that position with Consolidated after she had been so negative about every aspect of the company for weeks.

Taren exhaled noisily and then said, in a weak mimicry of Dr. Drama's stilted professional lecture voice, "I guess she's stressed beyond her ability to cope."

"I guess," I replied with an eye roll.

I did feel lucky that I was staying to work at the same hospital and didn't have to move from my apartment, but I was still anxious about the upcoming responsibility of being a staff veterinarian and equally worried about my decision to leave the support and structure of the intern/residency system. But I wasn't going to stoop to taking it out on my friends. I had let my ex-boyfriend Justin, not my missing mysterious current boyfriend Dag, but my former vet school boyfriend, mistreat me for years. Justin always had an excuse for his misbehavior: he was too busy, or too stressed, or too depressed, or too angry to be a normal decent person. It seems so clear now that I had been an idiot to believe him for so long, but I had a pretty strong need to help people, and he definitely needed boatloads of help. Melanie's sudden attack felt like Justin's habit of hurting me just to make himself feel powerful. And I was never again going to tolerate that kind of treatment. And yet by setting super strong boundaries against poor treatment, I didn't want to become as hard hearted and selfish as Justin had been. Now I was feeling guilty that I hadn't helped Melanie more.

I sighed dramatically just as Taren heaved a huge sigh of her own, and we laughed, first at our synchronized sighs then at the sheer absurdity of Melanie's outburst. Both Stretch and Taren also carried significant student loans, while I had arrived at the start of my internship with a weekender bag of clothes, my quilt and pillow, and an almost empty wallet as my only belongings. I didn't have any school debt because the trust fund from my deceased parents had lasted through seven years of college, but it hadn't lasted one day beyond. My move to the Indianapolis area had certainly been a fresh start, but one with very fragile financial resources. I'd only just recently paid off Max's surgery bills from last summer's rescue.

"So Stretch," I said with a funny slow drawl. "Are you really as calm and cool as you are pretending to be?"

He put an arm around Taren and replied, "I'm excited about my surgical residency with Dr. Drama. And Taren and I will be fine doing the long distance thing."

Taren looked up at him with such appreciation and longing that I had a twinge of envy, but when she looked away and her face was at rest it appeared like her underlying emotion was disbelief.

"So did you make up your mind about an apartment, Stretch?" I asked.

"I did," he replied with a smile. "I splurged for the one bedroom. Taren as one of my roommates this past year may be the best thing that has ever happened to me, but I couldn't take a chance that I'd get a roommate that could be as constantly needy as Melanie or as big a bully as Quickcut."

"Yeah, I hear you," I said nodding. "I'm staying in my apartment without a roommate, but I'll have to take over paying the rent now that the hospital isn't providing it."

"How big a hit is that?" Stretch said taking an appreciative look around the apartment. "I love this house."

"My landlord Phil worked out a good rate with the owner," I replied. "All of us housemates, including Phil, get along really well and I don't think he wanted to break up the band, so to speak."

"Yeah," Taren said softly. "I feel like we're breaking up the Intern band."

Stretch hugged Taren again and said, "After the next two weeks together moving and driving and visiting family, you'll be happy to get a break from me."

Taren smiled her beautiful smile, but it still didn't quite reach her eyes when she said to me, "I can't believe you aren't taking time off before starting your new position."

"Time off sounds great, but I really need the money," I said. "And I don't actually have anywhere to go."

"So is Melanie also working some extra shifts before her new job starts?" Stretch asked.

"I don't think so," I replied thoughtfully. "After talking to Melanie, Molly came back begging me to take more weekend shifts because they couldn't find anyone else to cover."

"That's why Melanie drives me crazy!" Stretch said, uncharacteristically agitated. "It's so frustrating! Everything in her life is so unbearable that she has to constantly whine and complain, but she won't ever do anything to fix any of it. Those extra ER shifts pay well, but while the three of us were fighting over every opportunity to grab an open shift this year, she just couldn't be bothered. Might rob her of some of her twelve hour's night's sleep."

Taren frowned and said, not for the first time I'd guess from her expression, "I think something is wrong with her. And we should be patient with her."

I nodded and said, "I'll try harder."

"I've had enough," Stretch insisted. "This morning she accused me of using more than my fair share of the milk. I flipped a couple quarters at her, but that didn't make her any happier."

"Lars!" Taren scolded.

Stretch rolled his eyes, but said, "I'll try to be nicer when I'm around her. But secretly I'll be counting down the hours until I'm out of the intern apartment and she's out of the hospital."

Taren shrugged, like the whole thing was too much to contemplate, and I said, "I can't wait to meet the new interns! Three of them this year, right?"

"Yep," Stretch said. "Hope they're good."

"Hope so," I agreed, and then a cold chill shivered down my spine.

CHAPTER THREE

Max cavorted around me in ecstasy. If we were headed to Dag's apartment with its fenced in yard, I would have picked up his regular lead. But because I had a bigger adventure in mind, I reached for his head collar, and he lost his mind with excitement!

I had mixed feelings about our outing. My time off was so precious that while I always made healthy plans, what I longed to do was to go take a nap! Or better yet I could snuggle up on my couch and read one of my borrowed mystery books while snacking on something sweet and buttery. Before I could change my mind, I grabbed the SUV keys and Max froze with his tail midway between happy up and dejected down. He loved the park, but still despised car rides even though I had worked hard on desensitizing him these past eight months. He had definitely improved because he'd fly out of the car ready to play when we got there, even though mere minutes before he would have been panting and drooling while plastered onto the back seat like a dog shaped rug.

Last year when Dag took off for his mysterious, but supposedly vital job, he left me his SUV, insisting that it would be horrible for any vehicle to sit unused for months and months. He claimed that I would be doing him a favor to drive it. It's another case where I couldn't decide if that was true or if it was all an excuse to help poor pathetic Kat who couldn't get herself a car. Or get any furniture if my housemates hadn't rustled some up for me, or get a whole lot of other things that normal folk have and I could only dream about. But I was worn out from trying twenty-four/seven to learn how to be a good vet, and using Dag's vehicle simply made that task so much easier.

I had a sling type of seat cover on the back seat for Max, and he lay scrunched flat with his cute fluffy Grinch paws wrapped over the seat edge trying to hold on all the way to Forest Park. I tucked his long lead into my pocket, put on my sunglasses, and vowed to enjoy every bit of my lone day off. The weather was cooperating, not an Indiana certainty; it was bright sun, but with a cool breeze so it was perfect for woman and beast alike! Max bounced out of the car and looked around expectantly. We started with a nice jog and soon I could feel all the tension leaking out of me.

Then I threw the ball for Max until his tongue was hanging low out the side of his mouth and I decided it was time to wrap up our outing with what Ethan and I call a sniffle snuffle walk in the cool shade of the trees. I chuckled to myself because Ethan and I had absolutely made up the overly cutesy name to drive Dag crazy. He certainly wouldn't argue about our need to communicate between an exercise walk, a bathroom break walk, and a scent/sensory walk, but it amused us to no end to think of hyper cool Dagger being forced to say the words sniffle snuffle.

I tried to copy Max and both notice and relish every nuance of the beautiful natural setting. I delighted in the trees the most: just amazed at the variety of leaf colors and shapes, and the way all the branches swayed and danced in the breezes. I realized I was mainly using my eyes, while Max mainly used his ears and nose, sniffing at everything on the path as well as pausing periodically to scent the air and listen to the numerous sounds. I loved watching him do it; compared to the information I might get from a whiff of something, I could tell he was getting so much more. His expression was what I imagine my face looks like when I'm engrossed in my favorite novel. It was like he was following an interesting story full of the most fascinating characters ever written.

During one of his air scenting episodes, his tail started a slow wag, then he looked around, interspersed with more focused sniffing. Finally sinking to the ground, his wagging sped up and he began to whine. After being so good all afternoon, he firmly set his front end and tried to pull me off the track and into the trees. His whining increased, he gave a yip, and then tucked his head down to his neck to combat the control of the head collar. He pulled so hard he actually did a somersault instead of relinquishing his effort to drag me where he wanted to go.

When I was helping him up, I let the leash go slack and he jumped into the underbrush behind a large maple tree. Following him I saw a moving shadow to my right. Last year I had been threatened in the parking lot at the hospital and shamefully all I had done to protect myself was a weak "no, no" while I tried to back away. After that I had practiced, in my head that is, shouting and fighting back somehow. So, I quickly looked toward the shadowy figure and screamed. Except I didn't actually make any noise because as I took a deep breath and opened my mouth, a large hand covered it. Then an arm wrapped around my waist and dragged me tight against his body. I stomped at his feet, tried to bite at his hand, and brought my hand up over my shoulder to scratch at his face, except all I connected with was air. My heart was pounding and I both hoped that Max would come to my defense and that he would run away and keep himself safe.

"Kat," a deep voice pleaded. "Shut up. And cut it out."

I dropped my hands down and stopped kicking at the sudden familiarity. Max yipped again and jumped up on us, not sure what our funny game was, but not wanting to be left out.

"Dag?" I asked tentatively.

"If I move my hand will you be very quiet?" Dag didn't even bother to confirm his identity, as if who else could possibly be hiding in the shrubbery and grabbing me.

I nodded my head and he moved his hand, then slid in front of me and slipped his arms into a much more pleasant embrace.

"Hey, pretty girl," Dag whispered. "Surprise!"

"What the," I started, but then stopped. After a couple of calming breaths, I continued, "Never mind, I have nothing sane to ask."

Dag laughed and shook his head grinning at me. "And I wouldn't know where to start. Nothing ever goes according to plan when you're involved. I think I'm being all cool and logical and the next thing I know I'm hiding in the underbrush and Max is tracking me."

I giggled and shook my head sheepishly. I don't know whether it's a good or bad sign, but one of the most common emotions that Dag and I share seems to be bewilderment at what the other one has just said or done. It's second only to such a powerful attraction that it makes me think about those magnetic toy dogs that click together any time they're close to each other.

"The hiding in the trees makes me think that you aren't back for good?" I asked.

"Probably not," Dag said. "I came back for the court case and if it goes to trial I'll be identified and my current job will be over. But the DA thinks the defense is waiting to make sure the witnesses show up, me specifically, to finally make an agreement. We really want the deal to go through. It'll have far reaching results for more than just these two mopes."

"Well, then I guess I'll hope for a deal," I said reluctantly. I accepted Dag's covert job and odd travel schedule, at least for the time being, because it was all set up before I met him. But as I transitioned from my crazy intern year into a staff veterinarian position, I certainly wanted to find a more normal work life balance. And that would eventually include my boyfriend being in the same state as me with a job he could tell me about!

Dag leaned over and kissed me warmly. Maybe because meeting Dag was a surprise and I didn't have a long anticipatory period of overthinking, I was able to relax and simply enjoy the few moments that we had. It felt so good to be in his arms again, safe and secure but oh so very excited at the same time.

Even as we lost ourselves in the holding and touching, I could feel him shift to look at his watch a couple times, and then he said, "I really have to leave now, but give me a two minute update on what's going on with you and the housemates."

"I'm good, Mei and Ethan are good, Phil has had some issues with his diabetes, but we're all eating as healthy as possible to help him, you'll miss Ethan's desserts at house dinners when you get back," I reported rapid fire. "Phil and Mei are really busy remodeling that weird two story garage building beside the house to make a new workout area for Tai Chi and karate classes. The hospital's good, I'm working an assortment of extra emergency shifts for a couple weeks, and then I'll start my new position as a staff vet in primary care and emergency. Stretch is staying for a surgical residency; Melanie and Taren are leaving and working their last day tomorrow."

"No desserts?" Dag said with a clownish frown. "Say it ain't so!"

"Birthdays are the exception," I replied. "Really? No desserts is the most important thing I said?"

"So everyone's good?" he asked, suddenly very intense, almost anxious.

"We're all good," I said with a reassuring smile.

"And you've heard from Issa?" he asked.

"She's been taking good care of me!" I assured him. "You bought me three really cute shirts for Christmas."

"I did?" he asked. "I asked her to get something practical, but really pretty."

"I got you a little something too, except I ate all your holiday candy when you didn't show up," I said. "Any chance you can stop by the apartment?"

"No," he said quietly. "There's a good chance they're watching both my apartment and Maisy's house. You're careful around that area aren't you?"

"Yes," I reassured him. "And I use your SUV when I go back over to the hospital at night."

Dag smiled and kissed me, rubbing his hands over my back and drawing me close again. He rested his chin on the top of my head for a moment, then pulled away and said, "I have to go, but I have something to tell you."

My heart clenched at his tone as he continued, "I wish I could

25

give you more information, but in the same way that I can't tell you where I've been or what I've been doing, I can't tell you where he is or what he's doing."

"Who's doing what?" I asked, bewildered once again.

"Your brother," he replied.

"Which one?" I asked.

"Your older brother," he replied. "Andrei."

"Andrei?"

"Yes, Andrei," Dag replied patiently, but with another look at his watch. "I knew this wasn't a quick conversation, but I really didn't want to just send a message out of the blue."

"Okay," I said a little despondently. "Is he okay?"

"He's fine," Dag replied, digging his hand into the front pocket of his jeans. "I have his email address for you."

"Does he want to hear from me?" I asked, with tears stinging my eyes.

"Yes," Dag said emphatically, obviously a little louder than he wanted because he continued in a much softer voice, "he's under the impression that you don't want to be in contact with him."

"Me?" I cried a little as I said it. "I'm not the one that left."

Dag held both hands up and said, "I'm sorry, but there really isn't much more I can share with you, even if I had the time. If you're interested, reach out to him. If you're not, that's okay too. I didn't give him your information, so it will be entirely your choice."

"Okay," I said and kissed him again.

"Gotta go, Sweetie," Dag said as he wiped away the tears clinging to my eyelashes.

"Should I leave first or do you want to sneak away?" I asked.

"You go first," he said smiling. "Act like Max got away from you, if anyone even noticed your trip into the bushes."

"Great," I said sarcastically and turned to leave, and then turned back and pulled him close to me for the briefest moment. After simply saying, "I miss you," I left.

CHAPTER FOUR

It was utterly surreal to be gathered for morning rounds with Taren, Stretch, and Melanie for the very last time. My intern year had been the most indescribably intense year of my adult life and it had flown by at supersonic speed. And yet that single year seemed to contain a decade of experiences and relationships; saying goodbye to my intern cohorts felt unnatural and wrong.

Our manager extraordinaire Molly bustled up to the assembled group and hesitantly asked, "Dr. Vincent?" which made Stretch smile and wink at me since almost everyone else had started calling our venerable leader by my Dr. Drama nickname.

"Yes?" he replied with a calculating look, like he was trying to decide if he was going to be gracious at the interruption or if he was going to throw a hissy fit about the sanctity of rounds.

Molly squinted her eyes right back at him. Somehow she never seemed to be intimidated by him or any of his theatrics, although she did work especially hard to accomplish any goal he set for her. She calmly said, "Before the storm rolls in our landscaper needs a decision on the tree for the center of our park. And there are multiple emergencies waiting."

He shook his head, sighed and said, "Kat handle the emergencies, Stretch take care of the surgery cases, Taren and Melanie, you're scheduled with Molly upstairs, and I thank you very much for a wonderful year. Please keep in touch," and strode away.

I was helping my friends pack up their apartment over the weekend so I didn't mind seeing the emergency cases instead of sticking around for their goodbyes. In fact I welcomed the distraction. As I picked up the first emergency file, multiple loud sobs echoed from the reception area and even muffled by the doors, the raw emotion within the cries tightened my chest.

I flew out to the front desk, the receptionist shouted, "Hit by a car," and I zeroed in on a wild eyed woman clutching a bloody dog. She was screaming unintelligible words while looking around desperately. It wasn't as if she was challenging the receptionist's patient instructions as much as invoking God and the universe to somehow help change what had happened. The owner was more than upset; she reminded me of an injured dog or cat that was so disconnected from their thinking brains that they viciously bite their beloved owners when the heartbroken people are just trying to help them. I gently spoke to her as if she was one of those wounded animals and her eyes slowly focused on me, but it seemed like she couldn't let her precious pup out of her arms, as if she could somehow keep her injured pet here on earth if she could just keep ahold of her. After a little bit of a wrestling match, I took the medium sized black and white dog from her, turned, kicked through the door, and ran into treatment. I could hear the owner's renewed shrieks, counterpointed with multiple low voices trying to calm her down.

I couldn't feel a heartbeat from my hand cupped over her chest so I shouted for help and we immediately started CPR. We never got the tiniest response so I finally pronounced her gone. It was difficult speaking to the family, but it was something I was slowly getting better at, and I stood quietly as they screamed out their despair. I don't know how people are able to cry and shout and sob and curse right when these heartbreaks occur. It wasn't a response that came naturally to me. I suspected that I would feel better if I could just let all the pain out right as it happened, but it felt like if I ever started I would never be able to stop. I simply went to my numb place so I could function with the next emergency.

We stayed busy the rest of the shift with the typical

summer injuries, usually hit by somethings, i.e. hit by car, hit by lawnmower, hit by baseball. All the trauma was interspersed with medical diagnostic puzzles that were my favorite cases since I got to play detective. But today there were just too many of them, and while I focused on staying composed and working efficiently, the sheer numbers of intense cases was overwhelming. And in the back of my mind I could hear that owner's screams echoing and no matter how I tried to relax the muscles across my shoulders or stretch my neck, my muscles tightened and cramped and a couple times I even caught myself grinding my teeth when I was trying to focus.

But I wasn't going to let my bad day, or the escalating pain, stop me from doing what I was absolutely determined to do today. I had even put it on the top of my to-do list in capital letters: SEND AN EMAIL TO ANDREI. I had been struggling to figure out what to say since Dag had given me his address. In multiple mental drafts I composed long rambling newsy letters and various bland moderate length versions as well as one short rude one that just said "why the hell did you abandon us?" The last few days it was like I had a program constantly running in the background of my mind trying to find a solution that was honest and heartfelt, but not confrontational. Somewhere in the middle of this horrible day I had accepted that while taking this first step was essential, there was no way that this was anything more than an initial step, the first baby step of what I prayed would be a prolonged conversation.

Thankfully the computer upstairs was free. I took a deep breath and quickly typed:

Dear Andrei,

I was so glad to get your address from Dagger; I hope this email finds you happy and healthy. I graduated from Purdue   School of Veterinary Medicine last year and now I'm a staff veterinarian at Hamilton County Veterinary Hospital Complex and live in Noblesville, Indiana. I love my job, but I'm unsettled about my future, there are so many possible paths I could follow. I'd really like to be back in touch with you and hear all about your life. I miss you.

Love, Kat

I sat there staring at the email in disgust. I had worked so hard and so long, only to come up with such a poor representation of my feelings. My head ramped up the pounding and a few hot tears spilled down my cheeks. Without really thinking about it, almost as a reflex, I started my measured antianxiety breathing while I stared at the screen and the offending email. Breathe in for the count of four, hold for the count of seven, exhale through pursed lips for the count of eight. No solution came to me and suddenly I only wanted it over with. As I reached out to hit send, I remembered how picture oriented Andrei had always been and added a favorite shot from my graduation and a cute picture of Max and me. Then I hit send, hoping adorable Max might soften Andrei's heart even if my poor words had no chance.

Before I left I double checked that everything was under control at the hospital and by the time I escaped out the back door, my entire body felt tense. As I dragged myself home my head started hammering with every step, but when I finally entered my apartment Max was his typical cheerful self. Normally that would be enough to vanquish a bad day, but tonight I could only function on autopilot, robotically taking care of his needs. And while all day I had looked forward to my healthy beans and rice supper, it looked so unappetizing when it was finally time to eat, I made myself some cinnamon sugar toast instead and then fell into bed.

I jerked awake and for the first few seconds I didn't know why I had woken up until the excruciating pain made it clear that I was in the middle of a severe migraine attack. My Grandma called them sick headaches while one of my doctors called them vestibular headaches, but no matter what you call them it's like having the worst attack of motion sickness along with the unbelievable agony of an exploding headache. With my world spinning and my stomach rolling and churning, I couldn't stand or sit up without immediately throwing up so I couldn't even get myself to the bathroom. But necessity was certainly the mother of invention and I'd suffered through enough migraines to know how to cascade over the side of my bed without jostling my head, then slither and slide across the floor like a snake to the bathroom before lifting my head and throwing up. And while that made my stomach hurt less, it ramped the head pain into the torture range.

Poor Max was immediately beside himself. There was not one part of my body language that was normal or familiar to him. I had certainly had a couple of headaches this year, but this was the first one anywhere close to this slithering and collapsing magnitude. I relaxed onto the bathroom floor, oddly comforted by the cold tile and the nearness to the facilities. My Golden Annie, the dog that my ex-boyfriend had given away behind my back, had always curled up next to me and licked at my hands when I was suffering, offering her own excellent brand of care and comfort. But Max's anxiety was so overpowering that he could merely pace back and forth outside the bathroom door and then run back to the bedroom, only to creep back and peer around the corner of the doorway at me to see if I was still acting bizarre. The night slowly ticked by, one long minute after another, with each of us in our own private hell.

As dawn started to lighten the sky, I reached the dreadful, but oddly magical, point where I knew the pain simply couldn't get any worse. Long ago I had stolen the imagery from an Air Force poem and named this time 'touching the face of God,' and I always surrendered myself to it. Despite medical advice to the contrary, I fully expected to die at this point, accepting it would be my last moment on earth as my brain actually exploded. But so far it had been instead the step right before blessed relief came. I stayed suspended in the pain for some unknown period of time, and then the pain ratcheted down, my stomach settled and I could consider standing up, getting a big cup of hot coffee, and maybe even being able to keep some medication down.

I would never willingly take the journey that would deliver me to this point, but there was a silver lining, a reward of sorts. The scientist in me would insist it was endorphins or neurotransmitters or increased blood flow, but it felt more like an otherworldly feeling much like the anticipation of gifts on Christmas morning or maybe falling in love. It was in no way worth the previous agony, but it was nonetheless life affirming and oddly delightful when the pain released and a weird joy flooded through me.

I stumbled through the apartment, trying to do what it would take so that I could make it to work later in the afternoon. Max cavorted in ecstasy, obviously still confused, but enjoying the moment because I was up on my feet and loudly imploring my coffee pot to hurry up, the same words I spoke every morning. He picked up a toy, but then immediately sought reassurance from me that everything was still okay. I told him he was a good boy and admired his toy, but I could tell that his anxiety continued unabated just below the surface. I felt sorry for him while at the same time I felt abandoned by his behavior toward me during the attack. He obviously cared that I was suffering, but he allowed his feelings to stand in the way of him actually doing anything that would help or comfort me. I filed the whole topic away to think about when I was actually getting adequate blood flow to my brain, but it definitely brought up feelings about my own empathy and anxiety. Could my deep whole-hearted empathetic feelings about everyone and everything create enough anxiety that it actually stood in my way of helping others? How horribly ironic would that be?

CHAPTER FIVE

"Welcome to our new interns," Dr. Drama said as we started evening rounds. "They've spent the day doing their orientation with Molly and will be ready to start, bright eyed and bushy tailed, tomorrow morning. This'll be an introductory week so they won't have specific patients of their own and will instead be attached to one of the staff doctors or specialists. Of course they'll be available whenever we need help, but they need to prioritize learning our computer, in house laboratory, and record keeping systems. I've sadly seen new doctors with top notch medical skills laid low by the paperwork."

The three of them nodded and smiled their unspoken compliance. After they trooped out and the emergency people got ready to start our shift, Dr. Drama said, "They seem alright."

"Alright?" I asked. "Is that what you said about us?"

"Probably," he said with a half-smile. "I always struggle with new doctor adjustment syndrome. By the way, I didn't assign you an intern this week because you're going through your own transition."

"Thanks," I replied. "I do feel a little off."

Dr. Drama took a deep breath and shook himself all over like a dog after swimming. He walked into ICU clapping and loudly asked, "Everybody excited about a great week? Gonna have some fun tonight?"

Starting with the ICU staff, new energy immediately infused through the entire treatment area. I certainly tried to be upbeat and encouraging at work, but my personal strength seemed to be my empathy. Some days it was difficult to stay positive on emergency shifts because there was always at least one patient or owner or staff member suffering that I could empathize with. But I appropriated some of Dr. Drama's energy, grinned, and replied, "Woohoo!" and danced over to my desk.

After my short night due to the migraine, I was actually relieved it was slow and happily settled into a chair in the library, but I was quickly bounced out of my seat by a particularly frantic page. I jogged up to the front office and Tessa, my favorite client service representative, called me over with a crooked finger. She leaned over the counter and whispered, "There's four huge boys and two bull dogs in room three. Something's not right about them."

"The dogs or the boys?" I whispered back.

"I meant the boys," she replied. "But the dogs definitely need help."

I silently repeated my key phrase for dealing with possibly impaired people, "stick to the facts, don't let the owner's problems influence the clinical decisions," and put another smile on my face. Two of the boys were pushing and shoving each other, fighting over the bench seat, one was sitting on the floor, and one was standing, but weaving back and forth. The weaving boy had a pattern going that would have been almost soothing except that each time he shifted to the right he bounced off the wall and each time he shifted to the left he hung there balanced for a second on one foot giving the impression that he might fall over instead.

"So, both dogs are vomiting," I started reviewing the history, but was promptly interrupted by one of the dogs loudly retching a couple of times and then profusely vomiting a huge pool of brown liquid dotted with what looked like popcorn and Doritos. One of the fighting boys clapped his hand over his mouth, moaned, and then vomited right next to where the dog vomited. This entire visit was not going to be pretty.

After Tabatha and I cleaned it all up, I had her take both bulldogs to the back to get vitals and draw blood while I tried to wrestle some kind of history out of these obviously drunk boys.

"Which one of you is the owner?" I asked with another,

and most likely my last, smile plastered on my face. The vomiting boy stumbled out the door to the waiting room, rudely slamming it behind him.

"We all are," weaving boy replied, holding still for a minute and then started his weaving up again. Only now his pattern was going front to back and when he weaved forward he'd precariously come up on his toes. I really thought he was going to fall flat on his face.

"Can you tell me what happened? What the dogs could've gotten into?" I asked.

They spoke at once, but it was some version of: I don't know, nothing to get into, everything was normal. It was so very obvious that the boys were impaired and there was a very good chance that whatever they all participated in, the dogs had gotten into it as well.

I decided that honesty was the best policy and said, "It's obvious that you all have been drinking and/or smoking something that could also make both of your dogs ill. But those same substances, that for you seems like a party, could not only make your dogs sick, it could kill them because their body size is so much smaller and their biochemistry is so very different than yours."

Weaving boy said, "We didn't give them anything."

"What was in the area that the pups could have gotten into? Some substances have very specific antidotes, while other substances cause very specific symptoms that I need to treat, for example heart arrhythmias," I continued.

Flailing his arms about, weaving boy insisted loudly, "We. Didn't. Give. Them. Anything."

"Okay, I hear what you're saying, but what could've been in their environment that they could've gotten into, without you knowing it, without you giving it to them?" My frustration and desperation started showing in my tone and I'm sure in my expressions, but now I honestly didn't care. "I need this information to save their lives. I don't care if you tell me that a neighbor threw it over your fence or it magically beamed in from space. I'm not here to get anybody in trouble. I just want to know what could be making them ill."

The boy on the bench seat slowly slipped forward onto his knees then stretched out on the floor. It was kind of a slow motion controlled dissent and he either immediately fell asleep or passed out. I watched his breathing for a minute and it seemed steady, but I had no idea what to do for him, or even if it was my responsibility to do anything.

Tabatha rapped on the door and told me that the boy who had left the exam room was now passed out in my waiting room. Weaving boy and floor sitting boy were now my only hope for information, and in this situation knowledge was the power to help the dogs. And I'd have to make a decision on what to do about the boys. Weaving boy poked his passed out friend with his foot then went out into my waiting room and started shaking his other friend and telling him he couldn't sleep there. Sitting boy slowly stretched out next to his friend and closed his eyes.

I looked back at the chart and realized that the listed owner's name was Elizabeth. And none of the boys here with me looked like an Elizabeth. And maybe she could be of help with both the dogs and the boys. With a quick prayer that she was in possession of her wits, I called the number we had listed.

"What?" Elizabeth exclaimed intensely after I explained what little I knew. "What the hell is happening?"

"I don't know," I replied honestly. "I need more information and the boys aren't making any sense. And I'm concerned about the ones that have passed out. Do you want me to call an ambulance?"

"I'll be right there," she said in a stone cold voice and hung up on me.

I went out into the waiting room and evaluated the boy passed out on my floor, until all the receptionists and the waiting clients simultaneously and very dramatically turned toward the entranceway. A tall, model beautiful, immaculately groomed woman came through the door with her eagle eyes actively surveying the scene. She paused just inside the entrance door, put her hands on her hips, narrowed her eyes as she chose a target, and then strode across the reception area, her high-heeled boots click clacking across the space. She paused again next to the sleeping boy, poked her pointed toe boot into his lower back, twisted it in a couple times and then delivered a sharp kick to his buttocks and said, "Get up Mike."

She strode confidently towards me and asked "Are you in charge?"

"I am," I said with a worn out smile. "Are you the owner of the two bulldogs?"

"I am responsible for them," she replied. "I'm also responsible for these boys. Tell me what you need me to do."

I considered delving back into the entire story, but then decided just to answer her simple question. "I need you to corral these passed out boys and get them the help they need so that I can help the dogs. And most of all, for effective treatment, I need to know what the dogs might've gotten into."

"Don't you have test for that?" she asked seriously.

"I can test for the most common things here rather quickly, but other tests I'd have to send out and there's a couple day turnaround time on those. It would really help narrow things down if I at least knew which class of drugs that I'm looking at."

"Okay," she said nodding. Then she'd turned to weaving boy and said in a frosty voice, "Tell me exactly what drugs were at the party."

"Ehhh," he sputtered, but then just repeated, "We didn't give the dogs anything."

Elizabeth drew herself up and said, "If you're going to spout garbage then just shut up. In fact shut the fuck up until you can tell us what we need to know. It's a crying shame what you four numb nuts did to yourselves, but it's downright criminal what you did to two innocent creatures."

She turned to me and said in a sugary sweet voice, "Why don't you give us a minute. You could go check the dogs, come back in a few minutes and I'll tell you exactly what the dogs have been exposed to."

As I was slipping out the door to the pharmacy I heard a loud crack. When I turned to check it out, weaving boy's eyes were bugging out in shock and he had a bright red mark on his cheek, but he was already speaking and Elizabeth was typing on her iPad.

True to her word when I returned a few minutes later she had a list of drugs that had been available, actually sitting out in a bowl ready for the taking, by boy or unintentionally by beast. She also got him to admit there was lots of booze available at the party, including a sweet fruit punch in a big pot left out on a low coffee table. Elizabeth signed the estimate, gave us a deposit without complaint, and then lined up the four boys in front of me and the reception desk, all of them semi awake and looking like they wished they were anywhere but there.

"I'm so sorry for my disrespectful behavior," weaving boy went first, speaking towards me, then including Tabitha and the receptionists. The other three boys followed the same script and then wobbled their way out of the hospital.

"Are we good?" Elizabeth asked.

"I'll call you with a report in an hour or so," I said confidently.

"Thank you," she replied graciously, then turned and marched out.

It might seem like an inappropriate response and maybe I should have been appalled at her behavior since corporal punishment seemed to play a big part in how she got me the information I needed. However I, more than anything else in the world, wished she could work with me on every shift, simply to handle all the non-veterinary weird shit that was constantly going on that I never knew how to take care of.

CHAPTER SIX

I snoozed through morning rounds; switching back and forth between evening, night, and day shifts was killing me. I stood there with an appropriate, but absolutely fake, interested look on my face, until it came time for me to report on my two bulldogs. "Thankfully it looks like my two partying bulldogs were mainly suffering from alcohol poisoning. There was a myriad of other drugs they had possible exposure to, but thank goodness we found no sign of significant ingestion of anything but alcohol. They're doing well and have stayed well oxygenated even though they both have some classic bulldog respiratory problems."

Dr. Harris, one of the new interns, asked, "Why did you monitor their oxygen saturation and temperature so aggressively all night?"

Dr. Drama's and Dr. Blackwell's heads snapped up at his tone or it wouldn't have even registered to me that his manner was rude, but I blew it off and answered his question. "I've learned that with short faced dogs in general, but especially with bulldogs, their anatomical issues can quickly turn any other illness or stress into a life and death fight to oxygenate and thermoregulate."

Dr. Harris shook his head derisively, "Overkill in this case, the dog was simply drunk."

I laughed him off and replied, "Just the right amount of no kill to my way of thinking. And alcohol poisoning is not the same thing as being drunk."

"And short faced dogs? You mean brachiocephalic dogs? With brachiocephalic syndrome?" he retorted scornfully.

I started to reply, but Dr. Drama shot his death glare at both of us. Then he did his classic come on hurry up hand signal and immediately rounds moved on to the next patient. As soon as we finished I hustled upstairs to use one of the more private computers to see if Andrei had replied to my email, and in all honesty to avoid Harris until I stopped wanting to slap his know-it-all face.

I so wanted Andrei to answer me, even if he was as rude to me as Harris had just been. Ever since I'd emailed him I couldn't stop brooding about why he had abandoned us. Of course I wanted to know where he was, what he was doing, whether he was happy; all the things a person would naturally wonder about a long lost relative. But deep in the core of my being I wanted to know what made him go from a loving brother to a complete stranger.

There was a message from Andrei! I was stunned by how much information he squeezed into a very brief email.

Dear Kat,

It was good to get your email. I'm still a Marine, now deployed overseas. Dagger must have told you that we can't give any details. My wife and kids live in North Carolina and we're in the process of buying a house. I only have a minute today and then I'll lose access to the internet, but you can answer anytime and I'll catch up as soon as I'm back. Love, Andrei P.S. Say hi to Stefan.

He included two pictures, one of him in his uniform in which he looked strong, fierce and absolutely wonderful and another that was a snapshot of his family. His kids were adorable, his son looked just like Andrei as a boy with a wide grin and half his shirttail hanging out. His two little girls were dressed in matching dresses and seemed to be twins. His wife was beautiful and appeared loving and kind the way she was holding on to everyone, obviously the heart of the family, but she was a complete stranger to me. I was filled with love and joy at the connection with my brother, but at the same time almost overcome with grief and regret for the time I missed with him and his precious family.

I quickly typed a reply, just wanting to keep the connection active.

Oh Andrei, what a beautiful family you have, I love them already. I'm so sorry about whatever happened so that we couldn't be together. I'd do anything to be a family again. Love, Kat

I no more than sent the message than the speaker called me downstairs with a page for any available emergency doctor.

As I stepped up to the shelf which held the pending emergency charts, I was startled to see Melanie waiting there, immediately grinned at her and said, "Long time no see!"

"What do you mean, it's only been a couple weeks," she replied, pinching her eyebrows together in mistrust.

"Just teasing," I clarified with a smile. "Happy to get to work with you for a shift."

"I bet you are," she said in an odd tone that I couldn't really decipher.

I heard a high pitched doggy scream from the reception area and hustled out front to help. A thin dog, maybe part Whippet or Italian Greyhound, was being awkwardly held by a frantic woman. Both her arms were wrapped around him, corralling everything except the most important part of him: his back leg which was attached to a decorative steel cover from a floor register. The woman was more stoic than her dog; he screamed every time he tried to shake off the metal piece, violently slamming the sharp corners into the woman's upper legs, while she only grimaced and bit her lip as it dug into her flesh. The dog was beyond frantic, terrified by the plate on his foot and seemingly convinced that only repeated shaking would free him from it. I grabbed the foot and held it close to the woman's body to take away the force of the blows and guided the woman with my other arm into an open room.

"Tabby!" I called to my technician. "I need a sedative for a twenty pound," the woman corrected me, "twenty two pounds," and I amended the order, "sedative for a twenty two pound dog, stat."

I took a brief history, but the problem was as simple as it

41

looked on first impression. The dog had been zooming around their living room, ran over the vent and jammed her toenail deep into a v shaped part of the decorative scroll and on the next step lifted the cover out of the vent. It was a quick fix after the sedative took effect, just a little bit of lubricant, a little work with a file, and little tugging in the right direction. I think the poor battered owner was going to have a longer recovery than the dog would have, although often dogs in the thrall of that kind of mindless fear could cause themselves all kinds of horrible damage. I reminded myself to educate the owner about wrapping up panicking dogs in beach towels or thick blankets to prevent self-harm and damage to others. Plus it's good general advice for her to know that applies to all kinds of emergent situations.

"Why do you always get the simple cases with appreciative owners and I get the convoluted no win cases that have no money?" Melanie whined, but with a half-smile that didn't seem to fit the rest of her expression.

"Lucky I guess," I replied, but turned away before I said something more real. I felt sorry for Melanie, but I couldn't be dragged down into her darkness and still do my job the way I wanted to. I left to get a minute to myself and to let her pick whichever emergency case she thought was the easy one, even though I deeply believed karma would make sure that any selfish choice of patients on her part would backfire horribly on her. At least that is how it always seemed to work for me.

In contrast to my thrashing screamer, my next patient was a silent sufferer, thank goodness his owner wasn't fooled by his stoicism. Sadly my sickest patients are often so quiet that no one recognizes how sick they really are since they aren't causing any overt trouble. He was quietly lying on his pink and blue crocheted blanket on the table and he and his owner had matching looks of agony on their faces, although his seemed to be rooted in physical pain while hers seemed to be based on some kind of embarrassment or shame.

"Tell me what happened," I started as innocuously as I could.

"Well," she said and then took a deep breath and rolled her eyes. "Rolo has become increasingly enamored of the blanket that my mother crocheted for him. My mother! She's ninety two!"

"And?" I asked encouragingly.

"And he wouldn't stop humping it. And Mom was due to get up from her nap and I didn't want her to see him going at it, so I locked him in the bathroom with it," she explained. "I didn't know anything could happen."

I shifted Rolo over so that I could see what was going on. He must have continued his enthusiastic humping after he was put away because his penis had slipped through the loose crochet stitches and then gotten trapped. It was red and swollen and raw looking and looked like his early efforts to free himself only made it worse.

"I'm going to take him to the treatment area and give him a pain shot before I try to disengage him," I explained to the worried owner. When I picked him up for transport the blanket moved with him and his breathing became rapid and his eyes widened showing wide white rings. I grabbed the blanket with the other hand to keep the weight from causing him any additional pain, and he looked at me with relief.

I quickly resolved his dire situation and managed to extract him without even cutting the blanket. But when I asked the owner if she wanted the blanket back she exclaimed, "No! Burn it! Burn it to hell!" And for some reason that absolutely cracked me up. I managed not to laugh in front of her, but as soon as I reached the treatment area I laughed until I had to lean on the wall, repeating "Burn it to hell!" whenever I started to wind down.

My merriment made Melanie and me an odd pair for the night. I was definitely wearing my rose colored glasses and everything seemed hilarious. Mel had, how do I say this, her shit colored glasses on and had a negative comment on everything and everyone. The technicians started to prioritize helping me and avoiding her which only made her feel worse, but honestly

I didn't blame them. Could she not see that she was causing half her own problems?

I couldn't imagine a way to broach the subject with her. I didn't want to confront her about her toxic attitude or challenge the veracity of each complaint in turn or be the idiot who tells her to cheer up as if that ever helped anyone. I did finally ask her "How's it going at your new job?"

"I read an article about different kinds of hospital cultures and it made me think," Melanie said. "It's a clue that if the general culture is supportive and prioritizes compassionate care, then you aren't even aware there IS a hospital culture."

"Huh?" I asked. "I don't get it."

"When management's basic values and priorities are the same as yours, you don't really even notice because everything fits and flows," she explained. "But when the culture doesn't fit with your feelings and goals, every single decision grates and stands in the way of staff harmony and good care and you feel it every minute of the day."

"That's really profound Melanie," I said appreciatively. "I guess it means the better the culture, the less you even consider it."

"Well, I'll tell you this," she said sadly. "You can't fail to notice the culture when it's horrible; it's like the air is foul with all the issues. The reason I came back here to work some weekend shifts is less about the money and more that I just need to remember how to relax and breathe at work."

"Oh, Melanie," I said. "I'm so sorry."

Melanie's tech started waving at her with a lab sheet and she ruefully turned away from me and said with a sigh, "I'm forced to literally take it one day at a time."

"It'll get better," I said hopefully, but Melanie just looked at me with such dead eyes that I wasn't sure she could feel anything but crushing despair. And yet deep inside I wondered why she couldn't see that while she craved our culture of compassion for patients and their people and each other, she was generating a negative, hypercritical culture around herself.

She was in fact forming a second epicenter of what she was so desperate to escape.

My shift was over so I tried to get away before I could gather any more negative energy, but Dr. Harris ambushed me as soon as I approached the back door and said, "You just hate bulldogs."

"I love bulldogs," I attempted to reply, but he continued speaking over me, "Everyone else loves those adorable faces, what's wrong with you?"

"I love how they look," I argued. "But I want them to be able to breathe easily. It's not a question of form, it's a question of function. We have a wonderful breeder that is working very hard to raise healthy individuals. Her stud has been certified free of hypoplastic trachea and a boatload of other genetic issues. But last night you could hear from across the room that these two dogs were in respiratory distress."

"Don't you ever read a scientific article? Bulldogs are too inbred, have too limited a gene pool to be saved," he said with an exaggerated eye roll.

"Make up your mind," I replied. "Am I too prejudiced against them or not prejudiced enough? Yes, they have issues, but there are solutions to every problem. And yes I read the article, but with further genetic testing and education of breeders and owners, and maybe even some judicious use of controlled outcrosses we can help."

"You're being ridiculous," he said raising his voice. "If you really cared about the dogs you'd know it's cruel to try. England is talking about banning the breeding of bulldogs, Norway has already done it, and the airlines won't let them fly."

"Well, it's not up to ER vets to make those decisions," I replied calmly. "We just need to help the patients in front of us and educate owners about how vulnerable their brachiocephalic dogs are."

"Go ahead," he said even louder. "Put your head in the sand. Not your problem."

I took a deep breath and started to turn, since simply walking away seemed like the right response, but he raised his volume

45

another notch, "Besides, you should never have agreed to see those dogs! You should have kicked them all out when those obnoxious boys showed up drunk and turned our waiting room into a circus."

"For goodness sakes," I begged. "Let it go. You're just looking for some reason to criticize me. Which is becoming increasingly apparent that it has everything to do with you and nothing to do with me!"

"You just think you're right because you're a year ahead of me," he shouted. "One year does not make you the all-knowing God of medicine."

"And yelling doesn't make you right! All your shouting proves is that you're louder than me, not righter than me! If you want to prove that you're right and I'm wrong, you must have actual proof. You can't just raise your voice or bug your eyes out and loom over me. You actually have to get evidence-based medical proof that what you're saying is right," I insisted firmly.

His eyes did bug out and he did take a step closer to me, but then he spun on his heel and stormed out. I took a deep breath and slipped into my antianxiety breathing pattern. I didn't want to spark another migraine headache, he certainly wasn't worth that. Then I remembered my client from earlier in the day and decided just to blow him and his argumentative attitude off. I said to myself, "Burn it all to hell," as I fled out the back door.

CHAPTER SEVEN

I was actually happy to see that the next chart on the emergency shelf was a skin case. The new interns were proving to be masters of criticism about everything and everyone, especially if it concerned the emergency department. I could only imagine what they would say about me looking forward to seeing a non-critical emergency. Dr. Harris seemed to be the vocal leader of their self-appointed complaint department. The other two seemed to be only concerned if they were asked to do any specific work that they didn't have any interest in doing right at that moment. But they needed to wake up and realize their student days of cherry picking what they were interested in was over. They were doctors now and it was all about what the patients needed not what the doctor wanted.

But I've seen a lot of dogs truly suffer with skin infections. They might not be dying, but they were certainly in pain and discomfort, and while I love being the hero and saving lives, relieving suffering gives me almost as much satisfaction. Plus there was usually a lot less drama during skin cases which would give my adrenaline levels a chance to chill out.

Of course if we ever opened the much talked about veterinary urgent care center on our campus, then we would send most skin patients there instead of the ER. I know many human hospitals use the acronym ED for emergency department instead of ER for emergency room. This certainly makes sense even for our veterinary facility since our emergency department incorporated multiple rooms and many kinds of specialized equipment. But we still use the abbreviation ER because people simply understand it better, and people under stress need everything to be as simple and intuitive as possible.

Plus personally I interpret ED as erectile dysfunction every time I see or hear it, which doesn't translate well in veterinary medicine and is just confusing. I was happy that the drug company released the most famous drug for erectile dysfunction in people under a different name to treat pulmonary hypertension in people and dogs. That way my owners didn't have embarrassing encounters at pharmacies just for trying to save their dogs' life. I suddenly realized that my mind was popping off on totally unrelated thought tangents, usually a sign that I needed to eat. I had more of Ethan's magic energy bites for my snack today so I took a brief break to see if that would help me stay more focused.

As soon as I was done snacking, I stepped into the room and while I only had one patient chart, there were two dogs patiently waiting. The look on my face was enough to make the owner quickly explain, "This is Bobo the patient," pointing at the smaller terrier, "and this is Rufus who's just here because he keeps Bobo calm."

I already knew that while sometimes having an emotional support dog for another dog does in fact work, it can also go atrociously wrong if one of the pair is overly protective of the other. I said, "Let's see how that works. If it's a problem you can run Rufus out to your car. I see that Bobo has been fighting skin problems for a few months and it got significantly worse this week?"

"That's right," she replied. "He's so miserable, he's tearing his hair out, and scratching nonstop even at night."

As I stood looking at the pattern of hair loss on his back extending onto his tail, Bobo snapped his head around and started chewing at a spot on the top of his thigh, then seemed to chase the itch down his leg in a twisting route, an action we call safari behavior. This behavior, along with his pattern of hair loss, pointed to this being an infestation of fleas with a resultant allergic reaction.

"Are your dogs on any flea prevention or," I started to ask, but she immediately interrupted, "Don't start that flea business. No one ever finds fleas on Bobo, my house is meticulously clean, and it's NOT fleas."

"Okay," I replied softly, but continued, "Is he on any parasite prevention, topical or oral?"

"He's on heartworm prevention," she stated emphatically, "but no flea poison. And the anti-itch medicine helps for a while and then stops."

"Okay," I repeated, and totally regretted thinking that skin cases weren't as emotionally dramatic as other cases. As I began to exam Bobo, I warned her about what I was doing to prevent confusion. "I'm going to examine the rest of Bobo's systems first, because once I start examining the skin I might get so interested in that I forget to do a full physical."

The owner nodded and the rest of the exam was unremarkable. I started the skin exam at the face and worked my way down, and everything I found reconfirmed that this was a flea allergic dermatitis, complicated by secondary infection and crusty seborrhea in the areas that he was self-traumatizing. The only thing that was missing was a flea to prove it to the owner. I checked the path that Bobo had recently been chewing, then quickly lifted the leg and looked at the belly. Fleas may prefer certain areas on a pet's body like the tail head, but once disturbed they will quickly move out of that region. I saw a flash of movement, but couldn't catch it. I knew in my heart this was a flea allergy, a situation where the patient will chew, scratch, and viciously traumatize the skin until they catch the flea or chase it off. But unless I could prove it to this owner I knew she'd never believe me. I started to look for the black flea dirt, the nicer name for flea excrement, which is also hard to find on a highly allergic dog because the relentless itching stops the flea before it poops or all the drool from chewing dissolves the evidence.

I stopped myself from gritting my teeth and relaxed my shoulders down, I didn't want a headache today with an important puppy class meeting to go to after work. I took a deep breath and Rufus leaned over and bumped my arm for attention.

And while there was a strong 'no two exams for the price of one' rule for owners trying to sneak an extra patient in, I knew that Rufus had to have fleas as well. And if he wasn't as allergic as Bobo, he would be allowing them to run around unmolested and I'd be able to catch one. I asked the owner for permission to check Rufus and I heard the owner gasp as I had him flop over for a belly rub and a multitude of fleas scattered in every direction. I nabbed one triumphantly, but the war to convince her that fleas were at the root of Bobo's problems was over.

We had a great discussion about fleas and flea treatment, including vigorous treatment of the environment, and emphasizing the difference between a flea infestation and a flea allergy and all the different ways that each problem can present. Treating fleas doesn't make an exciting story, any more than doing great preventative medicine does, but I felt like I really helped this dog and this owner. She was freaked out about having bugs in her home, but I took an extra minute to commiserate and honestly admit that as much as I know about fleas and how to treat them, I'd be anxious too if they were in my house. I also told her that all drugs have risks, but with modern flea treatments the risk assessment between tolerating flea bite issues for all the pets and humans in the house and the very low risk of the medicine made both treatment and prevention a no brainer decision for me.

The rest of my shift went well and I headed to the training facility for puppy class on time for once, in fact we all managed to arrive at the same time. I jogged over from the main hospital, Mr. Emerson slowly made his way from the parking lot with Chip, and Ethan and Max, Trev and Licorice, and Maisy with Roman arrived through the new garden. The neighborhood puppy club that we formed last year had mostly stuck together and been in and out of various training classes, but we decided that this was going to be our last formal class for a while. Mr. Emerson was struggling with the physical demands. My rotating schedule and increased responsibilities made getting to class reliably very difficult every week and Ethan didn't want to always come on his own with Max. Maisy was overwhelmed trying to put her life back together after her husband and son were arrested for drugs and assorted other crimes. And now she had to figure out how to run her kennel all by herself. Even Trev said he was going to be too busy for regular classes and he'd tell us why tonight.

Knowing that our trainer Gemma might be watching out the window we owners were on our best behavior, insisting that the dogs sit quietly next to us before we walked in one at a time. Then we let them off lead to play in the fenced in area. Some of the worse dog encounters that I have ever heard about, with the most horrible physical and behavioral consequences, have occurred in off leash dog parks. But these four dogs had been well supervised and well trained since puppyhood and letting them blow off steam before getting down to business worked well for us.

Gemma called us to order, we leashed our dogs and moved to the agility area. So far this was the favorite activity we had tried. After four or five months of basic training, we had signed up for all sorts of things as a group. At least once whenever we got together, one of us felt compelled to tease Trev about the time we all tried dock diving. Trev had been enthusiastically encouraging Licorice to jump when he slipped off the edge of the dock and belly flopped dramatically into the water. For some reason Mr. Emerson in particularly thought this was hysterical and could rarely talk about it without laughing until he couldn't speak and had tears in his eyes. Trev had lost his Dad a year or so ago and had grown very close to Mr. Emerson, so he was pleased to have this ongoing private joke, but still none of us humans were really interested in dock diving being their ongoing hobby.

Roman the Doberman was by far the best at agility, Maisy had hired Gemma privately to help her work on fine tuning his performance. Maisy was hoping to eventually compete with him at the dog shows. Chip and Licorice, the labs, were both good at it, although Chip could lose focus and miss his cues, while Licorice was so focused on going fast that he'd miss his contacts.

And then there was Max. After his initial hesitancy, he fell in love with the tunnel, and would do it over and over again. In fact Gemma started calling him a 'tunnel sucker' because he would seek out the tunnel from anywhere on the course. And he did it with such glee!

But he didn't feel the same way about some of the other obstacles. He acted like the weave poles were a form of torture and went through them hilariously slowly, like it was a slow motion video, or some kind of attempted mime performance. He hated the teeter and after a particularly resounding bang as it hit the ground, he refused to ever get on it again. I was doing these activities to have fun with my dog and develop his confidence, so I didn't want to continue an activity that caused him that much stress. Plus honestly, it was becoming clear that for my own sanity I needed to look for some time off activities for myself that were totally unrelated to my profession, not that I would ever neglect Max. So today I loosely went along with Gemma's instructions, but let Max do what he wanted, which was running through the tunnel.

The most productive thing Max and I did was provide some distraction for Roman while he ran the course; he was incredibly fun to watch. Then when Chip went for his last run, he got about half way through it, saw the pylon marking the order of obstacles and grabbed it. Then he zoomed around the course carrying it with a total look of exhilaration on his face. We all laughed so hard and his antics definitely stopped any sadness of it being our last class. When class was over, Gemma gave us certificates of completion and a little bag of treats, but then left us alone to figure out what we were going to do next.

"Well," Trev said with a grin. "Licorice and I aren't going to do another class because I'm going to be much busier now that I'm," he stood up and spread his arms wide, "going to be working as a veterinary assistant at the hospital!"

I jumped to my feet and said, "Congratulations! I'm so excited for you! Where will you be working?"

"I'll be working emergency mainly," he replied. "But they said

I'll be moving around some this summer, and then we'll see what works out when school starts in the fall. Gemma is making a push for me to become involved in training or daycare, but I need to see how my senior year activities unfold."

Mr. Emerson hugged Trev, having a little trouble with his balance in his exuberance, but catching himself with his cane. Once stable he patted Trev enthusiastically on the back, and said, "I'm so proud of you!"

Maisy hugged him next, and said, "I'll miss you at the kennel, but I know it's the right choice for you. Plus I'm cutting back so it will be easier to handle the workload by myself."

"You know you can call me any time you need extra help," Trev insisted. "I've learned so much from you and appreciate everything that you've done for me."

"I agree that it's time for us to cut back on weekly training sessions," I said. "But it's really very important to Ethan and me, and to Max, that we don't totally lose touch. What can we do? If we don't make a plan I know that I will continuously put it off just because I always think that tomorrow or next week or whatever won't be as busy as right now is."

"And time just slips away," Mr. Emerson agreed. "I need a plan too."

Maisy said, "Let's keep it simple. Let's get together once a month. We'll each host in turn. Trev with his magic computer skills can make a schedule, and the host can pick the details."

"Sounds good," Mr. Emerson said. "And if someone can't make it we can offer to pick up their dog."

"Is everyone still interested in exchanging occasional daycare and boarding as we go on?" Trev asked.

"Absolutely!" We all nodded our agreement as we began a final round of goodbye hugs and called the dogs in from the play area.

CHAPTER EIGHT

I was thrilled to be back on another daytime emergency shift, especially on a day like this that was starting off slow with everyone in a good mood! Dr. Drama was particularly happy with his eminently achievable surgery schedule full of interesting cases. So I was surprised to see Tabitha heading out of the surgery area with a frustrated expression.

"What's up Tabby?" I asked with a smile.

"No big deal," she said showing me a small grain of rice sized object grasped between her finger and thumb. "I tried to implant a microchip in one of the surgery cases and with a plink, loud enough for Dr. Drama to hear, it immediately fell out onto the metal table!"

"Oops!" I said sympathetically. "That's embarrassing!"

"Doc was in rare form with his response," she said with a smile, which widened into a grin as if she'd just had a really funny thought. "Oh well. I'd better go get another one from primary care."

I turned to head back up front and Tabatha added, "Don't forget there are cupcakes for my birthday upstairs!"

"Yum!" I replied. "Thanks!"

I had enough paperwork to obsess about that I forgot all about the cupcakes until I saw Tabby, Tessa and a couple other staff members delivering a sprinkle decorated cupcake to Dr. Drama's desk. Food wasn't actually allowed downstairs, but sometimes we cheated. When I saw Tabatha surreptitiously messing with Dr. Drama's lab coat, I was concerned that she had gotten pink frosting on it and it was hard to guess how many oops moments he would tolerate before his reaction was no longer fun and games. She was still grinning, as were the rest of the group, so I stopped worrying about it.

Dr. Drama ambled over and took a huge bite of his cupcake, smearing his face in the process. Then he proceeded to stuff the rest of it in his mouth and clownishly give a series of mumbled orders to the staff gathered around him. He winked at me as he pretended to grow increasingly angry that they weren't snapping to attention and fulfilling his unintelligible orders. Eventually everyone scattered back to work, but as soon as he put his lab coat on and started gathering his stethoscope and other equipment, they regathered around him.

Tabatha was carrying the microchip reader and as she waved it over Dr. Drama's midsection it started to beep and then read out a full microchip ID number.

"What the hell?" he asked belligerently.

"One of the sprinkles on your cupcake was a microchip!" Tabatha explained with a smile.

"You what?" he asked as his gregarious mood faded before our eyes. He snatched the microchip reader out of Tabatha's hands and ran it down his front. It beeped directly over his stomach, and his face deepened into a scowl.

Tessa added, "We'll be able to track it all the way out!"

He spun around waving the reader up, down, right and left and every angle in-between and it kept beeping, zeroing in on his midsection as the location. Emotions flowed over his face: disbelief, anger, fear, and I could tell he didn't know whether to let it go, get to work, and let it pass naturally or to get on the phone with the company and research if he was in any danger. The technicians' expressions on the other hand were not only relaxed and happy, they were universally gleeful.

When Dr. Drama's expression started to solidify into rage, I caught Tabatha's eye, glared at her and shook my head. She immediately held her hand up to quiet the crowd and said, "Dr. Vincent you should double check the inside of the back of your lab coat," pointing to where they had attached the discarded microchip inside his coat right about at stomach level.

His eyes bugging out, Dr. Drama whipped off his coat and examined the microchip where it was taped. After a moment's thinking pause, he put it back on and ran around the hospital pranking everyone else with his new toy. He made up an elaborate story of how he had gotten the microchip, saying that a technician had slipped and accidentally injected him with it.

When it was her turn, Melanie was mesmerized by his story and almost looked normal interacting with him. Her chuckles at his antics seemed real for the first time in months. She demanded to see where they had injected him and when he clownishly stuck his butt out and mimed pulling his pants down to show her, she actually laughed out loud while begging him not to. But a few minutes after she walked away from him, her face settled back into her typical grim expression, so the minute we had a break I asked Melanie to go upstairs with me.

"What's up Melanie?" I asked quietly. "I'm really worried about you. I wish we could have talked more during our last shift, but I got distracted by cases."

"Do you do social media?" she asked hesitantly.

"Not really," I answered softly. "I have to use the computer here at the hospital so it isn't worth it."

"Not on your phone?" she asked somewhat incredulously.

"Dag put me on his phone plan so that I could afford a phone, but I use it as little as possible," I replied. "I really just use it for work calls. I don't want to abuse his kindness or be any more beholden than I already am."

She looked at me in disbelief; her face totally bewildered and lost. It reminded of the time I was so frazzled that when my phone rang I picked up the handheld iStat electrolyte machine and tried to answer it instead. She shook her head and said, "Dag seems to be the type of guy that would have a pretty comprehensive plan so I bet you wouldn't affect him at all by using Facebook or Instagram."

Her attitude made me feel ashamed, both of my inability to afford my own phone plan, and equally of my irrational need to rely as little as possible on other people. I suddenly wished

I could get out of the conversation, but I was not going to let anything distract me from connecting with Melanie and finding a way to help her.

Melanie grimaced and continued, "Not that you SHOULD use any kind of social media. I wish I never had. Now I have an abusive client who is cyberstalking me and saying the most horribly toxic lies about me. And then she entices her followers to join in on the attack! After she killed her first puppy, she wrote disgusting things about me on social media, nasty vicious lies, all aimed at getting people to donate money to help her save the other puppies when it was all her fault they were suffering in the first place."

Melanie paused to wipe her eyes and blow her nose and looked at me with such agony.

"Not that she would ever actually use the money to help anybody but herself," Melanie continued, but in a diminished tone, as if the remembered pain sucked all the energy out of her. "After that first puppy got sick I got her free vaccines to protect the other puppies. I carefully explained how to isolate the sick puppy to keep the others safe. But she didn't take any precautions and didn't even use the vaccines. I think she was creating more tragic cases on purpose to wring more money out of kind hearted people. She even posted pictures of those poor unprotected puppies loving on the sick one supposedly bringing it a 'miracle love cure'. I could see on her site that people were sending her hundreds and hundreds of dollars, but she didn't pay a single penny of that to our clinic so I'm in big trouble with my manager on top of everything else."

"So the puppy made it?" I asked, happy that there was at least a favorable outcome.

"No," she said, shaking from the memory. "She refused hospitalization and took it home so she could do all the nursing care herself. Then later she tried to pass off a different puppy as the ill one to prove I was lying about it needing hospitalization. Of course then that second puppy got horribly sick and she was using him as the poster puppy on her begging page."

Melanie groaned and grabbed her abdomen as if simply talking about this woman caused her actual physical pain.

"Oh, Mel," I said with tears gathering, "I'm so sorry. What can I do to help?"

"Nothing," she replied despondently as she turned to leave. "There's nothing anyone can do."

After that grim conversation with Melanie the rest of the day unfolded as an ordinary emergency shift; no particular surprises and every case progressed appropriately. Patients with minor problems needed minor treatment and their owners were only minimally concerned. More severely compromised patients needed more treatment and their owners were understandably more upset. The ones I expected to do well did in fact do well, while the ones that I was worried about fought hard to improve their odds. But I still felt drained and a little depressed as I walked home from the busy shift. I wasn't delusional. I understood at a deep level that masses of healthy puppies and kittens accompanying super happy people singing my praises were never going to show up to an ER, but it was difficult to maintain an upbeat attitude without some kind of infusion of joyfulness into my day.

I turned towards the back door to head home for house family dinner night, but realized I had time to run upstairs and check the computer for a reply from Andrei. I usually did it on my lunch break, but I didn't get a break today although I couldn't complain since I was actually getting out on time.

I had received a reply from Andrei, but I sat there stunned and stared at the screen after I read it.

What do you mean 'whatever happened?' You never took my phone calls, answered my letters, remembered my birthday, or showed up on my doorstep. Then you made it impossible for me to even try to get in touch. What could you possibly expect after what you did?

I DO want to reconnect. And I'm not an idiot, I know that our demon uncle was the sole captain of the ship back then, but couldn't you find a way around him? Especially after you graduated and left the house to go to college? What happened then?

What I had done? What did that mean? I hadn't done anything to him. And how could I have prevented him from continuing to try to reach me? It didn't make any sense and I didn't know how to even formulate questions in reply. I reread my last email and all I had said was that I was sorry about whatever happened so that we couldn't be together. At the time I thought that I was being nonjudgmental about his abandonment, but maybe the apology was confusing. It's been pointed out to me that I say 'I'm sorry' too much, but I'm in no way taking blame. Rather I'm showing sympathy for the situation or someone's pain. I learned the hard way that I could never say it to Justin, my vet school ex-boyfriend, or my uncle for that matter, because they would immediately leap upon it as an excuse to blame anything and everything on me. But I don't remember Andrei being that kind of a person, I remember him responding as if I were showing him support. I didn't know how to reply and really didn't have much time to ponder it so I decided to keep it simple.

Andrei, what do you mean phone calls and letters? You never wrote, you never called. You left on your birthday and just disappeared. Of course we remembered your birthday every year, we but never had a clue where you were. I never forgot about you and never stopped hoping you would show up grinning your grin, wrapping your arms around me and picking me up off my feet. What happened to you?

I stood up so abruptly I knocked the desk chair over, took a deep breath, had second thoughts, but still reached over and hit send. As much time that had passed I knew that truth, as hard as it was to hear or to articulate, was the only way we were going to find our way back together.

CHAPTER NINE

I jogged a little and did some deep breathing exercises on the walk home to help transition from a cranky work-self to a fun relaxed home-self. And I deliberately blocked the deeper maelstrom of emotions that Andrei's email had evoked. It was house family dinner night and I wasn't going to ruin my favorite night of the week. Ethan had acted all 'I've got a secret' this morning when I dropped Max off at his apartment so I was guessing there was going to be something extra special served tonight, most likely a decadent dessert despite all of us trying to forgo sweets to help Phil to control his diabetes. And in spite of my supposed dedication to healthy eating, I was supremely happy about it!

As soon as I opened my door, Ethan sent Max bounding up the stairs to me and called out, "They're still working on the air conditioner so Phil and I opened your windows and set up a big fan in your apartment."

"Thanks Ethan, I'll be down soon," I called back. I heaved a deep sigh and groaned. Being hot would never, ever improve my mood.

Max didn't seem to care about the heat and wasn't a fan of the fan. Every time he walked across the room he dramatically took a wide circle around the noisy spinning monster. But his tail was up as he bounced on and off the couch with his eyes glued to my face, grabbing toys one after another until he found just the right one. Then he had an adorable case of the zoomies around the room with it!

I stepped into the bedroom to change out of my scrubs, but when I returned to the living room I was shocked to see

Max holding the cute little decorative pillow that Ethan had bought me for Christmas. Normally Max would let go of a forbidden object the minute I discovered him, before I could even order him to drop it. But for some reason, maybe being overstimulated, he danced in place instead, wildly shaking the pillow side to side as if he was trying to kill it. I moved towards him, but too late as the side seam of the pillow split and the microbead stuffing flew into the fan, creating an immediate microbead tornado. At first I was only concerned about the mess, but then I realized neither of us should be inhaling the microbeads so I held my breath and grabbed Max by the collar, dragging him into the bedroom. I found my bandana, quickly fashioned a mask and ran back in, shouting out unintelligible words of alarm as I ran towards the fan.

There was loud pounding on the stairs and then the door blew open. A powerful man rushed in, his aggressive body language making him appear ferocious, panicking me until it registered that it was Dagger, and I yelled, "Don't breathe them in!"

"Breathe what in?" he yelled back, but pulled his t-shirt up over his face and braved the swirling whirlwind of beads to pull the plug on the fan.

"The microbeads," I replied, suddenly way too loud with the fan noise shut off. The small white beads continued to fall and drift across the room, spreading startlingly far and wide around the living room, even into the small corner kitchen forming snowy cover on my counters.

I looked at Dagger, grinned dubiously and said, "Hi?"

"I was supposed to be your big surprise at dinner!" he said. "Should have known you'd find a way to outdo me in the surprise department."

I moved toward him with my arms open wide, but Max started whining from the bedroom as he heard Dagger's voice and then Ethan and Phil rushed into the apartment and demanded to know what was going on.

"Max is doing some redecorating," Dagger replied as Max

ratcheted up his response to a howl at hearing his name.

"Please get Max and head downstairs," I directed the boys. "I'll tackle this mess later."

Max cavorted around Dagger, translating his whole-hearted joy into jumps and play bows, with a series of spins thrown in.

Dagger seemed equally happy to see him and spoke to him with great affection as he guided him out the door, "What a good boy you are, you great big shaggy beast!"

I ducked into the bathroom to at least try to tame my hair, so Dag didn't call me a shaggy beast too. I also put a little mascara on and even used the pretty pink lip gloss that Issa, Dagger's sister, had recently sent me. She was a model in New York City and got all sorts of free product that she occasionally shared with me. More importantly she shared whatever news she received about Dagger's whereabouts and plans. Although during these past eight months of missing him she hadn't heard much from him either.

I ran downstairs to find everyone, the guys and Mei, our other housemate, already sitting at Phil's big table. Dagger bounced out of his chair and gave me a warm hug and then we took our seats.

"Was Dagger a good surprise?" Ethan asked with a grin.

"The best!" I replied enthusiastically.

"I hope you don't mind we were in your apartment," Phil said. "Not only did we set up the fan, we went ahead with the closet door project we talked about."

"Closet door?" I asked.

"We changed the panel in the back of your closet that leads to Dagger's apartment into a real door so that we could make it secure with a lock and security bar," Phil explained.

"I trust Dagger implicitly," I objected. "No need for all that."

"I was afraid someone could break into my apartment while I was out of town," Dagger explained. "I didn't want to put you at any risk."

"Thanks," I said with a warm smile. "So what's your news about the case?"

62

"Well," he said with regretful looks at each of us in turn. "I have good news about the court case, but that means bad news for travel plans. I'll be leaving early tomorrow morning."

I made an exaggerated sad face, but was able to ask in a normal tone of voice, "So the case is over?"

"Yep," Dagger said. "It was resolved without a trial. And they WILL be punished. Not as severely as they deserve, but at least they don't immediately go free and disappear into witness protection."

"And Maisy?" I asked without thinking, and Dagger shot me a warning look. The housemates knew my client and our neighbor Maisy had been married to a bad guy who had even involved their son in his crimes, but they didn't know about Dagger's involvement in catching them. Not that I even knew exactly how he was involved.

"The District Attorney tried to keep her out of it," Dagger explained. "And the divorce has been finalized so at least she can start over."

"That's good to know," I said with concern in my voice. I knew that money had been really tight for Maisy and that she would have difficult decisions coming up concerning her kennel full of carefully bred Dobermans and Yorkshire Terriers. But I trusted she would consider her dogs' wellbeing in every decision she made. And I could think about Maisy and her dogs tomorrow. Tonight I had Dagger by my side for mere hours. I was already planning on staying up all night if Dag was willing. I had skipped a night's sleep for patients often enough; it was my turn to choose to do the same for my personal life!

Ethan and Phil offered to do the dishes so Mei could show Dagger and me the newly remodeled workout space. I had meant to check it out long before this, but I had just never quite gotten over there. I liked the space. They had painted it a bright white, but retained some of the old wood around the doors and on the floor except where the mat covered the workout area. Mei handed me a rough flyer and schedule of classes, asked me to proof read it and hoped that I could share them at the hospital once they were printed. I was excited about it. I really enjoyed my dog training classes with Max, but I was looking forward to taking a class that focused on me for a change. I took the flyer and promised to both proof it and later distribute it, but tugged on Dagger's hand to let him know I really wanted to spend some alone time with him.

"I love it Mei," he praised. "You've done a great job. I'll tell Phil where I stored my weights so they'll be available for you."

"When you come back home," Mei said quietly, "you can have karate classes here too. I'm just going to teach Tai Chi and Qi Gong for now and maybe some self-defense later."

"Sounds really good," he agreed with a grin, "both coming home and running karate classes."

As Dagger and I walked back to my apartment I asked him, "You do karate?"

"I do," he replied with a smile. "And I'd love to teach you. But meanwhile I hope you take Tai Chi. It's really wonderful on so many levels and it would help you with the stress you're under."

"Stress I'm under?" I asked, trying to smile. I didn't want him to view me as stressed out. I couldn't imagine that would be attractive in any way.

"I can feel you pretty girl," he said softly. "You're wound very tight."

"Transitioning from intern to staff doctor, student to teacher is difficult," I explained. "But I'm so happy that I get to spend time with you that I'd hate to ruin a single second talking about any of it. I'll grow through it."

"Grow through it?" he asked as we entered my apartment.

"I'm not trying to downplay the experience," I said. "But I've accepted that while change isn't comfortable, it's the path to personal and professional growth."

Dagger nodded as if he understood and wrapped his arms around me, kissing me thoroughly, starting at my forehead then moving to my temple and then oh so very lightly to my eyelids. It was hard to breathe, as if the gloriousness of the sensations tingling across my body interfered with the normal process of breathing in and out. As Dagger's lips reached mine I moved even closer to him melting my body into him so I couldn't tell where my body started and his began. I could feel his hands on the small of my back pull me even closer as our lips met. My right hand was trapped between our bodies and I inched it up over his heart to connect with him on a deep visceral level. His heart pounded under my hand and I enjoyed the strong and regular beat for a few minutes, then slipped my hand up to his neck. I rubbed the back of Dagger's head and neck, the feel of his short military style haircut had always captivated me. I don't know if I innately loved the feel of it or if touching his short prickly hair was just such a Dagger related sensation.

We snuggled onto the couch and while I hated depriving Max of the reunion, I was glad I had left him with Ethan. With our time together so brief, I didn't want to share Dagger with Max any more than I wanted to share him with any of my day to day problems. Thank goodness we seemed to be on the same wavelength because we could have cleaned up the microbead snow all over my apartment, or discussed work issues or talked about Andrei, but we didn't. We talked nonsense, cuddled enthusiastically, laughed, shared our wildest hopes and dreams, and we even danced together holding each other close! The hours swiftly flew by making it seem like the shortest night ever, but it was irrefutably the very best night of my life!

CHAPTER TEN

The next morning I sat on a treatment table to wait for the day to begin, overtired and miserable that Dagger was gone again. But then Dr. Drama hopped up next to me and sat there swinging his legs like a little kid. We perched there enjoying the silence for a few minutes until the front door started to chime and the techs migrated past us to start the check-in process. It was an odd feeling; in a few short minutes I would be way busier than I could easily handle, but there was nothing I could do about it yet. I skootched to the edge of the table to get down anyway, but Dr. Drama put a restraining hand on my arm.

"Did I ever tell you about the two bulls standing on the hilltop looking down on their herd spread out in the valley below?" he asked.

"No," I replied, puzzled.

"Well, there were two bulls, one was an older veteran bull and one was a new young bull," he explained. "The young bull looked up at the older bull and excitedly exclaimed, 'Let's run down the hill and breed us some heifers!' The older bull looked down at the youngster and said leisurely, 'Let's walk down the hill and breed ALL the heifers.'"

I laughed out loud, actually it had a strong cackle quality to it because I was so surprised.

Dr. Drama grinned, hopped down off the table and said, "Energy conservation is important. We'll see all the patients, one at a time."

"Did I tell you that this guy, one of my clients, called ME a heifer last week?" I asked.

"No," he replied with a frown. "What did you do?"

"Well, I was kinda confused," I replied, "so I asked him how he knew that I had been interested in dairy practice in vet school. And that seemed to baffle him, so that's when I realized he was trying to insult me, but then it seemed way too late to be all affronted, so I just kept working on his dog. It's not the worst thing someone has called me."

"I'll never, and I mean never, understand why people say such insulting things to us. And sadly they are much more likely to pick on the ladies in the practice. Do they really think insults will change our diagnosis, or the price of the treatment, or how hard we try?" Dr. Drama said, making a face.

"It's like giving them any bad news hurts their feelings so they want to hurt ours even though we are the ones trying so hard to help them," I added.

"Classic shoot the messenger mentality," he agreed. "Insulting me never made me want to make life easier on that client, although I'm proud to say that it never once made me change the care I was offering the patient."

"Yeah," I said. "I guess that's all you can hope for, stay firm to what is best for the pet even though you wish you could avoid the client."

"Yeah, you're right," he said as he turned to go up front. "And make sure you don't let them steal your joy. Sometimes you just have to focus on the patient, walk away, and dismiss the owner and all their bullshit. Basically I just say fuck 'em! To myself of course! We certainly can't lower ourselves to their level out loud."

"Excuse me?" I said, not sure I heard what I thought I heard.

He turned back from the door and said with an evil grin, "You heard me."

The shelf was already stacked with emergency charts so I immediately jumped into seeing patients. Very quickly I was juggling four complicated cases, each at a different stage of testing and treatment, and then Melanie rushed over to me, clutched my smock and demanded, "You have to take the next case. You have to."

"I can't," I said as nicely as I could. "I'm already pulled too thin."

"It's that client that's abusing me," Melanie said with a whine. "She's demanding to be seen right away."

As soon as Melanie launched into her story, I thought about Dr. Drama's fuck 'em comment and wondered if I should cut her short and go right to his punchline answer. However Melanie was too distressed for snarky comments. She was breathing rapidly and wringing her hands as she spoke. I had often read stories with descriptions of people wringing their hands, yet I had never actually seen it in real life. But Melanie was repetitively and persistently wringing her hands, right hand with the left hand and then visa versa, to the point where her hands were red from the constant assault.

"You don't understand," Melanie insisted. "You've never had to deal with someone like this."

I didn't know what to say. How would she know what I've had to deal with? She'd stopped listening to me or caring about my feelings months ago, her own unhappiness blocking any interest or sympathy she might have for me or my problems. It obviously wasn't the time to address that issue so I went with a classic question, "What's the problem?"

"It's my cyber stalker, that Jade Peterson lady," she moaned. "She's here. And she's telling the tech a completely fabricated story which puts all the blame on her stupid regular vet! That's me! And nothing she's saying is true. She's crying that she has no money because she's spent thousands at my clinic, but she hasn't. She refused most testing and treatment and while her bill is hundreds of dollars she hasn't paid any of it."

"Is she just a con woman?" I asked. "I got completely fooled by one of them last year."

Melanie looked at me with anguished eyes and said, "I guess so. Before she turned the attack on me I thought she might be a Munchausen by proxy patient, you know one of those people with mental health issues who make their children, or in this case pet, sick for the attention. For sure she did absolutely nothing to prevent problems and then totally freaked out when her pets got sick! She constantly needed to be the center of attention of absolutely everyone. In fact one day she grabbed our poor cleaning lady and started crying and begging HER for help. Poor Sally didn't know what to do! What a monster, neglecting her pets terribly and then having a tantrum when her neglect causes these life-threatening problems. Talk about being totally disconnected to the consequences of her actions, or total lack of any action in her case."

"Okay I'll see her," I agreed reluctantly. "But you'll have to wrangle my cases back here. Promise me you'll keep up with their lab results and radiographs and treatments. And look at my slides!"

"Argg," she groaned. "I'll never enjoy microscope work like you do, but I promise to do whatever you need!"

"You need to find something in the science side of practice that you do enjoy," I advised. "It's a break from all the emotionally charged person to person interactions. And best of all it provides a little order in the chaos; a bit of time where your brain can make sense of the world."

"Whatever you need," she repeated, but didn't act like she agreed with me or had any interest in my advice.

As I walked down the hallway toward the quarantine exam room, I saw Diane Tate, one of my favorite people, checking out at reception. She waved to me and mouthed "Thank you," as I passed by. I smiled and tapped the file I was carrying against my forehead in a mock salute. Diane was a domestic violence survivor who'd stayed with her abuser until he almost killed her, all to protect her cat. Her abuser had been killed and now she ran an informal rescue operation in her home, taking in both dogs and cats of women who had to escape to domestic violence shelters that weren't set up to take pets. I helped her out when I could, like stopping by her house the other day to exam a new rescued kitty and then arranging for her to pick up some antibiotics. Diane was always so appreciative and never abused my help. If I had told her she needed to bring the kitten in, she not only would have done it, she would have been good natured about it and paid her bill.

After donning full protective gear, I walked into the exam room and was beyond shocked and disturbed. The poor puppy was blown up like a balloon. At first I thought there must have been some kind of chest trauma and it was air under the skin, but as soon as I touched the pup I could tell it was fluid. It wasn't blood, but I couldn't imagine what it was until I found a needle hole on the back of the neck leaking a watery fluid. Obviously someone, most likely Melanie, had set the woman up to give the pup sub-Q, i.e. under the skin, fluids at home, but this lady had given way too much or given it way too often.

In horror, I spun around to face the woman who winced at my expression and immediately whined, "I kept giving her the fluids, but she's not getting any better. It's what that stupid doctor at Consolidated said to do."

Before I could think of a proper retort, the receptionist told me through the door that a woman was in reception and wanted to pay for the plasma that the pup needed. Dagger's constant use of colorful language had ruined me. The only words I could think of for this entire odd, and getting odder, situation was shit show! There was no way this was going to work out well for me or the clinic. And worst of all I couldn't imagine a way it was going to work out to help the poor puppy.

The client overheard enough that she demanded that this woman be allowed into the room so she could speak to her, but I explained that she had already contaminated our reception area once by dragging the virus laden puppy inside, even though we instructed her to wait with the puppy in her car. We surely weren't going to compound the damage by allowing additional people in and out of the contaminated room to spread it further.

I tried three different ways to explain how complicated the situation was now. I emphasized that while plasma may certainly be part of the therapy that this puppy needed, like she'd been told days ago, it was a tiny part of the overall care the critical puppy needed now. The Good Samaritan was at least smart enough to come to the hospital and pay directly for the treatment, ensuring that her money didn't disappear into the con woman's pocket, but without commitment to the entire treatment plan it wasn't going to help the suffering patient.

The client didn't pay attention to my explanations and simply kept arguing, her voice rising louder and louder, but she was actually making less and less sense with every word. Finally I held my hand up and demanded, "Stop! You are not in charge and you can't be in charge because you not only don't know what you are talking about, you're showing no care and concern for any of the other patients. Right now you focus on getting control of yourself. I will speak to this woman who is offering to help. I will make a plan to help the puppy. If you refuse the treatment plan I will call for official help because you are torturing this puppy and that is against the law."

"You can't tell me what to do," the woman sneered.

"No I really can't," I said softly. "But they can if I report you. And you have exactly fifteen minutes to make a plan to resolve the issue."

I sometimes wished I could 'escape' from an exam room, maybe because I just needed to be by myself for a minute to think without interruption, or to get treatment started for a critical patient, or because I was anxious to see some pending radiographs or bloodwork results. But this time I truly felt like I had to escape from this owner because she was simply unbearable to deal with. No wonder Melanie was so overwhelmed by her. She had a retort to anything I said, each statement less reality based than the remark before and, even more bothersome, more aggressive as well.

When was a person's behavior so bad that I could say no, I will not deal with them any longer? This poor puppy desperately needed us, but being entangled with this person, who either had mental health issues or substance abuse problems or was simply a money hungry evil con woman, made me feel complicit in the puppy's ongoing torment. More and more people seemed to be taking out their pain and despair on the very professionals trying to help them. I sure didn't know how to change their behavior. Plus after dealing with my mean spirited uncle and my emotionally abusive ex-boyfriend I must have repeated the mantra 'the only person's behavior you can control is your own' a thousand times. If I accepted that I couldn't change her then when could I morally and ethically decide that enough was enough and fire them as a client and totally ban them from the hospital? We could treat the patient if she could find family or friends that would take responsibility for the care, but people like her had usually burned their bridges with family and former friends long ago and no one that knew them wanted to deal with them any more than I did.

I blessed the fact that I worked at a large multi-doctor practice with numerous support staff and solved my immediate dilemma by turning her over to my hospital manager. I updated Molly on all the craziness, gave her a detailed medical plan for the puppy, and told her she had fifteen minutes to negotiate a solution before I reported the woman for cruelty.

I took a huge deep cleansing breath and returned to the treatment area to help my other patients. I couldn't find Melanie and it turned out that she had left the minute her shift was over. I couldn't believe that she had not chosen the much more expected and socially appropriate response of waiting to check in with me, the person who had done her this huge favor. The good news was that all my tests were done and written up in the records, and all appropriate treatments had been initiated. I still had to communicate with my owners, but I was happy to do that. Not only would the clients prefer the continuity of hearing from the same doctor; it allowed me to reconnect with them now that I had more answers, so that we could review our plans together. But I wondered if Melanie had even considered the owners or my feelings. If I thought that I wanted to escape this one horrible client, it seemed like Melanie was constantly trying to escape everything and everyone associated with her profession.

When I finished my phone calls, Molly bustled up to me and,

rolling her eyes, exclaimed, "Oh my gosh! Unbelievable. She has to be the most appalling human being that I've ever had to deal with. She made my stomach turn."

"I'm so sorry," I commiserated. "I would have held on longer, but I have all these other patients."

"Well," Molly said with a surprising grin. "I think I arranged a miracle. The Good Samaritan lady took ownership of the puppy and agreed to the entire treatment plan. The puppy's already out in isolation on an IV!"

"They both signed all the legal forms?" I asked in complete disbelief.

"Yep!" Molly said. "It felt like I was making no headway with her and then two police officers in uniform walked in to pick up K-9 officer Mace after his knee surgery. Then suddenly she couldn't sign quick enough to resolve the problem."

I chuckled, wondering if she thought that I had made good on my threat to call the authorities, and if that had anything to do with her sudden bout of conscience, and said, "That was beyond lucky timing!"

CHAPTER ELEVEN

"Dr. Kat! Dr. Kat!" I heard the loud call as soon as I left the exam room. I scanned the waiting room...I mean the reception area. We weren't supposed to acknowledge that waiting was a part of emergency practice, even though it definitely was and always would be. Patients in crisis come in unpredictable bunches no matter how much we try to schedule and control the flow. I saw Suzie frantically waving at me from across the room and then she raised Puff up into the air to demonstrate her limp body.

"Did you give her the pred?" I inquired, jogging towards her, checking if Puff had already started her emergency drugs.

"Yes," she replied desperately. "And when she didn't respond I repeated it because I didn't know what else to do for the drive down here."

"I'll take her in back, get her electrolytes running STAT as well as the other bloodwork, and give her steroids IV," I explained in shorthand. Puff had been diagnosed with Addison's disease a year ago and had suffered with a particularly fragile form of the disease so Suzie had become an expert on her dog's problems and treatments. Suzie was another one of my favorite clients, so kind, nurturing and attentive to the changing needs of her fluffy little mixed breed dog and yet equally warm and thoughtful to me and my entire staff. That combination made her the perfect advocate for a pet that suffered with complicated and at times rapidly changing medical issues. But today was a little frustrating because it was the third Addisonian crisis we'd had to deal with in the last few months. After the second crisis I had even called my endocrinology professor at Purdue, who, after reviewing my diagnostic and treatment plan, gave me wise advice and practical suggestions, but basically encouraged me to proceed on the course I'd set.

I turned Puff over to Tabby with instructions to come get me the minute the electrolytes were available, and went back to Suzie to put our brains together to figure out what was causing these crashes.

I started with a basic review, "Addison's is an endocrine problem in which the adrenal glands no longer function. The two adrenal layers do two different jobs, one makes the hormones that help deal with stress while the other makes the hormones that regulate the body's electrolytes."

"Right," Suzie nodded and then held out her hands in a classic questioning pose and asked, "And?" Her expression saying that I had given this explanation more than once in the past.

"And we'll know in a couple minutes which hormones we aren't compensating for properly," I replied.

"And if her kidneys are failing again?" she asked anxiously.

"Remember that her kidneys aren't exactly failing even when her kidney blood values are sky high," I explained. "They just can't do their job when Puff gets low electrolytes because without the sodium and chloride the body can't process the water correctly. But the kidneys will respond very quickly as soon as we start her on the proper fluids. Of course if you weren't as attentive as you are and the crisis went on too long, then her kidneys could be permanently damaged."

"So what's been going on with Puff? And with your household?" I asked. "Sam out of town again?"

"Things have been pretty normal," Suzie answered thoughtfully. "Sam's been out of town for a week, but he's always traveled a lot and Puff doesn't seem particularly stressed when he's gone. She likes to sit in his lap, watching TV and sharing his snacks, but she always seems perfectly happy to sit in my lap instead when he's gone."

"Hmmm," I responded, wracking my brain. "Am I right? Was

Sam out of town during the last two crises?"

She said, "I think so."

"But she doesn't seem stressed?" I asked.

"No," she replied. "Plus I gave her a little more pred like you told me to last time."

"That's right," I started to reply, but Suzie excitedly interrupted, "Absolutely he was out of town during each crisis, because I always have to drive down here by myself!"

"So what does he do differently with Puff?" I asked triumphantly. I was certain this was a key question even though I could not imagine what exactly could affect Puff so profoundly.

Tabby rushed in with raised eyebrows and shoved the electrolyte report under my nose.

I nodded at Suzie and held up a finger, turned to Tabby and instructed, "Start the saline solution. I'll be back there in a minute."

"So it's the mineralocorticoid that's off? The one that we tested and tested?" Suzie asked confused.

"Well, we'll have to evaluate that medication, but I think it's something else," I replied, rerunning everything Suzie had said in a loop in my mind. Snacks. She had said Sam shared his snacks with Puff.

"Snacks?" I asked. "What does he give her and do you feed her the same thing?"

Suzie blushed and replied with a low voice, "Potato chips. He shares his potato chips. And no, I don't. I might give her a couple of pieces of her dog food, but I don't give her any people food. I was told not to when she was a puppy."

"And that's great advice nine hundred and ninety nine times out of a thousand, but in this one very rare case, the potato chips must be giving her the added salt that she needs. You can either give her the same number of potato chips when he's gone, or you can stop the chips altogether and salt her food if that is easier."

Suzie started laughing, half in relief and half in the absurdity of potato chips being our answer. I soon joined in and we laughed together until I had to go check on Puff. I really wanted to grab a pad and actually write out a prescription for 'ten potato chips' daily, just to forevermore be able to brag that I wrote an Rx for potato chips! But sadly, while Dr. Blackwell told stories about the old days of writing prescriptions for all sorts of things like 'keep splint clean and dry' or 'feed only the special prescription diet' to elevate the instruction's importance to the status of prescribing a drug, i.e. giving the orders additional gravitas to force compliance. But now the seriousness of the drug crisis in humans precludes that practice. Prescription pads are numbered and tracked and we can no longer use written prescriptions in any other way. Too bad, no Rx for potato chips for me!

Everything abruptly slowed down after Puff was stabilized. Suzie even ran out to the nearby drug store and bought a bag of her husband's favorite brand of potato chips which led to another round of hilarity as I made a big deal out of adding potato chips to Puff's treatment sheet.

I took advantage of the break in the action and checked my email. I tried to keep any personal problems from impacting my professional hours, but since I never even attempted in any way to keep my professional concerns from impacting my personal time I felt it was only fair to risk a little long lost brother drama during my down time at work. If more emergencies arrived I had already proven that I would immediately leap into action and leave my personal concerns behind.

Andrei had given a brief but pointed reply:

Kat, I was in the Marines. I wasn't that hard to track down if you had ever tried.

I immediately replied:

Andrei, I knew you wanted to join the Marines, but I never heard that you did. I was so desperate that Jane (my best friend) and I tried calling both Parris Island and San Diego multiple times, but they wouldn't tell us anything. Finally someone told us recruits can't get phone calls and we'd have to call the Red Cross if it was an emergency. We didn't want to get you in trouble if we lied about an emergency to get their help so we assumed you'd call us as soon as the phone restriction was lifted.

I was so surprised when Andrei replied right back:

Kat, I called the second we were allowed to. I called the house at all times of the day, left messages, until finally the landline was disconnected. Then I wrote letters. I tried. What's wrong with you, of course I know who Jane is. I even wrote to you once in care of Jane's Dad. I don't doubt that Uncle Evil tried to control my access, but some of it must have gotten through before you legally blocked me from trying. The only reason I can even legally email you now is that my lawyer found out it's no longer valid.

Legally blocked him? What did that even mean?

Tessa called up the stair well, "Dr. Kat? We have patients and a gentleman who refuses to talk to anyone but you."

"I'm coming," I replied as I quickly typed back to Andrei.

Uncle got so weird after you left, we never knew what he was going to do. We were never allowed to use the phone or touch the mail. He told us that we had messed up some important financial deal and could no longer be trusted. Then he changed and said it was for our own safety, to keep us from being hurt. And what do you mean I blocked you? I had no way to block anyone. I have to go now. I have emergencies. I may not get a chance to write back until tomorrow.

I hit send without reviewing it and flew down the stairs two at a time to make up for the moment I took to answer Andrei. I recognized the man in the waiting room as someone I had taken care of on my last shift. He had vociferously and rather obnoxiously blamed his regular veterinarian for selling him flea medication that didn't work because he, the owner, was getting bit by fleas every time his dog sat in his lap.

It hadn't been a real emergency, since the dog was perfectly fine, so my guess was that the owner had been using us as a simple second opinion. Dr. Whiney Lazybones (or as others called him intern Dr. Harris) hated having to see second opinions through the emergency service, but I didn't mind. Most of the time I could reassure anxious clients that therapy was on track, and explain that full recovery simply takes longer than any of us would like. Although sometimes the failure of a patient to respond to an appropriate treatment was the very clue we needed to solve the mystery and diagnose a rare disease. Of course there also could be the frustrating situation where the owner didn't give the prescribed medication, or didn't follow instructions like using an E-collar or restricting activity, etc., and questioned the diagnosis instead of facing the reality that treatment can't work if it's not given.

In this case the dog's skin had been pristine, no sign of inflammation or self-trauma, and on a detailed exam including scrapings and cytology, I had found absolutely no evidence of fleas or any other parasite. So I had tried to talk the gentleman into going to his own physician to check out his own skin issue, but he acted disgusted by my suggestion and pointedly stopped listening to me, pouting silently until his paperwork was done and he could leave.

When I entered the reception area, he raised his right hand high into the air with his thumb and forefinger pinched together and excitedly shouted across the room, "I caught one! I have it! You'll have to believe me now!"

I hustled across the room and softly said, "I believed you, but it wasn't safe to double up on flea medication since your dog was already on modern parasite control and I couldn't find proof it wasn't working! Remember we talked at length about the fleas spending most of their time in the environment?"

"But I only get bit after he's been on my lap," he replied querulously.

I reached over the counter and grabbed a piece of clear tape. I didn't want the bug escaping before I could determine what it was. As soon as I trapped it out from between his fingers I knew it wasn't a flea, definitely wrong shape and size, and with a brief explanation I headed to the back and my favorite microscope. He made as if to follow me but I shook my head, held up my hand in the classic stop sign, and simply said, "No!" I'm the least confrontational person I know, but I swear people have no boundaries anymore and use no common sense. I had told him I was going to exam it microscopically and that I would be right back. In no way was that an invitation to go with me!

I put the tape on a slide, relaxed at the microscope, and took a deep cleansing breath. This guy's persistence and need to be proven right was really frustrating.

I put the tape trapped bug under the lens and adjusted the focus. It wasn't a flea, it was a louse! Which was just as confusing because lice are so much easier to kill than fleas so that modern flea control medication controls them as well. Some companies test for their products ability to kill lice and some don't bother, so it may or may not be listed on the package, but I could still be confident the dog wasn't the source of the infection. The owner swore there were no other pets in the home so I decided to identify the exact species so I would have more information. For example if it was a swine louse I could ask him if any of his friends had a pet pig. Our parasite identification book showed it was a sucking louse (versus a biting louse) and I noted it had an almost round body and two pairs of very thick legs with large claws. I flipped between the pages in the identification book looking for those features, starting with the dogs and cats and then expanding into all the other species, but none of the lice had the proper anatomical features until the very last page. Under the heading of 'human sucking louse that can be misidentified as a veterinary parasite' was *Pthirus pubis*, the human pubic louse, and it was the exact picture of the louse under my microscope.

I straightened up away from the eye pieces, took a deep breath, and then looked again. Yep, it was a pubic louse. This guy had crabs and was trying to blame his dog who had absolutely nothing to do with it. Lice are very species specific, which meant there was no catching it from anything except from some other human. I started to laugh quietly. Potato chips to save lives and telling obnoxious people that they have a sexually transmitted human disease, this didn't feel like practicing veterinary medicine. Instead it felt like being a player in the theatre of the absurd. I soberly made my way up front and quietly said, "Let's step into the exam room to discuss this."

He not only didn't follow me, he stepped back away from me and loudly proclaimed, "I'm right aren't I? And you don't want to admit it where everyone can hear. That expensive flea medicine is worthless and you're just covering up for them."

"No," I said softly. "It's not fleas. And your dog has nothing to do with it."

"Then what is it?" he retorted.

"Let's step into an exam room," I repeated, taking a couple steps toward the room.

"No! Tell me now what my dog has!" He glared at me and childishly stamped his foot in emphasis as he spoke.

"I told you it's not your dog's problem," I said emphatically. "It's a human parasite. Please step into the room."

"No!" he shouted, foamy saliva gathering at his lips. "Tell me!"

"You sir have crabs!" I stated loudly. "Pubic lice."

He stood in stunned silence and then in a more conversational tone asked, "Then why was I getting bit when he was in my lap?"

"I truly don't know," I replied quietly. "My guess would be something to do with his higher body heat activating the lice to move."

"Then where did I get them?" he asked in an oddly accusatory voice.

"From a human," I said quietly. "It's a human disease."

"I need a handout about this," he said in a demanding tone.

"I'm sorry," I said as I turned to leave. "I don't have handouts on human diseases. Call your physician."

The rest of my shift, as Dagger would say, was straight and normal. Puff responded well to her therapy. We had a great plan to hopefully prevent any more crises from occurring and she would go home in the morning. I chuckled my entire walk home. It may have been theater of the absurd, but I still managed to help both pets.

CHAPTER TWELVE

I happily strolled through the undeveloped outdoor space situated between my apartment and the main hospital, the same area I used to call the badlands. I had discovered poor Max discarded here, wounded and starved, so I was impatient for the land to be healed and flourish just like my sweet boy had! I try to think of it as 'the garden' now, although tons of work had to be done before it deserved that title. But a lot of us had put sweat equity into the transformation effort and slowly we were making progress against piles of trash, abundant rocks, and rampant weeds.

The only reason I was heading to work at six in the morning was to catch up on a bunch of paperwork from my last few shifts. After a single month splitting my time between primary care and emergency shifts, I was switching to strictly emergency work because one of the doctors was off work recovering from a car accident. I was happy to help out my colleague and the switch to a single service would certainly simplify my life, but it still felt important to start my new schedule fresh with all my primary care paperwork done.

But first I had to retrieve my notebook from the training building where I'd left it after a meeting I had attended. And while all of the doctors and many of the techs used an iPad, financial issues forced me to work old school and take handwritten notes and carry them around in actual folders. But the research collected there was equally necessary for my productive day to day case management.

I was surprised that the training facility was pitch black. I guess I'd never beaten the trainers to the building before. I had my keys so it was no problem and Gemma told me last night that she left my notebook on her desk so it should be a quick in and out. I slid my key in and turned it as usual, but didn't hear the classic click, so I turned it the other way and felt the latch catch and the door wouldn't open. So I turned it back again and it swung open. It was beyond weird that it was unlocked; normally everyone in the entire complex was very security conscious.

The bank of light switches by the back door was huge, so I just started flipping them on and off in order until I finally lit up a couple of small lights in the area by the desk. As I walked over, the hair on the back of my neck started to raise, but I dismissed the warning and berated my hypersensitive self for worrying about every miniscule thing. I wished Max were with me. Not only would I have some protection, I would have his more sensitive ears, eyes and nose, so if he alerted I would at least know I wasn't imagining things.

After a couple more careful steps, I noticed Gemma's chair pulled out from behind the desk, moved awkwardly close to the wall, and I fearfully reacted, startling to the point of even throwing my hands out like I was about to fall. There was someone just sitting there, not moving, with their arms uncomfortably pressed into the arms of the chair, head drooping yet still staring past me to the right. I spun around, but there wasn't anybody there, and then I spun back, but the figure hadn't moved.

"Gemma?" I asked quietly, not wanting to surprise her, then continued louder. "Gemma, what's wrong?'

I took another couple of steps closer and demanded, "GEMMA! What are you doing?"

I wished I had turned more lights on. I wished I had turned all the lights on. I took another step and could just make out that it wasn't Gemma. It was Melanie and I swore she was taped to the chair with pink self-adherent wrap and white medical tape, but that couldn't be true. I looked over my shoulder again, picked up one of the bars used in the agility jumps and held it in front of me in some attempt at protection, and then took another step closer. Her face was so odd, angled to one side, her eyes wide open and unblinking.

One more step and I reached up to my neck to grab my stethoscope, only it wasn't there because my day hadn't really started yet, and all I could think was that she wasn't breathing. I dug through my pockets for the stethoscope and slipped it into my ears as my chest heaved with shock and concern. I took the final two steps up to her and placed the stethoscope over her chest, hearing no heartbeat or breath sounds. I let it fall and then jerked it out of my ears, trying to make some kind of sense out of what I was seeing.

Her arm wasn't just taped to the chair, there was an IV stand behind her with an IV line running from a bag of fluids. And what was it with the tape? It was if the IV line had been taped into her arm and then the arm of the chair had been wrapped up as well, as if the person who had done this had just gone insane. There was an empty measured injection port as well, and the line leading from that medicine reservoir showed a blue medicine. That didn't make any sense. None of it made any sense. I couldn't even think of one IV medicine that was blue. The euthanasia solution we use is blue, but it's specifically and artificially colored blue so that no one ever mistakes it for something else. I touched her neck since I couldn't get to her wrist to take a pulse. Oh my God, she was so cold. And no pulse.

I tried to take a couple deep breaths to somehow bring my shocked brain back into use. I told myself that Melanie was a person so I needed to get her people help. Then my brain tried to stop me, to bring me back to the reality where I knew that there was no help for Melanie, but the idea had lodged inside my brain that I had to call 911 and they would help her. I grabbed my phone, fumbled with the lock a couple times to open it and then was finally able to punch in 911.

When the dispatcher asked, "What is your emergency?" I struggled to speak, then finally begged, "I need an ambulance. Right now. I need an ambulance right now. No, maybe I don't need an ambulance; I think she's dead. I don't want her to be dead. She wasn't dead yesterday. I worked with her yesterday. I think I need the police. I think someone did this to her, she's all taped up."

The dispatcher asked for the address and then started to talk me through first aid response until I told her she was cold and stiff already. She asked if she was deceased, beyond help, and I said yes as my heart broke. She directed me to wait for emergency services outside the building so that I could direct them through our parking lot maze. I was glad she told me to stay on the line, because it served as a lifeline for the emotions that were threatening to consume me.

I stepped just outside the door and took deep breaths of the fresh air. Dr. Drama was getting something out of the trunk of his car when he caught sight of me. He grinned and came over to me whistling a jaunty tune. I dreaded speaking, knowing how deeply hurt he was going to be that this horrible thing had happened. It was even worse knowing that it had happened at the hospital complex that he had created out of his dual love of animals and medicine, knowing that as soon as I spoke he wouldn't be whistling jaunty tunes again any time soon.

As he got closer my face must have told the story because his song abruptly stopped, his expression changed to mirror my despair, his step faltered and he simply asked, "Who?"

"Melanie," I answered bleakly.

"Melanie the person?" he asked awkwardly. "Our Melanie?"

I realized he figured out a disaster had occurred, but assumed it was one of our patients that had suffered some kind of accident.

"It's bad," I said. "The police are coming. Don't go in there."

He stared at me as if my words were incomprehensible, then slipped through the doorway into the training facility. I considered following him, but I could hear the approaching sirens and decided to stay put to direct them to the correct building like the dispatcher told me to. And then I screamed and screamed and screamed. I wasn't trying to call for help; I was simply trying to let the pain out before it devoured me from the inside out.

The police arrived first, and then so many more people came to help, but as I told my story over and over again my reality started to warp, nothing felt real. Everything, not just the training facility, was shut down except as the only ER department in the region they allowed confirmed emergencies through one ER entrance. In the beginning I mainly acted to answer technical questions for the detectives, giving them information on equipment and personnel and protocols. The police were kind, but extremely persistent, and the relentless questions made me feel worse and worse. I kept asking questions in return, but no one could or would answer any of them.

The rational part of my brain knew that they were trying to get vital information as quickly as possible to figure out what had happened to Melanie, but I hated the process. I could tell that many of my clients hated answering my questions when I was taking my histories, even when I explained that those facts would form the very vital foundation of our testing and treatment plan. I realized it was the same for police questioning, but it felt intrusive, like they didn't trust me or they wanted to judge or accuse me. I hope my clients never felt that way, I swear every question I ever asked was to gather information crucial to help their pet. I told myself that the police were doing the exact same thing, but it felt like their words were stabbing me in the chest. The hours ground by until Dr. Drama insisted that I be allowed to go home.

The walk home was torture, each step a marathon. All I wanted to do was talk to my house family, but the authorities had asked (demanded?) that I speak to no one. So then all I wanted was to get home, but I dreaded being by myself. I finally made it inside the house, but stopped in the foyer. The single flight of stairs stretched out in front of me and seemed much too tall and steep to tackle. I pictured Max waiting to love on me, the comfy chair I could snuggle up in, the great book I could get lost in, the yummy dessert I could indulge in and absolutely none of it motivated me to take a single step forward. Shame at the possibility of being found frozen downstairs by my housemates started my feet moving, but each step seemed more than I could possibly handle, my energy ebbed low and my legs felt wobbly. And it didn't fit the usual challenge pattern of it getting easier with every step forward; every step was as momentous as the step before.

I let Max out of his kennel and when I saw a note from Ethan saying he had taken Max out for a walk an hour before, gratitude flooded through me that I didn't have to leave now that I was safely home. Then tears filled my eyes and trailed down my face. My legs turned to noodles as I tried to go back to the living room and my entire body started to shake. I slowly sank down next to the wall and slumped forward, my elbows on my thighs and my head in my hands. Then I sobbed as unbearable pain washed over me. Melanie was dead which was unimaginable. Inconceivable. Time distorted around me as I wept and moaned. I struggled to hold on, but I couldn't stop. I wasn't conscious of anything going on around me and only started to come back to time and place when I had to fight to breathe. I focused on my breathing pattern, even though I didn't have enough energy to actually feel anxious, and finally I could feel just a touch of control return.

I sat up and rested my head back onto the wall and discovered Max sitting directly in front of me as still as a statue with an expectant expression on his face. Between us was every single toy that we owned: soft lovey toys, hard chew toys, outside balls, rope tug toys, toys I'd forgotten we had. I wish I could say that I was organized and they all lived in a basket somewhere in the apartment, but I had never gotten around to it. The toys were perpetually scattered in every room, under every piece of furniture, buried in chairs and sofas, hidden in closets. He must have single-mindedly hunted them all down, trying desperately to find the one that would bring me back to normal. I had always given him lots of praise and warm regard when he had a toy, in part because he was adorable, but mostly because a dog with a toy in his mouth doesn't have room to have something of mine in there instead. My past behavior must have convinced him that toys were very important to me as well, and thus would be the proper offering in the face of profound grief and heartache.

Max swept his tail across the bedroom carpet in a cautious wag, opened his mouth in a gentle pant, and locked his gaze on my face.

"Thank you, Max," I said softly.

He jumped up in relief, searched the toys in front of him, picked his favorite lovey toy and presented it to me. I threw it feebly a few times, and praised him as best I could, but I knew I wasn't fooling him. He tried to up his game, tossing the toy over his head, even batting it with his foot which usually made me laugh. I tried as long as I could to convince him I was okay, but finally gave up, crawling into bed and curling up into a tight ball. Max jumped up on the bed with me, snuggling close, and I passed the rest of the day and night surfing wild waves of grief and pain.

CHAPTER THIRTEEN

The first days after Melanie's death passed in an excruciating surreal state of flux. The hospital complex was still partially shut down, but my shifts in emergency continued. While I didn't make any mistakes or fail to complete any paperwork, I couldn't actually remember half of what I did. Our owners, Drs. Vincent, Blackwell and Tolliver, were being supportive of all of us. They even shortened our regular emergency shifts and joined the rotation so we didn't feel smothered by the weight of the entire complex.

The shear shock of finding Melanie's body was slowly wearing off, but the sorrow of her loss and the fear that none of us were safe grew with every passing day. Not only did we feel like we needed to use the buddy system any time we went outside, many of us brought our own dogs to work and tried to include our canine protectors on every outdoor trip, especially at night.

The authorities instructed us not to discuss anything to do with Melanie or her death, but Stretch and I couldn't help confiding in each other. We'd both been questioned by the police at the hospital and then again more officially at the police department in downtown Noblesville. I had felt judged and maybe even suspected of something nefarious on the first day, but since then they made me feel more like I was simply being helpful to the investigation. Stretch on the other hand was becoming more and more anxious every time they wanted to speak to him. He felt that their attitude was increasingly accusatory, and complained that they had him repeat the stories of his recent exchanges with Melanie over and over again.

"Did the police ask to speak to you again today?" I asked Stretch when we had a quiet moment after rounds.

"No," he replied with a puzzled look. "Did they ask you?"

"Yes," I said. "They said they had more questions about the IV equipment. But at least they want to do the interview here so that I can demonstrate on the machines."

"I don't understand what their thought process is," Stretch said miserably. "I swear they suspect I had something to do with Melanie's death. They keep coming back to the fact that I threw quarters at her after she accused me of taking more than my fair share of the milk."

I grimly chuckled, or maybe it wasn't so much a chuckling sound as more a series of snorts of disdain, and said, "I doubt they truly suspect you. I think they're just stirring everybody up to see what people say under stress."

"My Dad told me not to speak to them again without a lawyer," Stretch said softly. "I know that's the smart thing to do, but it makes me feel guilty of something just to ask for a lawyer."

"I never thought of a lawyer," I said in surprise. "I guess there comes a time when you do need someone on your side. I wonder if I need one too."

We exchanged miserable expressions, shrugged, and then Stretch headed back to the surgery suite. A question dawned on me and I called out to him, "Hey! Did you tell them you threw the quarters at Mel?"

"No, why?" he asked.

"You mentioned the incident at the Interns meeting," I explained. "But you and I didn't tell the police, Taren hasn't been questioned, Melanie couldn't have, so who told them?"

"Well, it happened at the apartment," Stretch said, obviously deep in thought. "So the only other person who could have told them was Quickcut."

"Why would he bring that up?" I asked. "It was such a minor incident."

"I have no idea," he said, exhaling noisily. "I don't know what to think about any of this. Or what I think about anybody. Except you of course."

I sighed heavily and then attempted a smile. I settled for squeezing his arm before he headed back to the surgery area.

There were no emergency cases waiting and my police interview wasn't scheduled for a couple hours so I felt untethered. I couldn't decide what to do. I considered texting Andrei again, just to vent about losing Melanie. But I wasn't sure I could handle facing family issues at the same time I was trying to come to terms with Mel's death.

I decided to work with my collection of blood and cytology slides. It felt calming to lose myself in the microscope work. When a report from the cytologist came back, I tried to reconcile my opinion on the slide with what the specialist described. I had learned so much in just one year doing this and I was determined to keep it up no matter how busy I got.

After studying ten slides, I paused to do a couple neck exercises. Turns out microscope neck was right up there with tech neck for, well, being a royal pain in the neck for me. I stretched my neck from side to side and caught Dr. Blackwell's eye from where she was working at her desk.

As Dr. Blackwell walked over she said, "I'm glad you love hematology and cytology like I do."

"You're good at it," I said.

"I wasn't when I started, but ever since one of my vet school professors challenged me to make a slide for every blood test I sent out, I've done exactly that," she explained. "Plus I find microscope time gives me a moment's peace in the middle of the chaos of practice. In the weirdest way it helps emotionally sustain me."

Speaking of weirdness, tears gathered in my eyes and I had to carefully hold my eyes still without blinking so that they didn't spill out. After a brief pause I said, "Well, you're the mentor that taught me to do that a year ago," but didn't explain that Melanie had resisted the advice and felt quite differently. And now I'd never have a chance to convince her.

Without having a clue about what was going on inside me,

Dr. Blackwell chuckled and said, "I guess that makes my mentor your grand-mentor! I was so fortunate to have the best clin path instructors, but it was my own Dr. Drama worthy moment that sealed my love of cytology."

"Tell me," I urged as I relaxed on my stool, smiling at her creation of the grand-mentor concept as well as her use of my Dr. Drama nickname.

"I was in my equine rotation," she said leaning back, obviously happy to reminisce. "I was assisting the equine surgeon in the large animal medicine barn and we were working up a beautiful dapple grey gelding. The poor horse was pawing and leaning in the stocks, obviously suffering, and we suspected some kind of colic, a true abdominal emergency. So the surgeon took some fluid from the abdomen for cytology and to speed things up he had me hand carry the sample to the clinical pathologist."

I nodded to urge her on and she continued, "So I took the sample, jogged through the corridor, entered the main building, went down the hallway, up a couple flights of stairs, down another hallway into his office. I explained what was going on so he dropped what he was doing and prepped the slide, then we both sat at the double headed microscope. He explained everything he was seeing, using the pointer to be sure I saw every detail including the toxic cells, which were particularly bad news for the horse. I took meticulous notes as he spoke so that I could repeat every point to the surgeon, but as I started to leave, the clinical pathologist added, 'This is severe toxicity. I'm surprised this horse isn't dead.' So in concern, I ran back down the hallway, flinging myself down the stairs skipping steps, through the hallway, into the corridor to the large animal clinics, but as I rounded the corner and entered the procedure room, I saw the horse shudder and collapse in the stocks. I hurried over to help pull him out and we attempted to do CPR, but he was dead."

I shook my head in amazement and asked, "What did you do?"

"That's the best part of the story," she said. "The minute the surgeon pronounced the horse dead, I lit out through the large animal hospital, back to clin path at a dead run, yelling 'The horse is dead! The horse is dead!' like I was Paul Revere reincarnated. I ran all the way back down the hallway, up the stairs, through the hallway, and into his office still yelling, completely out of breath, but not stopping because it was such an epiphany that the cells on a simple slide could really have told him so much information. I never fell out of love with looking at slides after that experience."

"I love it too," I agreed. "And while I haven't had a case that exciting or perfectly timed, I have been able to get patients specific help long before the reports were back. And I agree with you, I get that same oddly peaceful feeling during microscope work as well."

Dr. Blackwell patted my shoulder, smiling regretfully, and said, "We all must find ways to take care of ourselves and each other."

"Someone had to have done this to her," I replied, leaping to the conclusion she was referencing Melanie.

"Yes," she agreed. "But somehow it has to be connected to her mental health issues. I don't know how. Maybe the choices she was making put her in jeopardy?"

"Do you think so?" I asked.

"I don't know what to think," she said sadly as she turned to go upstairs. "I really don't."

I went over to the pharmacy area to see if any emergencies were waiting, but we were still caught up. I thought about calling Phil and asking about the whole lawyer situation. He may be my apartment manager and housemate, but he was also my go to person for all things law and order related. Then I realized that I might be able to catch him out in the parking lot. Phil, being exceptionally protective despite his advancing years and health challenges, had reacted to our situation by patrolling our parking lot area every morning and evening instead of taking his usual walking route down the alley. He insisted that a lifetime in a service profession like police work, dedicated to taking care of people, did not end with retirement. He needed to do what he could to keep us all safe.

I let Tessa, my favorite receptionist, know that I would be out in the parking lot and went looking for Phil. He was at the far end of the lot and looked like he had a gang of helpers with him. Last year Dag had befriended three semi-homeless veterans that he called the Jays because they were named Jim, John, and Jack. After Dag discovered drug dealing and other dangerous criminal activity in the alley behind our houses, he and the Jays had worked hard to physically clean up the area, focusing mainly on discarded drug paraphernalia, specifically to keep the neighborhood children safe. They also helped him clean up the neighborhood in another way by gathering the evidence that led to the arrest and prosecution of the dealers. Sadly two of the people arrested were Maisy's husband and son, and while I felt sorry for Maisy who knew nothing about their criminal behavior, it was difficult to have any sympathy for her husband who had maliciously hurt so many people. I didn't know what to think about her son. He was an entitled ass hat, in Dag's colorful lexicon, but I had to believe he wouldn't have done it if his father hadn't entangled him in that despicable world.

When Dag left for his vital secret mission, or his wild vacation of debauchery, whichever it was, Phil had taken over watching out for the Jays. He gave them jobs at the apartment complex and after that went better than expected, he let them rent one of the complex's apartments at a special rate. It looked like now Phil had roped them into watching out for us as well.

As I headed in their direction, the large automatic ER doors whooshed open and two technicians pushed a wheeled stretcher outside with a large German Shepherd securely strapped to it. The poor dog was breathing so hard that I could still hear him even though the man was shouting on one side and the woman was screaming on the other side. I quickened my pace as the technicians' expressions beseeched me for help.

The woman turned and aggressively screamed at Tabitha in

an unexpected personal attack, "You're a liar! You don't know what's wrong with him so we're going to take him to someone who can fucking figure it out. You stupid, ugly, fat ass girls don't know what the hell you're doing."

Her husband continued the tirade, shouting an even more disgusting rant, chock full of profanity and body shaming attacks, but actually making no sense. Not one word had anything to do with their dog or veterinary medicine. It was pure venom whose only purpose was to stop Tabitha from repeating whatever she was trying to tell them. And worst of all, the unreasonable attack was successful because there was absolutely nothing relevant or appropriate that I could reply to or clarify, so I was effectively rendered mute as well.

"How about you shut the fuck up," Phil bellowed at the surprised man as he hustled up. The Jays strategically placed themselves around Phil and glared aggressively at the couple, who immediately ducked their heads, shut their mouths, and sheepishly tried to get their dog off the stretcher and into their truck.

I asked Tabatha, "What's going on?"

"They've refused all tests and treatments, then demanded to leave against medical advice." she replied sadly. "I started the AMA paperwork and they turned their fury on me! Why did they come to the hospital in the first place if they were just going to refuse all tests and treatments?"

The Jays hissed their muffled commentaries in the background, "Idiots!" "Bullshit!" "Fucking stupid shit!"

The owners finished loading the poor dog and screeched out of the parking lot.

The technicians and I stood there defeated and trying not to cry, while Phil and the Jays were red faced and shaking with anger. We stared at each other, all of us realizing what an impossible situation it was. It felt so hopeless; no response by any of us would do anything to help the dog.

Proving that the men's protective responses did however help the technicians, Tabitha turned toward them and said gratefully, "Thank you so much for standing up for us."

Phil assured her, "You didn't deserve any of that. I don't know what their real problem is, but their behavior simply can't be tolerated in a hospital setting or you won't be able do your job for the rest of your patients. Nobody could."

"Thank you," Tabatha repeated. "I just can't imagine what I could have done or said to have them feel such hate for me."

Phil snorted and said, "As someone much smarter than I said, 'Never attribute to malice that which can be adequately explained by stupidity.' Not your fault, they didn't actually feel hate for you. They had absolutely no desire to understand what you were saying because then they'd have to admit they'd made mistakes and were now suffering the consequences."

Tessa came to the door and motioned for us to come inside. I gave Phil a quick hug and then thanked him and the Jays one more time. I dejectedly entered the hospital. I was ashamed that I had not stood up for my technicians, and even more frustrated that I really hadn't even considered saying something like Phil did at the time. I had tried to weed out any medical issues from what they were saying so that I could address those concerns, possibly clarify our recommendations. I was confident I could explain medical facts or hospital protocol to them. But I never once considered that I was allowed to tell them to shut up. I really wish that the wonderful pets we take care of could bring themselves to the hospital to see us when their owners were so self-absorbed and hateful.

CHAPTER FOURTEEN

The fuzzy brown puppy was adorable! In fact he looked like an itty bitty version of my Max, but he wasn't acting like a typical rambunctious doodle puppy. He was lying on the table and looking up at me with soulful eyes when he should have been wiggling and bouncing and biting me with his little razor sharp teeth. Of course I love working on easy patients, but I'd learned the hard way that an extra quiet, easy-to-exam puppy was often a very sick puppy.

I discovered rapidly that the sweet puppy had pale mucus membranes with a rapid heart rate and I made a presumptive diagnosis of anemia. And while I could be fooled by a couple other diagnoses, statistically in a puppy a likely cause was a rampant case of intestinal parasites that were sucking out way more red blood cells than the baby blood system could replace.

"Has the puppy been dewormed?" I asked the worried owner. "Or has he started heartworm preventative? I mean parasite protection."

Everyone in the veterinary world was trying to switch to calling the multipurpose medication, which both prevented heartworms and treated intestinal worms, parasite protection instead of the old fashioned restrictive term of heartworm prevention. I was absolutely dedicated to controlling intestinal worms, which had important human health significance since they are the second leading cause of preventable blindness in children. But I still struggled to make the title switch!

"Yes," the owner replied, pulling out the puppy's record to show me. "He was dewormed as a baby and we gave him his first preventative pill the day we brought him home."

"Hmmm," I said. "We'll need to take a blood sample to get more answers."

"Whatever it takes," she said with a worried smile. "I already love him like he's one of my kids."

Tabitha took the pup while I went over the initial plan with the owner. She was pretty certain he couldn't have eaten anything dangerous, but quickly agreed we could take X-Rays to be absolutely sure.

I settled in on the tall stool at the microscope to evaluate the blood slide, but it only took the first view of a deformed cell to pop me back off the stool to hustle back into radiology. I took the container of comparison coins out of the drawer as Tabitha brought up the first images of the puppy's abdomen.

"How did you know?" she gasped in amazement, pointing at the four dense white objects on the screen.

"The cells told me," I said with a grin, holding the coins up to match size to be sure one could be a penny. "Yep, it looks like a quarter, a dime and two pennies."

"This one?" Tabitha asked, pointing at the perfectly round one of the proper size.

"Maybe," I said. "I'm more worried about this one, the one that appears to be dissolving. When they started making pennies with a zinc core in 1982, zinc toxicity in pets and children started showing up in large numbers. People mistakenly call it copper toxicity because the pennies still look copper, but the zinc core is the villain. You could take a chance of an old penny passing, but you can't do that with modern zinc pennies. We'll have to stabilize the pup and then head to endoscopy and maybe even to surgery. But we have to get the pennies out as soon as possible."

Dr. Blackwell walked into radiology and I pointed at the penny on the image and said, "You should see the slide!"

She gave me a high five and said, "Nice! You should be happy with that catch! I was coming over to check on you. You looked so sad earlier."

I told her about the nasty couple yelling at Tabitha in

the parking lot and asked, "What's wrong with people? It was such a personal targeted attack. Is it because we appear vulnerable since we're so empathetic and trying so hard to be compassionate? Or are they being horrible just because they assume they can get away with it? Or is it just because we're women?"

"I don't know," she said sadly. "I don't know if trying so hard to be accommodating and compassionate has contributed to the increased abuse or if the feminization of the profession makes us appear defenseless. Or maybe it's not about us at all and it's just the deterioration of society. But it's getting unbearable."

"You were part of that first wave of significant numbers of female vet students," I said. "Was there abuse of the women graduates back then?"

Dr. Blackwell paused to consider her answer and then explained, "It was definitely different for us in the 70s. Women were just starting to be accepted to veterinary school in higher numbers, more than the occasional female acceptance that was," she paused to make air quotes, "the exception to prove the rule that veterinarians needed to be male."

"And how was your experience?" I asked with a frown, remembering some stories I'd heard.

"It was mixed," she replied with a sad smile. "Medical schools were a bit ahead and I was actively being recruited by the medical school professors at the University of Vermont, so that helped my confidence. It used to make me laugh to think of some future mother finding out that her pediatrician desperately wanted to be a veterinarian, but had to settle for being a physician because she was a woman!"

"That's hilarious, and really quite disturbing," I replied. My vet school class was 80% women as were many of my professors, so I had a completely different experience.

"I was extremely lucky; I was accepted by more than one vet school," she continued. "But I was still shocked when one school sent me a provisional acceptance. The letter clearly stated that if the Equal Rights Amendment passed, then I was accepted. But if the ERA did not pass, then I was not accepted! Can you believe that? What acceptance committee had the balls to write and send a letter like that? I had close to a 4.0 average, back when there was nothing higher than 4.0, and I received a 100% on my VATs! Plus I had experience in a small animal practice, a mixed animal practice, on a dairy farm, and I had exposure to my uncle's farm that raised beef cattle, pigs, and sheep!"

"Very broad experience," I said, impressed. "But what are VATs?"

"An old fashioned admission test for veterinary school, like SATs for college, or the MCAT tests for medical school," Dr. Blackwell.

"And you got a perfect score?" I asked impressed. I had taken GREs for my application process.

"Not exactly," she explained. "It means I scored higher than 100% of the other applicants."

"So how could they have given you a provisional acceptance?" I said. "How could that be legal? How could they live with themselves? Did they feel no shame?"

Dr. Blackwell ruefully shook her head and replied, "It's difficult to explain the culture of the time. It wasn't illegal and everyone, men and women, said that women couldn't be vets. It was just so common that we all begrudgingly accepted it. I wanted to be a veterinarian since I was four years old and it wasn't as if one or two people told me I couldn't do it; hundreds of people over the years told me I couldn't! Even odder they usually added something about how I'd have to like math and science. Maybe I wasn't a huge math fan, but I had always loved science especially biology. No one ever bothered to ask me what subjects I enjoyed or which I was good at. They simply assumed a girl wouldn't be interested in any kind of science."

I shook my head and asked, "How did you stand it?"

"That's the part that is so difficult to explain," Dr. Blackwell said, her face lacking her usual confident expression. "Those comments were expected. If we refused to be discouraged and applied anyway, we certainly weren't surprised or even offended by the rejections because these opinions were so widespread."

"What did you do about that school with the provisional acceptance?" I asked.

She replied, "I had multiple other choices so I refused them outright. With a certain amount of glee."

"Were you treated well in vet school?" I asked.

"Generally I was," she replied. "Some professors were extraordinarily accepting and inclusive, while other individuals made it more difficult. I was still very interested in large animal medicine at that point, but the clinician that took the students out on farm calls didn't want to take the females on call with him. And those farm calls were tremendous opportunities to learn practical large animal medicine! Maybe more importantly they were vitally important to learn what large animal practice was really like. That clinician would take off without the women students, even resorting to sending us on fake errands to make his escape and leave us behind."

"What did you do?" I couldn't imagine being treated like that for any reason at a professional school, much less for being female.

"Well, one of the senior women told me to get to the ambulatory clinic early every morning that I was scheduled with him, steal his medical case, and then take it everywhere I went so he couldn't leave without me," she said with a grin as she remembered.

"Seriously?" I couldn't believe it.

"Yep," she replied. "And it worked. Towards the end of my rotation, he actually taught me a lot. I wasn't picking up on how to palpate cows so he stood right there with me, gave me the time and constant direction until it finally all connected in my brain. It may be why I'm so good at abdominal palpation in dogs, once that fingertip feel/brain connection clicked, it never left my skill set. Which helped me my entire career and there are dogs that owe their diagnosis, maybe even their lives to him. Even though I'm sure he thought his help was completely wasted when I didn't end up in dairy medicine."

"I'm sorry it was so hard for you," I said gently.

"I wasn't an angel in response," she replied with a grimace that transformed to more of a smirk as she remembered. "Large animal veterinarians neuter animals in huge numbers. It became almost a reflex to threaten harassers with some variation of a castration joke! Which was usually told enthusiastically while waving a sharp scalpel around!"

I laughed out loud for a long minute.

"My crowning achievement was portraying one abuser in a skit by waving around a huge electroejaculator that we used on the dairy bulls," she said with a grin.

This time I belly laughed.

"Vet school was quite an adventure back in those days, both in and out of class," she replied, but then her expression turned dark. "And yet I sometimes wonder if it made us more ready for the harshness of practice. These days I worry about the young women in our profession, especially with the problems of suicide and drug addiction, which are such classic indicators of despair! While I'm glad the school environment is now so inclusive and supportive, maybe it makes their later adjustment to practice all the more shocking. They haven't had the experiences that help develop the resilience they need to combat the public's abuse."

"I never thought about it that way," I said. "But I'm still glad the school environment has changed."

"Absolutely agree! Abuse wounds the abused and steals a piece from the soul of the abuser," she said mournfully. "And traumatizes anyone who witnesses it and doesn't do anything to stop it. It injures everyone involved and must be stopped."

I nodded in agreement, but then said, "On the other hand, I had a really rough senior year for other reasons so it would be comforting to think that I'm tougher and more resilient because of it. It would make all that pain seem worthwhile, at least in part."

Dr. Blackwell said warmly, while patting my arm, "I accept that we'll never be able to stop all the abuse out in practice. It's simply people being people in a selfish world, dealing with their own traumas, mental health problems, and addiction issues. So we unquestionably need to stop what can be stopped, but then we should put the rest of our energy into not only surviving, but thriving in the face of what remains."

"That's good advice," I said appreciatively.

"Yes, acceptance is certainly a part of the solution," she agrees. Then she stood up straight and tall and her expression got tougher, "It's also time to start having consequences to bad behavior in our hospitals. The only way to protect our patients is to protect our technicians and ourselves from the truly abusive people. I can promise you this: the era of the fired client has come to this hospital. There's going to be a list of zero tolerance offenses, and another list of three strike offenses, but mark my words we are going to start protecting our people. We'll refuse to serve those that abuse any of us. It may not stop all the abuse, but at least our people will know that we'll stand up for them."

CHAPTER FIFTEEN

"Where are you going to meet with the detectives?" Tess asked, with a weird combination of fear and respect in her voice. "They're waiting in the reception area now."

"I'll see what works for them," I replied calmly. "But I think they want to go to the training facility."

"Do you want me to come over in a bit and check on you?" she asked anxiously.

"No," I assured her, smiling as I headed to the front. "I'm not confused about who the good guys are. They want to find out the truth about who hurt Melanie and I want to know who hurt Melanie even more than they do."

I walked up to the two men in dark blue pants, white shirts, and guns in holsters on their hips, and the taller gentleman asked, "Dr. Kat?" I smiled and he continued, "I'm Detective Strickland and this is Detective Warner."

"Nice to meet you," I said, and then grimaced because I think I met them the day Melanie was killed. When experts say that stress and anxiety blanks out your short term memory, they sure know what they're talking about! I'd seen it often enough in exam rooms after I had to give people bad news, but after finding Melanie's body it feels like I lost even bigger chunks of my memory than was normal.

They both smiled and nodded and I asked, "Did you want to head over to the training facility?"

"Yes," Detective Strickland replied. "No one has been in there, correct?"

Patting my pocket for my keys, I headed toward the front door and replied, "Bunches of your people have come and gone, but none of us as far as I know."

As we approached the training facility door, my heart suddenly started pounding and my mouth went dry. I really did not want to go back in there. I forced myself to keep walking, but I couldn't stop my breathing from becoming louder and increasingly rapid. I tried to do my measured breathing, but I didn't want to be so precise about it that it made me look weird or guilty somehow.

"Let me go in first," Detective Warner said as he appeared at my elbow and took the keys out of my shaking hand. He entered in a way that made him look like Dagger when he was being protective, and immediately flipped on all the lights. He scanned the room intently before moving out of the way so that Detective Strickland and I could come in. Of course, Melanie's body wasn't there, but I didn't realize that the entire IV setup and the chair and all the tape etcetera would be gone as well.

I turned to the detectives and asked, "I thought you wanted me to go over the IV setup again. Where is it?"

"It's all evidence," Detective Strickland replied simply. "Everything is being processed downtown. We assumed you'd have another similar setup you could show us."

"Sure," I said. "But not here. This really isn't part of the medical facilities. Well not exactly. Although more dogs do lose their homes due to behavior issues versus medical problems, so I guess training is a type of preventative medicine. But not the kind of medicine that uses IVs or other medical equipment."

When I looked up at them, they were staring at me with slightly tilted heads like confused puppies, obviously wondering what in the heck I was talking about. I quickly apologized, "Sorry, never mind" took a couple deep breaths and then asked, "Why are we here then?"

"We're going to release the crime scene and let the entire facility open back up today. We want to take this last chance to be sure we understand how this all works," he said. "So where did the IV apparatus come from?"

"Many of our IV stands are portable," I replied. "So it could have come from ICU, or surgery, or cardiology, or even one of the wards. If we're slammed our techs fight to keep their hands on them for their own patients, but on a really crazy day with multiple critical patients they can end up moving around quite a bit."

"Have you ever seen an IV stand here in the training facility?" Strickland asked.

"Never," I replied thoughtfully. After replaying the set up in my mind for a minute I added, "On the other hand, we only have a few measured injection ports and use them mainly in ICU and oncology. Have you checked to see if they're all accounted for?"

This time both detectives looked like dogs who froze and pricked their ears up when they alerted on an important scent or sound. I wondered if they were really reacting like dogs or if I was imagining it all to make the whole situation seem less intimidating to me.

"We should check on that when we go back over to the hospital," Strickland said. "Before we're back in that crazy circus atmosphere, we'd like to hear what you think. Who do you think would want to harm Melanie?"

"No one," I answered quickly. "She is," I had to pause for a second, "she was a really good person. She was going through a hard time, but it's the kind of thing you might roll your eyes over if she was getting tiresome. No one would want to hurt her feelings much less physically harm her."

"How about Lars Larson?" he asked.

"Stretch would never, ever hurt anyone," I insisted. "And at the very worst he was mildly irritated with her. And his very worst response would be to avoid her."

They nodded thoughtfully and Strickland asked, "How about clients?"

"According to my more experienced mentors," I said ruefully, "people in general are getting meaner and more disrespectful. And that includes some of our clients, especially in emergency. We had some creepy guy screaming at our techs just today."

"Did Melanie know him?" he quickly asked.

"I don't think so," I replied slowly. "He was one of those people who wanted to blame us for all his dog's problems, but who in fact rarely brought his dog to the vet. He had waited to seek care until it was way too late for anybody to be at fault for what was happening except himself."

"Hmmm," Strickland said tapping his lip as he thought. "Might still be worth checking up on him. Oh. How about Jade Peterson?"

I made a disgusted face and groaned. "Now that lady's a piece of work. Terrible, terrible person. Tortures dogs. Uses people. But she never seemed physically threatening. Why do you ask?"

"That's part of our ongoing investigation," Strickland replied and oddly didn't look me in the eye, staring off instead to the far corner of the room.

We kept walking and I meant to file the entire conversation away to think about later, but then in a sudden burst of self-concern I asked him, "I really want to fire her as a client. Would anything you know stop me from doing that?"

This time his eyes locked with mine and he said forcefully, "Call me immediately if she comes in again. Hold off doing anything official for now, okay? And don't be alone with her. And call 911 if she does anything."

What? That was utterly alarming, but we were walking in the back door of the main hospital so I had to let it go. I took them to ICU and showed them how the injection ports work. The setup allows us to piggyback a drug onto the main IV line and give a measured amount of that drug over a set period of time automatically, i.e. without having to tie up a technician to stand there and inject it. They are used very commonly in human hospitals, but less often in veterinary hospitals.

"Did you figure out what was in the drug reservoir?" I asked. "Is that what killed her?"

"We're still investigating," Strickland calmly replied. "We might need your help again after we get more answers."

"I'm happy to help," I said. "Anything else I can do for you now?"

"We're going to pick up some records before we leave," he replied. "We may need to have you interpret them at a later time."

"Sure," I said with a smile.

As soon as they left to go up to Molly's office, Dr. Drama hustled over and asked, "What are you doing?"

"Not sure," I replied. "I was scheduled out to speak to the detectives and it didn't take as long as I thought it would. Hey! Did you know they are planning on letting us open back up today?"

"No," he said, totally uninterested in this vital piece of news that I had just given him. "I need help."

His disinterest left me stunned, but I jumped right in and asked, "What can I do for you?"

"I have to take that Sheltie in ICU into immediate abdominal surgery, an exploratory laparotomy," he said. "Looks like a gallbladder mucocele and she's in an acute crisis."

"Sure," I said. "Do you want me to talk to the owner?"

"No," he replied, obviously exasperated. "I need you to discharge the Lab that you saw through emergency and then transferred to orthopedics. The one with the fracture and the external fixator? Come on, tell me you've kept up with the case."

"I know who you're talking about, no problem," I said reassuringly.

"There IS some problem," he snapped back. "The owner's freaking out about seeing the pins or something."

"I'll handle it," I said confidently. "Go save the Sheltie, I've got this."

The Lab had been hit by a car and part of the repair had been internal, but Dr. Drama had also needed to secure, via pins through the skin into the bones, a metal rod on the outside of the leg. The owner was a nice woman, but she confessed to me that she was not very medically oriented and insisted that she really didn't want to be involved with the medical details, declining to even hear too much about what was going to be done. She kept saying that she trusted us to do whatever was best for her puppy.

Her year and a half old, ninety pound puppy that is.

I gathered up Reginald's records and discharge instructions, but left him sleeping in his kennel. The owner would do a much better job listening to me if he wasn't there demanding all her attention, especially if the sight of the external fixator was going to freak her out even more.

When I entered the room, she met me with rapid fire questions, "What's wrong? Can't he go home? Where is Dr. Vincent? What happened?"

I smiled and said as calmly as I could, "Everything is good. Dr. Vincent was called away to an emergency surgery, just like I had to call him away from other patients when Reginald needed him. But these are his specific discharge instructions and I'll go through them with you."

She took a deep breath and apologized, "I'm sorry. I'm just not good with illness or blood or needles or any of this."

"And I bet I'm not good at whatever you're good at," I said with another smile.

"I'm an interior designer," she said with her first smile. "Even do a little renovating."

"That's perfect," I said. "Think of orthopedic surgery as carpentry instead. It's all about weight bearing and force, but that part is all done. The vital part that you have to deal with is to keep Reginald on a leash and quiet so that it can all heal and get strong. Like keeping kids from swinging on curtain rods you just installed."

"I can do that," she said confidently.

"The part that you'll see on the outside are really just metal tinker toys," I said. "Like a super fancy double curtain rod install."

She shook her head, but laughed companionably. I looked contrite and admitted, "I actually don't know that much about interior design or carpentry, but I played obsessively with the original tinker toys and erector sets at my grandparents' house."

"My sister and I did too!" she said with a soft laugh.

"Great!" I said. "It's exactly what you'll see on his leg. You've got this now!"

I went through the rest of the instructions and when I brought Reginald back into the room and pointed out a few additional details, she handled it all very well. She balked a bit at the E-collar, but then took a deep breath and told me, "I'll keep it on no matter how many sad eyes he gives me! We can't have him chewing up these precious tinker toys!"

CHAPTER SIXTEEN

It was already a bad morning and I'd only been awake for twenty minutes. First Max was distracted by the neighborhood noises and couldn't concentrate on taking care of his business, which was just so infuriating. It's not like it wasn't the exact same thing we did first thing every morning. Maybe tomorrow I'd sit down and drink my coffee first and then he could be the one waiting impatiently on me? I stood in the fenced in yard blowing each breath out of pursed lips, trying to literally blow off my frustration. Then when I was finally able to chill out and enjoy that most precious first cup of coffee, Max slimed my favorite work pants right before I had to walk out the door. Worst of all I forgot that I should have left early because we had blocked off the paths through the new hospital garden so that the nursery people could plant the new trees. I quickly jogged to the hospital to make up lost time, but I was shocked to find that Dr. Drama was already in the middle of a colossal rant about people being late. It turns out he hadn't even noticed I wasn't there yet. The new emergency technician Ellie, the one he was so excited about, was almost an hour late and wasn't even answering her phone.

"Late on your first day of work?" Dr. Drama asked the rounds crowd incredulously. "Seriously? So she's dedicated and focused enough to get specialty training, but she can't get herself to work on time?"

"Maybe there was a communication mix-up?" I tried to placate him. "Maybe we told her the wrong time or date?"

"I told her myself," he hissed as he fixed his angry glare on me. "What the hell."

I told myself to shut up and keep myself out of trouble, but even as I thought those self-protective thoughts my eyes flicked over at the swear jar. I tensed as Dr. Drama took a huge intake of air and stepped closer to me. He was really all bark and no bite, but his theatrical build up still scared me sometimes. My Uncle had rarely physically punished me, he was much more into taking away privileges with ongoing loud verbal abuse. But he did often grab my arm and would grip it harder and harder as he spilled his particularly vicious venom louder and louder over me. His words would get very personal and more and more intense as the pressure of his hand would increase, and the threat of even worse physical violence seemed to always be there. And it always ripped me up inside.

So because of my Uncle, I had trouble standing up to Dr. Drama's verbal onslaught, despite the fact I had never seen him physically touch anyone, human or animal, in an unkind way. As a point of pride I forced myself to stand firm in front of him. Dr. Drama immediately backed away, which made me wonder if some of what I was feeling showed on my face. He started to speak, but the door to treatment blew open and our manager Molly called out, "Code red! A dog has dug out of a run, popped a gate and is loose."

"You've seen him?" Dr. Drama asked hopefully.

"No," Molly replied. "And the back gate is open for the tree delivery. He's a medium sized fluffy white dog with a red bandage on his right front leg."

"Shit. Shit. Shit!" Dr. Drama said rushing toward the back door just as the campus wide intercom announced, "All available personnel assemble at the boarding kennel entrance. Loose dog." As he walked past he knocked the plastic swear jar off the shelf in a fit of temper and it bounced dramatically a couple times, then continued to roll around on the floor for long minutes afterwards. We all studiously refused to look at it.

Molly separated us into small groups, sent some people searching the immediate area on foot, instructing others to take their cars to comb the surrounding areas. I called Ethan and asked him to get our neighbors, specifically our group of puppy friends, to scour the area around our houses, since it was the closest neighborhood to the hospital. I suggested he take Max with him to search; some dogs are attracted to other dogs or at least will give themselves away by barking at them.

My group made a big loop around the new garden as well as searching all the dumpster areas, but my despair and my stomach ache grew as time passed and there was no sighting of the canine escape artist. We worked so very hard to keep our patients safe with double doors and extra fences, but no matter how strict our protocols were, this rare canny dog managed to come up with escape tricks we'd never thought of.

Molly sent me back to emergency to see patients and my constant prayer was that I wouldn't see the escapee as a trauma patient coming in my front door. In fact I got nervous whenever I went to the reception area for fear I would see a fluffy white dog bleeding or collapsed on the floor there. But this trip to the front all I saw was a pretty young woman that I recognized, her black hair in disarray above a visibly sweaty face, her scrubs marked with dirt and rips at both knees. She was agitated and trying to get the attention of our single remaining receptionist.

"Ellie!" I called out. "What happened?"

"Dr. Kat! I'm so sorry I'm late!" she apologized as she spoke excitedly and waved her hands around for emphasis. "You're never gonna believe what happened! I was on 31, traffic buzzing every which way and there was this dog, this fuzzy white dog with a red bandage on his leg, running down the side of the road. I just had to try to save him, but he wouldn't come to me so I kept having to run after him. I know I should've called, but I left my phone in the car and I just kept thinking he'd get tired and I could catch him and he kept almost getting hit, a couple different times, it was horrible!"

"What happened to him?" I asked frantically.

"I made a flying tackle and I got him," she said with a proud smile. "Tore my pants though. He's in my car out front. He seems okay, but can you check him out for me?"

"Absolutely!" I said grinning. "Do you need a slip lead?"

"Nope," she replied. "I always carry one in my car. I sure hope Dr. Vincent isn't too angry at me for being late."

I laughed and assured her, "No way. That's our lost patient you just saved! Dr. Vincent will probably do something embarrassingly congratulatory and appreciative!"

Dr. Drama burst through the door just after I finished speaking, he had to have been listening to our exchange on the security feed. Running towards Ellie he threw himself down on his knees, athletically sliding towards her, and came to rest directly in front of her. He lifted his hands up in the air in classic prayer position and gushed, "Thank you! Thank you! Thank you! Most importantly you saved a sweet boy, but you also saved all of us because we would have grieved forever if he had gotten hurt."

Ellie laughed and grasped his folded hands with both of hers and said graciously, "I didn't have a choice. I had to help him. But I felt so bad about being late!"

Dr. Drama jumped to his feet, laughing loudly and truly joyously, and said, "You had absolutely perfect timing to my way of thinking! Miraculous timing I'd have to say!"

I headed to the far back to have a brief minute to myself before I got back to work. It felt good to be knocked out of my dazed emotional state for the first time since Melanie's death and fully feel the ecstasy that the dog had been found safe and unharmed. But at the same time, all sorts of suppressed emotions were pushing to the surface, demanding to be allowed through that open door into my consciousness and none of them were positive. I didn't want my trip to the kennels to be a completely selfish break so I made sure to check on all the hospitalized patients on my walk through. As I approached the quiet far back, I heard voices from the dog food prep area.

"I can't believe I got stuck here doing all the work while Dr. Vincent's pet doctor got to run around supposedly looking for the dog," said the oddly pleasant voice of Dr. Harris. It wasn't the tone of his voice, but his constant criticizing and complaining that made me wince and react like I was hearing nails on a chalkboard. I tried to silently back myself out of range, but couldn't escape hearing the rest of the conversation.

"The joy of being on the lowest rung of the ladder," Dr. Nash, one of the other interns, said.

"It's more than that," Dr. Harris replied harshly. "Whenever I make a great point she has to nitpick it apart. Especially if Dr. Vincent is around. She couldn't make it in surgery and now she wants to keep me from succeeding when she couldn't."

"Then why is she his pet?" Dr. Nash asked.

"Who knows?" he said with a sigh of disgust. "Probably feels sorry for her. Maybe he likes touchy feely weirdo doctors. I'm surprised she didn't need to take all sorts of time off for her friend's death. And what's with that? Is it even safe around here for those of us actually doing all the work?"

This wasn't the first time I had caught people talking about me behind my back. In fact the last time it was in this same spot! But I was stunned because I hadn't even had any interactions with Dr. Harris since the bulldog fiasco. Well, of course we had interactions, but I didn't regard any of them as important or impactful. Was he just making stuff up so he had an excuse to complain about me? Or did he take any minor correction as an attack on his obvious perfection? If I had pointed out an error of his, it was in part to save him from a tongue lashing from Dr. Drama. What was wrong with Harris? I honestly didn't even know what to think or how to feel. Maybe numb was a better way to operate around here.

I went up front to let them know I was available and heard a shout from across the reception area. It was Reginald's owner, the person who was initially freaked out about her dog's external fixator until I convinced her they were just fancy tinker toys.

She motioned for me to join her and handed me a huge box of Cookie Cottage cookies from Fort Wayne. How did she find out they were my favorite cookies of all time? And how did she get them here in Noblesville?

"I love these," I gushed, hugging the box to my chest.

"I know," she said with a smug look on her face. "I had to be quite the investigator to find the perfect gift for you!"

"So I heard that Reginald is doing very well," I said, turning the focus back to her pet.

"Yes," she replied. "But that isn't the only reason why I owe you such a debt of gratitude. My sister was in a bad accident, broke some of the bones in her face, and they had to use an external fixator to repair it. On her face! She was freaking out!"

"Is she okay?" I asked.

"Yes!" she replied. "But the first time I walked into her hospital room, she was petrified that I would faint or scream or throw up. But I was cool as a cucumber because I knew all about external fixators. I even made tinker toy jokes and offered to get the old erector set from Grandma and Grandpa's house in case her doctor needed some extra parts. It made all the difference in the world to her to have me react this way. And I credit you. You could have shamed me for being a complete wimp, but instead you gave me the gift of understanding and acceptance. Which then made all the difference to her. If I wasn't freaked out, she felt like it just couldn't be that bad! Thank you."

"Thank you for telling me," I said gratefully. "I do love these cookies and I love getting to share them with all the wonderful people who work here. But more importantly, by letting me know that something small I did grew into such a blessing, it gives me hope that other things that I've done could have grown as well."

She grabbed me up into a warm hug and I couldn't stop myself from clinging on to her so tightly, like I wanted to hold on to this feeling long after I had to throw myself back into the hospital chaos and stress. I hadn't realized when they said it, but it had half worried me and half hurt my feelings when two experienced police detectives investigating a murder had been so negative about our hospital's circus atmosphere. Was it just so new and unexpected to them or did it really compare unfavorably with human emergency departments and, even worse, murder scenes? It reminded me of the time my friend Jane, who was studying to be a Psychologist and working at the university counseling center, had visited me when I was working an emergency shift senior year. Jane had remarked that she had observed more people in crisis in our waiting room than she had seen at her own counseling center! I wasn't sure how to take that statement at the time, and more than a year later I still didn't know what I thought about it. Was the pain and stress and responsibility of having an injured or seriously ill pet just too much for average people to handle? I'm confident that I was both educated and trained well enough to be able to take care of the pets' medical issues, but I'm not at all sure I was prepared to handle all of the owners' psychological problems.

CHAPTER SEVENTEEN

Now that my frozen feelings seemed to be thawing, I was able to acknowledge that I had put off emailing Andrei for way, way too long. So today I headed to work early enough so I could check for a reply from Andrei and still have time to email if it was there. I was ecstatic to see a message from him until I read it.

Oh Kat, what do I mean? What do YOU mean? The minute you got a lawyer involved there wasn't anything I could do about the situation. I sure didn't dare break the order of protection, I could have gone to jail for just trying to talk to you. And that would have been the end to my military career. And while I never trusted our uncle, your signature on those legal papers sure looked real to me.

I was stunned, but forced my fingers to type.

Andrei, I truly don't know what you're talking about. I never went to a lawyer and the only legal papers I ever signed were to do with the financial stuff. Uncle would sit me at the dining room table and bring out a pile of forms for me to sign. He never let me read any of the forms, and if I tried to look at them at all, he'd have a fit about having to put all this effort into our financial affairs for us and then threaten that I could do all the work all by myself if I wanted to complain about how he was handling it.

As I sent the message, a band of pain suddenly formed around my head and started to squeeze. What had I done back then? What had my uncle done? What had I let him do in my name? I certainly never trusted him. I knew that my happiness and wellbeing was simply not a concern for him. But I honestly never thought he'd waste his precious time and energy to enact some elaborate plot to what? Keep Andrei out of my life? The only thing my uncle ever seemed to care about was his prestige and his money and getting his own way about everything. He had seemed glad that Andrei was out of our lives since he was the only one of us that would challenge him in any way. I distinctly remember Andrei asking him about our financial situation and how angry my uncle would always get at any attempt at a discussion. After Andrei left I made sure I questioned him as little as possible about anything.

I'm sorry Andrei, this is all so devastating to me. I have a terrible feeling that maybe I did fall for some horrific scheme of Uncle's, but I honestly remember nothing. One of my friends was just murdered at the hospital and I feel afraid all the time, like I did after Mom and Dad died and then again after you left. I don't know who to trust or what to do. Only now I have patients that need me so I'm trying to focus on them. I never wanted to lose you and I'm so sorry if I did anything that caused that.

I took a couple deep breaths and hit send again. It was a mistake to face these kind of feelings here at work. I should just bite the bullet and use the phone that Dagger got me for these kinds of personal interactions at home. Although oddly enough I was glad that the minute I walked downstairs I'd be way too busy to worry about my personal problems. My fear was that if I were at home I would absolutely lose myself in the emotions and waste hours suffering without any possibility of distraction or redirection.

The first person I saw in the reception area looked so distraught that I was reassured that I would very quickly lose focus on my own problems. I stopped in front of her and patted her arm as comfortingly as I could and asked, "Is there something I can do to help you?"

"Do you hear that?" she asked frantically. "That dog is obviously suffering. It may not be my dog, but someone has to help whoever it is. You have to do something for its pain."

The door to the back was propped open to move some equipment in and when I concentrated I could hear a dog crying/howling in the back. It had a very recognizable pattern and tone, and she was right we were all 'ignoring' it.

I turned to her with a gentle smile and said, "I'll certainly go to the back and double check on this patient, but let me reassure you that it's most likely not pain that they are expressing, but simply the excitatory phase of anesthesia instead."

I pointed my finger and used my hand like it was a conductor's baton to beat out the rhythmic cries as they occurred and explained, "Hear how regular it is, more like trying to chant rather than a quick sharp sound like yelling ouch. It's actually the opposite of pain, it's from the pain killer they give them and is a sign that they are just high, but in the excitatory phase."

She looked at me with deep anguish as I jogged away to make sure I was right. The rhythmic whines were classic, but I'd be absolutely sure when I could see his body language. I laughed when I saw the dog, a beautiful red husky, a classic breed for this response, resting quite comfortably while whining on the beat, once even raising his nose in the classic wolf howl position.

I chuckled as I returned to the woman and initially thought that I did a great job at explaining once again that the dog was fine and not suffering in any way. And on top of it all, it wasn't even her dog. And yet she was still distressed and in fact continued to become more and more upset, crying harder to the point of gasping for breath and holding her stomach and kind of writhing in place.

She finally managed to gasp out, "Does that happen in people?"

"It does," I replied. "I'm sure it sounds different, but I know it's very common in children waking up from anesthesia. When I had my wisdom teeth out as a teenager, everyone in recovery that day were rowdy criers. Our mouths were all still totally numb so the group was suffering from zero pain! Yet we still sounded like some kind of wild wailing chorus."

I so wanted to get back to my schedule, but this woman's anguish was so sharp and so real I just couldn't walk away. I softly asked, "What's the matter? The dog is fine. In fact you can hear him winding down."

"It's not the dog," she said as she snuffled and gasped. "My son sounded just like that when he woke up from surgery and I begged and cried and shouted for someone to help him until they kicked me out. He has special needs and I've been scared to death that he'd need another procedure and have to suffer that much pain again and not be able to tell us."

"Well, of course talk to his anesthesiologist if he needs another procedure, but I wouldn't worry," I said with a smile. "Maybe bring it up with your doctor on a regular visit when everything isn't so emotionally charged, but I think they'll tell you the same thing I'm telling you now."

"Thank you," she said gratefully. "I can't explain how much that memory has been torturing me."

"And just think," I said. "You might be able to warn your friends if their children have to have anesthesia for some reason. It's not so shocking if you've discussed it before hand."

The rest of my emergency shift passed smoothly, steadily busy, but everything, and everyone, stayed orderly. I even walked out pretty much on time. I was extra happy about that since I was hoping to make it to Mei's Tai Chi class. I'd not only get to go to class; I'd have time to get a snack beforehand. Life is good!

It was only the fourth Tai Chi class that I'd been able to attend with my crazy schedule, but I was totally committed to getting there if there was any way I could. The Tai Chi movements seemed very simple when I checked them out on the internet, but when I tried to actually do them it was way harder than I ever imagined it could be. And doing everything so deliberately slowly was shockingly difficult.

Before my parents passed away I had taken all sorts of classes like gymnastics and dance and also played Little League and volleyball. After my Uncle moved in and took over, all my fun activities evaporated. Although I did manage to continue playing volleyball with my friend Jane, probably because my Uncle was always trying to sell something, insurance or whatever new job he was working on, to Jane's rich Dad. So when

I joined the Tai Chi class I felt confident that I could do well in a beginner's class since I had done well in other sports. Well, I was not excelling, in fact I was barely keeping up! It was enough different from everything I had ever attempted, that I really had to concentrate just to follow simple instructions, including how and when to breathe while doing it. But the hardest part, and it turns out the best part for me at this time of my life, was that the very necessary concentration and focus drove every other thought out of my head. And if my mind did wander off to think about finding Melanie's body, or worry about Dr. Harris's nastiness, or wonder what had happened with Andrei, or honestly any other tiny random thought, I would completely lose track of what I was doing and be noticeably out of synch with the rest of the class. Or even worse I'd be heading the wrong way or standing still like a dope having no clue what I was supposed to be doing! So while working emergency was definitely teaching me multitasking, Tai Chi was forcing me to really be in the moment and learn to focus on just this one thing I was trying to learn.

Today I totally enjoyed class. Mei was a wonderful teacher and created an informal, warm, and fun class. But she still kept us all focused on what we were trying to learn. One of my classmates called us a motley crew, which made me laugh, but we were for sure diverse, although retirement age ladies made up the preponderance of our members. What I liked the best was there were no other veterinarians and on purpose I didn't talk about veterinary medicine during our social times. I love my profession passionately, but sometimes it felt like it was eating me alive. I was happy that I changed back to using my real name Kat at the end of last year, but I felt like I had lost the ability to change back to my original sparkling Kat personality. I think it was because of the total devotion I had to my patients that I desperately needed conversations and relationships that were just for the parts of me that had nothing to do with my life of service.

As I walked back to my apartment, I tried to wrap my

brain around the feelings that class had brought up. I felt full of energy, yet so much calmer, which you'd think was an impossible combination. Running at the park with Max certainly made me calmer, definitely helped any feelings of excessive anxiety. But running made me tired, didn't fill me with energy like Tai Chi did. They both stopped me from replaying and overthinking every recent conversation, and turning every little feeling into some kind of major catastrophe, but they were definitely different experiences. Maybe my fourth lesson was too early to make this determination, but I think Tai Chi was going to be a really important part of my life, especially that part of my personality that was occasionally forced to deal with crippling anxiety.

After giving Max my complete attention while I fed him and took him for a long meandering walk, I sat on my bed staring at my phone, arguing with myself about whether I should or shouldn't check for a message from Andrei. I really didn't want to chance my good mood on reading an unwelcome response and yet it seemed cowardly not to look. At one of our house family dinners we had had a really good conversation about different kinds of cowardly behavior. Of course, there is the most common kind that people talk about, physical cowardice, but there are all sorts of other kinds of cowardice and I personally don't want to suffer from any of them. Finally I had to acknowledge that not checking would make me an emotional coward so I took a deep breath and pulled up my email account, but Andrei hadn't replied. Of course then I was oddly disappointed.

Having broken my rule about using my phone to check my emails, it was easy to go ahead and check in on social media. My senior year at vet school, more than a year ago now, had been brutal due to my lying cheating ex-boyfriend. At the time I had outwardly blamed only him, and maybe his new secret girlfriend to a lesser extent, but deep down inside I was most eviscerated because my friends and mentors had believed his lies and stories. In the same way I knew that Stretch didn't/

couldn't/wouldn't hurt Melanie, why didn't they know that I couldn't possibly think/say/feel any of the negative things Jason accused me of? Why didn't one of them come to me and ask why he was making up these wild lies? So I mainly just lurked, checking out what people were doing without liking or commenting on anybody's post, but it did make me feel oddly comforted to catch up with their lives. Then I checked out some veterinary sites, learned some new techniques, which was very cool except it made me ponder how fast knowledge was being added in my profession. One of my professors said that the knowledge base of medicine doubled every eighteen months, meaning that if I graduated knowing every single thing that I needed to help every patient that by now I'd only know half? That was pretty overwhelming. I finally went to bed, hours later than I should have, but I had gotten lost down the rabbit hole of information. And Andrei still hadn't replied.

CHAPTER EIGHTEEN

"I'd love to assist in surgery," I declared, "but where's Stretch?"

"With the police," Dr. Drama snorted in exasperation. "Again."

I sighed in commiseration. "I'm sure they'll clear him soon."

"I know," he said quietly. "I trust them to do whatever it takes to find out what happened to Melanie, but it's just all so inconvenient. And even when Stretch is physically here, he's walking around all depressed that they could possibly suspect him."

"It's been tough on him," I said somberly. "We know he didn't hurt her, couldn't hurt her."

"Did you tell the detectives that?" he asked.

"I did," I replied. "Did you?"

"Of course I did," he answered with a scowl and a step toward me. "Why wouldn't I?"

I threw my hands up to placate him and said, "Just checking. It seems like someone has to be saying something that implicates him or we'd all be questioned the same way he is. I know Quickcut had to be the one telling stories about things that happened at their apartment."

"Why would he do that?" he asked as he gestured that we should head over to the surgery suite.

"I have no idea," I replied. "I know Quickcut gets jealous every time you praise Stretch. Maybe he didn't think that some stupid little derogatory story would make Stretch look so bad to the detectives."

"I think there's something more to it," Dr. Drama said, his

face taking on an expression as if he were pondering deep thoughts. "The detectives keep referring to all the tests they're waiting for."

"Yeah," I agreed. "I heard them complaining about how long DNA test results take to come back, and about how everyone expects results back in a flash like it happens on television."

Dr. Drama looked like he was going to reply, but then we approached the surgery prep table and he did his magical personality transformation to what I privately refer to as 'super surgeon'. He becomes outwardly calm and controlled, but intensely focused on the patient. He nodded once and the surgery technicians began giving concise reports on the present status of fluids, blood products, and medications. He sent me ahead to scrub so I could get the surgery instruments ready while he did a final quick ultrasound scan of the dog's abdomen.

I'd done my detailed surgical scrubbing procedure so many times that I could slip into autopilot mode and think instead about everything I knew about bleeding tumors on spleens. The statistics are well known; approximately two thirds of bleeding tumors are cancer and without chemotherapy the patient only survives one to three months after surgery. But this dog was younger than the typical middle aged patient and was a smaller terrier mix, i.e. not the classic Golden Retriever, Labrador Retriever, German Shepherd or Boxer, so we were hoping it would be better news. Of course the weird signalment, e.g. the patient's age, breed, and reproductive status, for this medical presentation might also mean a bizarre diagnosis, maybe something none of us had ever seen. Statistics certainly pointed us to a probable diagnosis, but that's not the same thing as a definite diagnosis.

I still passionately loved abdominal surgery, so standing at the surgery table and readying the instruments made me reconsider my decision not to try for a surgical residency. Of course confronting just one orthopedic surgery would make me equally sure that I had done the right thing. I loved seeing orthopedic cases on emergency: stabilizing the patients, diagnosing the problems, doing the required testing. The only thing I didn't like was the surgery itself. Which is a huge problem if you are the surgeon.

Dr. Drama joined me and asked, "What's wrong? Everything ready?"

"Everything's great," I said with a smile. "Just having deep thoughts about career paths."

"Sorry we pulled you out of primary care," he said regretfully. "But we really needed you in emergency. And we still do."

"I'm actually loving emergency," I said. "But standing here I was thinking that I could be happy doing abdominal surgery all day long."

"I need the variety," he replied with a wide grin. "Although I agree with you that it's easy to deeply feel what a miracle life is when you're in the abdomen or chest."

"Yep, I do feel that way," I said. "But lots of thoracic and abdominal surgeries are true emergencies. It's not like I'll never get to do them working ER. And I love wound repair almost as much, which I also get to do all the time in emergency as well."

"How's Max doing?" Dr. Drama asked. "Speaking of wound repair."

Dr. Drama had done substantial surgery, including a skin graft, on Max after his despicable former owners had dumped him in our back lot with massive untreated burns. I replied, "He's doing great. It took a while, but the pigment is moving into the scarred areas and that makes them so much less noticeable. Not that he cares, but I get tired of all the questions I get when we're out in public. Although questions are better than the people who just assume I'm the monster that did this to him. Talk about getting looks that could kill!"

Dr. Drama made his initial incision, carefully working around the spleen, and we stopped chatting. I was in charge of the suction, but it wasn't the huge job that we expected since it wasn't still actively bleeding. There was a huge clot on one end of the spleen and there was some unexplained scar tissue on the other end.

"That looks way more like trauma to me," Dr. Drama said in a disgusted tone, although then his face contorted into a semblance of pleasure as he realized that removing the spleen would be curative if it was in fact a traumatic injury instead of a cancerous tumor. So really it was bad news that someone probably hit or kicked this dog, but good news for his recovery and prognosis. Of course not telling us about the trauma make it look less innocent, so something nefarious probably happened and we'd have to figure out the mystery.

After we removed the spleen, Doc did a careful examination of the abdomen to make sure no other organs had been injured, and thankfully we found nothing else significant. The area of old scar tissue on the spleen hinted that there may have been a previous trauma as well, but we would know more after sending samples of the spleen to the pathologist to check microscopically. In an effort to protect myself, I tried to have as few feelings about this patient as possible, since the case wasn't even my responsibility. Plus Dr. Drama seemed angry enough for both of us, but all I could think was: what's wrong with people? How could a normal sized person not realize that hitting or kicking a little terrier sized dog would cause significant injury? Or do some people just not care?

I closed the incision, did the paperwork, and transferred the patient to ICU while Dr. Drama brought the owners to his office for a heart to heart consultation. I definitely got the easier job. We really couldn't assume who did what to this poor dog, but we had to find out enough facts so we could help prevent it from happening again.

Yawning a jaw cracking yawn, I ran upstairs for a big mug of coffee before returning to my duties in the emergency service. Regretting my late night wasting time bouncing all over the internet, I added lots of sugar and cream, hoping the combination of energy boosters would keep me going through the challenges of the rest of my shift. Then I walked up front to tell Tessa that I was available for patients. Yes, I know I forget and call them receptionists all the time. I'm not trying to be disrespectful. It's just an old habit from the very first practice I worked at when I was in high school, when I was in fact doing that very job. Actually at one time or another I worked at most of the jobs in a vet hospital on my long path to have the occupation that I had long dreamed about. In the midst of the chaos, I sometimes forget to be grateful that I was living my childhood dream.

I was abruptly startled out of my reverie as a slightly built man and woman staggered in carrying a large limp German Shepherd. The woman banged on the open button to the sliding door, mouthing help as her wide eyes darted from one to another of the three of us rushing to assist them. Tabby peeled off to get the stretcher and cart as Dr. Lane and I helped the owners support the animal's weight as the woman screamed, "Choking on a ball! We live only a block away, he's been unconscious for a couple minutes."

Hearing that, Dr. Lane, one of the daytime emergency vets, laid the dog on his stomach on the floor right where we were and tried to reach the ball through his mouth. Sometime last night, on my long internet binge, I had watched a video of a new way to save a dog from choking. In fact the patient they had saved in the video had been choking on a ball and looked a lot like this dog.

I had never done the procedure. In fact I had never even heard of doing it this way until last night, but it had made sense. They had shared a very clear video so I said to Dr. Lane, "Let me try a new way to do this. Flip him over on to his back."

Dr. Lane gave me an odd look and sent one of the techs to put surgery on alert, but quietly warned, "One try."

"Flip him on his back," I ordered, then climbed on top of him, keeping my weight on my knees. I arranged my hands around his jaw and neck with my thumbs just behind the easily palpated ball in his throat. I pressed down and then up like they showed in the video and the ball just popped out. I've never been so shocked in my entire life! I climbed off him and turned him on his side, calling for oxygen and readying myself to do CPR, but he immediately started to breath on his own, first gasping oddly and then loudly retching to clear his throat.

Dr. Lane moved the dog and his owners into a room with the tech, and then followed me into the treatment area and asked, "What was that?"

"I just saw it last night on my phone," I replied breathlessly. "They're calling it an external extraction technique or the Heimlich maneuver for dogs."

"I've never heard anything about it," he said shaking his head.

"I hadn't either," I said. "I've tried the chest compression type of Heimlich before, but it didn't work."

"That was so incredibly slick!" he said with a grin. "I want you describing that at rounds, and get that video to show. No, don't do that, directly email that video to every single person in the hospital, okay?"

Oddly enough when I walked back into the room, the dog looked fine, he was on his feet and checking the room out. The owners on the other hand were partially collapsed on the bench and looked very much the worse for wear.

After I finished with them, I couldn't settle down and paced around the treatment area. I can't begin to describe how extraordinary I felt, saving the dog with a simple inexpensive maneuver. Every so often medicine isn't all that complicated. You just have to do the exact right thing at the exact perfect moment in time! That's what I did and I felt like a superhero! If Dag walked in the door right now, I'm not sure I would or could feel any happier. It's probably why I use the word passion for my profession, because of this depth and breadth of emotions that it can evoke, both positive and negative.

CHAPTER NINETEEN

Max and I took our time walking to work. I was working second shift, scheduled for three to eleven, although let's be realistic I never get home before midnight. I had promised Dag to use his SUV whenever I worked these late shifts, but I'd lent it to Ethan to use for work while his car was in the garage. Max and I would be fine running home. Max was huge and had a tendency to rise up onto his back legs like a person when he was nervous, which made him very intimidating. If anyone else happened to be out that late, I wasn't worried.

I realized that I was still on a happiness high from saving the choking dog yesterday. Sadly however, after only a year in practice, I was also cynical enough to predict that today I would somehow have to experience the negative side of practice. It might be people arguing about their bills or refusing recommended testing and then complaining when we couldn't give them a diagnosis. Or my most recent complaint, owners angry that we didn't think to trim the nails on an emergency patient after we had stopped everything else we were doing and used all our skill and resources to save him from bleeding to death. As I opened the back door, I told myself I would absolutely resist every one of these common annoyances and hold on to my glorious superhero feeling, no matter what anyone said. And that included any comments from our trio of hypercritical interns. I think I took their constant negativity so much worse because they knew better. So it not only affected my mood, it stole my belief that if I just worked harder at explaining everything then people's attitudes would improve. Certainly if everyone understood the reasons we do what we do, they would love and appreciate us! Or to use one of my favorite expressions, they would realize that there's always 'a method to our madness.'

Of course, the first person I saw was Dr. Harris, or my private nickname for him Dr. Whiney, and I laughed at the accuracy of my cynical prediction for my day. At the first sight of me he frowned and started to speak, but I just grinned and blew past him. He couldn't say anything to ruin my day if I didn't allow him to catch me!

Tessa hustled to join me as I headed into the locker room to dump off my stuff. I not only had an armful of clean laundry to put away, but I was also carrying a big bag of yummy food. I had made myself a really nice bento box for supper, but Ethan and Mei had surprised me with a multicourse picnic dinner as well. I reassured them that my scheduled eight hour Friday night shift often stretched into ten or twelve hours and doubling up on meals would definitely help me handle it better. Tessa promised to put it all away for me if I would go up front and speak to an owner who was upset over the appearance of the post op patient that she was attempting to send home.

I doubled down on my commitment to keep an upbeat attitude and grinned again. This situation might turn out to be hard to handle, but I was determined to do it. The last time someone was complaining instead of listening to instructions, the dog was wearing an Elizabethan collar to prevent him from self-traumatizing his surgical incision. The minute our technician had left the room, the owners had whipped off the collar and stood by while the poor dog chewed out all his sutures, right there in the exam room. And of course she threw a second hissy fit when Dr. Drama charged her to replace the missing sutures with staples.

I walked in and was happy that the E-collar was still on and the stitches were intact! Plus there was no swelling or redness so I asked gently, "What are you concerned about?"

"Look at the size of the incision!" she exclaimed. "It's huge. It wasn't that big a lump!"

The incision seemed perfect to me, given the recorded size

and suspected tumor type, so I decided that it was probably a simple case of failed expectations. I took one of the trifold paper towels and drew a picture of an irregular circle portraying the tumor and then drew margins around it, and finally drew an ellipse around all of that, explaining as I drew. "First, Dr. Vincent had to remove a border around the tumor to be sure that he got it all out. If the lump is cancer, then the edges will be checked to be sure that they are free of cancer cells. But then he had to make an elliptical incision which is way longer than the tumor, even including the borders, because if he made a circular incision he could never get it to close. The edges have to sit right next to each other to heal as quickly as possible. Even with the elliptical incision there can be a bit of puckering, but with a circular incision there would nothing but puckers and no way could it easily heal across the gaps."

The owner stared at my drawing and, sounding unconvinced, said, "It's so long, so many stitches. It will take forever to heal."

"We have an expression in surgery," I said comfortingly. "Incisions heal side to side, not end to end. So a two inch incision," as I made a small two inch representation with my thumb and finger, "heals in the exact same amount of time as an eight inch incision," as I made a much bigger representation with both hands.

The owner sat down abruptly and appeared to deflate, "I guess I thought it wasn't a big deal because the lump was relatively small. This makes it seem like a much bigger deal."

"The pathologist will tell us how big a deal it is," I replied. "Not the number of stitches. Dr. Vincent did the right thing to give Rowdy the best chance for full recovery. We'll call you as soon as the results come back."

The discussion didn't count against my cynical prediction for my day, because this client truly didn't understand the surgical decision making process. I didn't understand it before I went to veterinary school. When I worked as a part time assistant in high school, one of the surgeons at the practice bragged about how small her spay incisions were and I believed that fact made her the best surgeon. Then one of my professors explained it meant that she either didn't remove the entire uterus or she had to put undue pressure on the attachments and their vessels to tug them out of the inadequate incision. And for what? A tiny incision didn't heal any faster than a bigger one.

The owner actually seemed happy when she left, although I was embarrassed when she carefully folded up the paper towel I had drawn on and placed it in her purse. The techs and assistants had already started teasing me about my quirky little paper towel artistry. Of course I used handouts with great pictures drawn by skilled medical illustrators for all the big things. But some questions that people seem to care the most about are the smallest and/or most general things that aren't usually covered in any handout. And the paper towels are the only thing I can reliably find in that moment to draw on. And if we tried to write a handout that included every single detail for every little question, it would be so long that either no one would read it or they would lose the very essential instructions in the overabundance of explanations.

My shift proceeded well and I was actually caught up by the time Stretch came in. I was really happy to see him and promised myself not to quiz him about his interview. I asked, "Hey Stretch! Did you hear about the choking dog I saved?"

"I did!" he replied. "That video is really cool. Thanks for sending it to me."

"You're welcome," I said. "Dr. Lane had me send it to everyone."

"Well," he said with a smile. "You might have helped me out with the police as well. I had to go back this morning because I finally got a lawyer like my Dad wanted. While I was waiting at the station, I showed the video to one of the K-9 handlers and it seemed like everybody's attitude lightened up about me."

"That's good," I said. "I hope you're not too stressed. No one believes you had anything to do with what happened to Melanie."

"Yeah," he said somberly. "But the detectives seem to think that it has to be someone that knows all about the medical equipment. So they think it's one of us, some kind of inside job. I did try to explain to them that we're really dedicated to client education so we often share all sorts of details about the equipment that we're using to our owners. And shamefully I threw physicians and nurses under the bus as well since they use them way more than we do. But the hardest part is that when we were discussing it, the detectives brought up the fact that someone could have coerced Melanie into being their inside person. They asked all sorts of very specific questions and every question just made me sadder and sadder to think that someone may have forced her to assist them."

A wave of horror washed over me as I contemplated someone forcing her, probably terrorizing her, into setting up the equipment that would ultimately kill her. It didn't make sense to me. I just couldn't fathom any part of it. I could imagine someone like Jade Peterson hurting Mel, but never in this weird complicated way. Jade was obviously a horrible person. Frankly she made my profoundly narcissistic uncle look like a rank amateur, but I couldn't see her being smart enough or organized enough to pull this off. So if Mel had been thumped with some heavy object in the heat of a physical confrontation, I'd be the first to blame Jade. But not this. Plus why would Mel ever go with Jade into the training center all by herself?

I heaved a psyche clearing sigh and locked eyes with Stretch, but as I started to share all these questions and feelings with him, I was paged to an emergency. I jogged down to the hallway behind the exam rooms, but Tabby gestured for me to come out to the reception area. As soon as I saw it was the owners of the choking dog I panicked and my heart pounded in my chest. What possibly could have gone wrong? Did I do something that compromised the dog's airway? I don't think what I did could have hurt him, but what else could have happened overnight? I looked at the dog collapsed on the floor and realized it wasn't even the same dog. It was a Labrador, not even the same breed.

The dog shakily forced himself up on his feet and projectile vomited across the floor. It literally shot out like a water cannon turned on full force. I placed my hands on his abdomen and gently attempted to palpate it, but he was tight as a drum and unbearably painful. He looked at me with soulful, suffering eyes as his legs buckled and he fell back down on the ground.

I called for the stretcher and cart but Trevor, on one of his first ever shifts, insisted, "I can get him. I pick up my Labs all the time."

The dog groaned and his mucus membranes turned even muddier so I agreed, warning Trevor, "Protect your back."

He did a perfect squat and slipped one arm around the dog's chest, but the Lab was too big for him to scoop him up under his butt, so he carefully slipped his arm at the most caudal part of the abdomen near the pelvis. He gently hoisted the suffering dog up and took a couple steps toward the back treatment area. The dog shifted, Trevor tried to maintain his proper hold, but even with my help there was a brief moment when it looked like he was juggling the patient, but he finally got a safe grip.

There was a sound, like a weird mix of a soft pop and, not trying to be funny in any way, a long fart, then there was a splat and out of the corner of my eye I saw a bright pink ball bounce across the reception area floor. I stared at it, actually stunned in disbelief as it bounced a couple times and then rolled towards the door. Every single person in the lobby: clients, CSRs at the front desk, techs and assistants on various missions, the dog's owners, and me, stared at that rolling ball like a magical being had sprung into existence. I wouldn't have been more surprised if it had been a baby dragon or a unicorn skittering across the floor.

The dog struggled to get down and Trevor carefully set him on his feet. The dog looked up at me, certainly not acting normal, but obviously a lot more comfortable. The stretcher arrived and I gave Trevor instructions about X-rays and bloodwork and IV fluids for the techs. As I sent them on their way to the treatment area, I put on gloves, collected the ball and turned to the owners.

"Is this one of yours?" I asked, reasonably I thought.

"Yes," she replied, laughing softly, but with an out of control frantic edge to her tone. "We're throwing them all away. Both dogs love balls so much that we got them a child's ball pit without paying attention to the size of the balls. What a colossal mistake!"

"You've had a lot of excitement in the past twenty four hours," I said calmly.

"We could have lost them both," she said, tears gathering in her eyes and then spilling down her face. Her husband put his arm around her and pulled her close.

"Duke is fine," he said reassuringly. "And now I have hope that Major will be too. What's next Doc?"

"We'll know a lot more in the next few hours," I said with a small smile. "The obstruction by the ball may be relieved, but the gastrointestinal tract has undeniably been stressed. We'll have to manage his electrolytes and fluids and blood sugar and a boatload of other things. But I have a really good feeling."

CHAPTER TWENTY

The remainder of the shift was demanding and busy, but my double food offerings certainly helped me keep good energy going throughout all the ups and downs. I stepped into the next exam room and, like I'd been doing all shift, immediately apologized, "I'm so sorry for your long wait. Thank you for being so patient."

"No problem," the young man said with a wan smile. "Benny is certainly uncomfortable, but I don't think it's a life and death emergency. The dog that got in before us was bleeding all over everything so I definitely wanted him rushed to care ahead of us."

"Thanks for understanding," I said with a bright smile. "That dog's doing so much better already."

"Good," he said with a matching smile.

"Tell me what's up with Bennie," I said.

"Well, your nurse said that it might be his anal glands?" he replied. "But I thought dogs scooted when they had anal gland problems. Benny's just been licking his butt obsessively and not wanting to move around."

"Different dogs react differently," I said. "Scooting and licking are the most common signs, but my Aunt's dog would run across the room and simply sit down real quick, which is an odd presentation and made diagnosis difficult. And I've seen pugs spin around on their bottoms while licking the air, which is even odder. But I'll check the whole area and we'll figure this out."

I opened the door and called Tabby in to hold Benny for me. Usually I'd already have her in the room, but she was trying to work on all the busy day paperwork that was threatening to crush me. After doing a complete exam, I put on a glove and did a rectal exam. Thank goodness the answer was simply very full anal sacs and not anything more serious. Plus Benny had horribly self-traumatized his skin trying to scratch the uncomfortable, but unreachable, anal sacs. So as itchy as the underlying problem was, the resultant skin infection was now even more painful and would definitely need to be treated as well. While I was completing the rectal exam I emptied the anal sacs, diagnosis and treatment all in one, and applied a liberal amount of multipurpose topical medicine to the affected skin.

"E-collar?" Tabby asked as she left the room. "And topical to go home?"

"Yes," I agreed and turned to the owner to ask, "Do you have any questions?"

"Yeah," he said. "What causes the problem? Is it the food we feed?"

"Probably not," I answered. "Sometimes people recommend high fiber food to cause a bulky stool to help push scent material out with every bowel movement, but I don't find that usually helps. Sometimes it seems like allergies can make them more sensitive, or concurrent infection can complicate things, or even the scent material can get all dried out and need medicine instilled inside. We'll get you a handout that discusses it all, but usually having your groomer or one of our techs empty them on a regular basis helps the most."

"Oh," he said, seeming a little confused. I realized that I hadn't asked about Benny's history of trouble in the past and asked, "Has he had any trouble with anal sacs in the past?"

"Ahhh, not that I know of," he replied with an embarrassed look on his face, as a slow flush colored his cheeks. "There are a couple of unneutered male dogs next door that he plays with."

I didn't understand what that had to do with the topic we were discussing. He looked at me awkwardly, and I felt like there was something important that I was missing. I knew it wasn't just a random comment. I could tell he was trying to answer the question that I had just asked. I replayed it in my mind on repeat until it finally dawned on me.

"Oh sorry," I said. "So sorry." I pulled one of my famous trifold paper towels out of the dispenser and wrote down the words anal sacs in large print and explained, "I get that it might have sounded like I said sex, but I said sacs. Teeny tiny glands produce the scent material that fills the sacs. The sacs are what need to be expressed when they become overly full. The proper expression therefore would be empty the anal sacs, but many people use the term anal glands instead, because while technically incorrect it does stop this kind of miscommunication from happening."

"Well," he said, "I think I'm going to call them anal glands from now on."

"Well, my professors and my mentors here at the hospital might be disappointed in me for my inexactitude," I said, feeling my own cheeks turning red. "But I am never, ever calling them anal sacs again for the rest of my career."

He gave a shy smile, then started to giggle, and I couldn't help myself and joined in. The louder he laughed, the louder I laughed until Tabby came back in to check on us. Neither of us felt like explaining so we simply continued laughing until I finally pointed at the medication, the E-collar, and the handout and then, with tears in my eyes, gasped out, "Thank you for your patience and your understanding," and left the room.

It was way past midnight before I even thought about going home, just like I had predicted at the start of my shift. Max loved coming to the hospital, it was like a second home to him. It had been the first place I had rushed him to after discovering him so close to death in our badlands, abused and abandoned and neglected by monsters. We all worked so hard to save him and comfort him that night, and he loved the hospital and the people here as a result. But this late at night he had had enough, just as I had, and we were both supremely ready to go home.

I packed up my bag of empty food containers, snapped Max's leash on, and said goodbye to everyone. It was crisp out, but I savored the cool air because it smelled clean and fresh compared to the constant disinfection odor of the hospital. We crossed the first parking lot and Max rumbled a low growl beside me as his hair, growing in weird patches due to his extensive scarring, stood up along his back. I held the bag of containers in front of me like a shield, but didn't see or hear anyone in the area. We headed through the first parking lot as Max continued to alert toward a cluster of cars on the far side.

I kept us moving and Max settled down until a man popped up right in front of us. Max promptly backed up, but then leaned forward and took a hesitant step, raising his head up in the odd way that he has, stretching his neck up and tilting his chin to the side, the action he did right before he'd rise up on his back legs. The man stood silently but expectantly, and he did look vaguely familiar, but I couldn't quite place him, which wasn't that uncommon for me. The way my brain worked I had a better chance of recognizing a pet first.

"Can I help you?' I asked in as calm a voice as I could muster.

"You killed my dog," he snarled in a low aggressive tone.

"I'm so sorry for your loss," I said gently. "Would you like to step into the hospital where we can talk about it?"

"No," he snapped, getting louder with each word. "What good would that do?'

"Well," I said quietly. "We're not going to keep talking in a dark parking lot in the middle of the night."

"It was good enough for you and your little army of crusty old men to yell at me in this parking lot," he retorted.

Now I recognized him, he was part of the pair of owners that had screamed at the technicians as they were helping them get their suffering dog to their car, even though they were removing the poor dog against medical advice. Uncle Phil, and the Jays, had stood up to them, and while his actions had made me have lots of thoughts about how to handle toxic clients, I didn't actually know this man.

"I'm sorry, but I wasn't your doctor so I'm not the person you should be talking to," I stated and turned away. It was becoming obvious, by the smell of his breath and his demeanor, that he was drunk and spoiling for a fight. I had a firm grip on my phone and on Max's leash and thought the smartest move was to walk off as if I was going to continue on my way home. But my plan was to suddenly cut back after a couple steps and run to the hospital instead. My encounter with Dag at Forest Park had shaken my confidence a bit since he had easily countered all my self-defense moves, but I was planning on giving them another try if this guy touched me in any way.

I don't know how he moved so fast, but he appeared in front of us again and shouted, "Why didn't you help him?"

"You refused everything we offered," I said quietly, but then raised my voice as the fear and anger took over. Something had broken inside me last year and I just couldn't allow myself to be abused again. Not because I couldn't withstand the pain of the abuse, I'd already proven I could, but because I couldn't stand the shame of not standing up for myself. I shouted, "What did you expect me to do after you abused my people and dragged your poor dog out of here? I'm not magical! I don't have a magic wand to wave around to fix your dog! I wish I did, I'd cure your dog and then make you disappear. And you wouldn't like where I sent you!"

The man looked at me with as shocked a look on his face as I have ever seen. Max rose up on his back legs, steadying himself with one paw on my side, and barked a deep staccato woof down at the man. Then he stared at him with wide anxious whale eyes and his huge mouth hanging open as if he couldn't decide just what to do with it next. I know my Max well; his puppyhood of severe abuse and neglect made him much more likely to run away than anything else. But I had the sense that maybe he too had reached a point where he was willing to stand up for himself, or maybe a more reasonable explanation, stand up for me.

I couldn't dial 911 without looking at my phone, and I didn't feel safe looking away from this disturbed man, much less turning my back on him to make a dash for the hospital. I patted

Max, then guided him down onto all fours, took his collar in my hand and started to back away. The man stared at me like a dog watching a rabbit, trying to judge when it was the right time to spring into action. This was going to happen and I readied myself to simultaneously scream for help and to fight back the second that he moved any closer to me.

"Hey Doc," a voice shouted out as a car rolled up towards us. The driver carefully, and slowly, cut between us, never putting Max at risk, but getting pretty darn close to the man.

When I got a good look at him, I asked, "Oh no, not another catastrophe with a ball?"

He grinned, but with an ice cold expression, and kept a steely glare toward where the man had last been standing and said, "Nah, I just brought some chicken and rice to feed Major. I know you have that special bland diet, but he loves chicken and rice and we were feeling so guilty. Whatcha doing out here?"

"I live really close," I said, trying to see where the other man had disappeared to. "Max and I were walking home."

"How about I give you two a ride home?" he said. "Major and Duke would never forgive me if I let someone hurt you."

"Thank you," I said with a big sigh. "I would love a ride home."

I helped Max into the backseat and climbed into the front seat with another sigh. I wish I could remember my savior's name, but I had thought of him as Major and Duke's Dad throughout both emergencies and no matter how hard I concentrated, that's the only name I could come up with now. Somehow mid rescue it seemed like a socially inappropriate way to address him though.

He asked for directions, then pulled out of the hospital complex, smiled rather shyly, and asked, "Does stuff like that happen often?"

I said ruefully, "That was my third scary parking lot encounter," and suddenly felt like crying from the humiliation of admitting to that fact. It couldn't possibly be the way working in a service profession was supposed to be.

"That's totally unbelievable to me," he said, and we exchanged similar expressions of chagrin and regret.

"As Mr. Rogers said, 'when bad things happen, look for the helpers,' so I look to you," I said with a smile. "I really appreciate you coming to my aid. It made all the difference in the world, not just to the outcome, but to the way I feel about human kind in general."

He smiled back as we pulled up in front of my house and said, "Sounds like the pets treat you better than their owners."

"They generally do," I agreed. "Pets may bite, scratch, and rake me, or pee, poop, and vomit on me, but at least they are straightforward and honest about it. I appreciate that."

He laughed as I got out of the car and retrieved Max. I said, "Thank you so much. I hope Major does well tonight and gets to go home in the morning."

"Thank you for saving Duke and Major," he said with a deeply serious tone to his voice.

"Thank you for saving me and Max," I said just as seriously, then chuckled and shook my head. I couldn't make this stuff up.

CHAPTER TWENTY-ONE

It's vital both for my wellbeing and my identity to see myself as an emotionally courageous person. But this morning I was having the most bizarre reaction to the crazy man in the parking lot incident and I had no idea where it came from. I've lived through some hard, hard times. I've been hurt by obviously bad people and I've been in other situations with people that I thought were good people where I never saw the painful betrayal coming. But I have always reacted by keeping my feet marching forward, trying to find the positive where I can, and continuing to do my best even in the worst situations. Yes, maybe briefly I would turn inward to minimize any additional painful encounters, but then I'd quickly bounce right back out of it. In the best of times I prided myself in being both open and honest. And in the worst of times I never lost my dedication to being honest, but a couple of times I had to temporarily curtail my openness, but only to the extent that I needed to survive. But from the minute I woke up this morning, through my first cup of coffee, and during the rest of my morning routine, I knew that I had to call Dr. Drama and tell him what had happened in the parking lot and I simply didn't want to. I didn't want to move forward, or look for positives, or try my hardest. I didn't want to deal with any of it. It dawned on me that this may be the exact definition of an emotional coward, but I just really didn't care. I didn't want to do it.

It's been pointed out to me numerous times by multiple people that I don't have much of a self-protective nature, and I have to agree. But I undeniably do have a very strong protective response when it comes to the people and animals that I care about. So the second I realized that everyone else could be at risk at the hospital if I kept my mouth shut, I knew I had to alert them to the possible danger. The image of Tessa or Tabby or Stretch being confronted and possibly hurt flashed into my brain, and provided the motivation I needed to immediately dial the hospital and ask to speak to Dr. Vincent. I almost called him Dr. Drama, but I caught myself at the last minute.

"Dr. Kat," he said with a suspicious tone. "Can't live without us even on your day off?"

"Yeah," I replied, "Max doesn't uphold his end of our conversations like you do."

"And?" he asked, obviously wanting me to quickly move the conversation along.

"There was an incident in the parking lot late last night when I was going home," I said. "That abusive owner that took his dog home against medical advice and yelled at our techs a couple days ago? He threatened me. One of my owners interrupted the confrontation and drove me home. But I'm afraid that creep may come back to cause more trouble."

"Did you call the police?" he asked.

"No," I said. "He disappeared as soon as my rescuer drove up."

"Kat," he said in a gruff voice. "That's not acceptable."

"I'm sorry," I said defeated. "I don't know why I didn't call. I just didn't want to bother them."

"You didn't want to bother them?" he asked caustically. "At the only time when they actually had a reasonable chance to do something about it?"

"He was drunk," I said.

"That just makes it worse," he said "You let him drive away drunk?"

I didn't know what to say. I know I messed up, for me and for the hospital. I sure didn't want to be treated like a victim, but I really, really hated being treated like I was the bad guy here. But I guess the joy of being a talker like I am is that when you're struck silent people who know you well recognize it's a bad sign.

"I'm sorry," Dr. Drama said sincerely as the silence stretched out. "I'm sorry that happened to you. I'm not upset with you, just upset this is all happening. Why don't you call one of the detectives and ask what we should do now? They have the information about that asshole. I gave them everything we had just in case he had something to do with Melanie."

"Okay," I replied softly.

"It's going to be okay," he said confidently. "We'll figure this all out even if we have to hire security."

"Okay," I said. "I'll call Detective Warner."

"Keep me in the loop," he said. "Did you tell Phil?"

"No," I replied reluctantly.

"Let him know so he can watch out for you at home," he insisted. "While I figure out what we're doing around here."

"Okay," I agreed, and quickly asked, "How is Major, the dog that bounced the ball out his butt in the waiting room?"

Dr. Drama chuckled and said reassuringly, "He's great! Eating well, acting normal. He'll get to go home today."

"Thank goodness," I said. "He's a wonderful dog! His owner is the one that saved me last night."

"Glad to know that," he replied and with a quick, "gotta go," he hung up on me.

I jumped off the bed and froze in place. I really didn't want to make that next phone call, but I knew I had to. I felt like a spring deep inside me was being successively and painfully tightened and I wanted so badly to find a way to relieve the tension. I finally decided to do what I could remember of the Tai Chi form we were learning in class. I didn't want to be completely freaked out when I called Detective Warner, but I didn't want to procrastinate any more than I already had, so I only did it for a couple minutes. Oddly, since I only remembered about half of the form, it still managed to settle my nerves.

I got the card Detective Warner gave me with his cell number on it, and took a couple more deep breaths as I contemplated what I should tell him. Then I decided that while I was becoming an expert in taking a medical history, it was his job to know what information he needed to know in this situation and I'd just need to answer his questions. I've trusted him ever since he noticed how scared I was to go in the training facility and went in ahead of me in a protective manner. The longer I worked with animals, the more I relied on people's actions and their body language to help me judge what type of people they are. It was much better than relying on what they said, which had never worked particularly well for me since time and again I believed my lying and manipulative uncle and ex-boyfriend. So the way that Detective Warner had reacted made me think he was a good guy that I could personally count on.

He answered quickly and after identifying myself I told him, "I need some advice about a situation that occurred last night. I was confronted in our parking lot and afterwards I didn't call 911 like I should have and I've already been chastised by Dr. Vincent."

"Who was it? Did they hurt you?" he asked in an intense tone.

"No," I replied, feeling tears sting my eyes and wobble my voice. "One of my dog owners chased him away. But by his body language I'd swear in a court of law that he was about to physically attack me."

"Who was it?" he asked again in a rough voice.

"It was that guy that was verbally abusing my techs and was confronted in the parking lot by my neighbor and my four veteran friends," I replied. "Dr. Vincent said he gave you his name and information already, but I don't think I ever even heard his name. I didn't have anything to do with his case. I just came over to protect my techs that day."

"Okay," he said. "We'll swing by his house and have a chat with him."

"Please be careful," I said anxiously. "If I ever call someone an animal or a beast, you need to know that from me, that's a compliment. But I'm telling you this guy is a vicious predator and he could hurt you."

"I hear you," he said reassuringly. "We know what we're doing."

"I still don't think he had anything to do with Melanie," I said, trying to be fair.

"Maybe not," he agreed, "but I'm still interested in what he's up to. I'll make initial contact, since I want to speak to him anyway, but someone else may contact you to make the report on this latest incident. I'll let you know."

"Thank you," I said with relief. "Anything new about Melanie?"

"Not much that I can share," he said. "But we're collecting good information. You haven't heard from that Jade Peterson person have you?"

"No," I said. "Her dog's care was taken over by a Good Samaritan and we've seen them, but there's been no problems or interference by Jade."

"That's good," he replied without further explanation.

"Thank you for giving Melanie's death the attention she deserves," I said gratefully. "She was a good person who just wanted to help animals."

"You're welcome," he said, and it sounded like he was going to say more, but then said, "We'll talk soon," and hung up.

You'd think I'd feel better after speaking to Dr. Vincent and Detective Warner, but I actually felt even more agitated. I decided to run downstairs to finish my penance and tell Uncle Phil.

As soon as I told him he enfolded me in big hug and I could finally relax. More than that, I felt like I could breathe freely, and bits of tension left my body with every exhalation. Phil patted my back a few times and then let me go after a final tight squeeze.

"Thanks, Phil," I said. "I'm finding all this pretty overwhelming."

"I'm sorry," he said. "I have no clue about a long term answer for what the fuck is wrong with people, but I do know what to do in the short run. We're going to have the best ever house dinner tonight and make sure you feel safe and cared for. And then we're going to figure out a way to assure your safety when you're outside this house."

"Thank you Phil," I said with a weak smile. "Dr. Drama said something about getting security."

"I'll give him a call," Phil said. "I have some ideas."

"I have some ideas too," a soft voice came from Phil's kitchen as Ethan peeked around the corner. "I have some products entering the testing phase I could contribute to the cause."

"I thought you worked with computers," I said after giving him a quick hug. "I'm confused."

"Video surveillance systems and drones with cameras and all sorts of smart products are just computers in different shapes and sizes," Ethan said grinning. "One of my jobs is to develop new applications, so I might be able to get you some sort of tech on my research and development budget."

"That's cool," I said appreciatively. "Lots of good ideas, and thanks for the support, but those are questions for another time. Right now the most important question is: what's for dinner?"

CHAPTER TWENTY-TWO

Early in the day, when I first thought about emailing Andrei to see if he had received my last email, I reacted by hustling into my kitchenette and vigorously cleaning every surface instead. But this time my displacement behavior didn't stand up to the strong inner voice that kept reminding me of my new commitment to immediately tackle any task that I was reluctant to face. No cowardly procrastination for me! So I made myself comfortable in the living room, with my feet propped up and my phone on a pillow in front of me, and typed another email to Andrei. He probably didn't have access to the internet wherever he was, but since I didn't know where he was, there was still a chance that my last email had been lost in security precautions and/or various countries' censorship.

Hi Andrei! I'm in no way trying to pressure you, but I haven't heard back and I'm afraid something went wrong with my email. I'm pretty desperate not to screw up anything with you now, because the more I think about it I must have somehow screwed it all up after you left for the Marine Corps. I certainly knew that our uncle repeatedly lied to us. And believing anything a liar says, after that first batch of lies are discovered, is insane. A rational person would have to be an idiot (Me!!) to keep believing the liar time and time again.

Uncle changed some after you left; he stopped actively criticizing me all the time. Stefan was still the golden child, but I was no longer the constant family scapegoat. He acted like I was invisible more than anything else, like anything I said was totally inconsequential, not worthy of critique or rebuttal or even reply. When I'm talking to people who have rescued neglected dogs, I emphasize how horrible neglect can be, even compared to overt abuse, but for me his neglect was almost restful compared to the years where everything I did was wrong and everything I said was misinterpreted. For long years he had to let me know that every single quality I possessed was just so inherently wrong; it felt good when it stopped.

If money (especially the trust funds) were involved, he could be almost pleasant to me. Looking back he had to have been doing something shady with our finances and was trying to keep me from suspecting. I can't remember, did I tell you that he was always involved with any of my big purchases, like my car and computer? At the time I did suspect some kind of selfish motive. I decided he was doing it so that he could earn cash back rewards on his credit card while I paid for the original total from my trust fund. It didn't feel fair, but I kinda accepted it, like it was worth it to get his help. Then when he kicked me out of OUR house he claimed that he owned all those things that were precious and necessary to me. And of course he could prove it with his credit card receipts. Every time I see a meme that says something like, 'Love people and use money, don't love money and use people,' I think of him. There's no better way to describe him. And I'm so ashamed that I never realized it at the time that when he was even a little bit nice to me it was because he was plotting to use me in some way.

I'm not saying all this so that you'll feel sorry for me. I have somehow found the most excellent group of people to work with and another incredible group to live with and be my pseudo family. But I miss you and I want things to be right between us. I'm deeply sorry for our estrangement, but I honestly don't know how it all went wrong. You talk about an order of protection. I have no knowledge or memory about that, but I googled it so I at least know what it is now. One of my housemates is a retired police officer and I'll follow up with him and see what I can do about that.

I'm praying for you. Be safe. Kat

I closed my eyes, said a little prayer and hit send.

I went to the kitchen and put together another bento box of snacks to take to work to supplement my left over pasta from this week's house dinner. My housemates were still sending the majority of the leftovers home with me after every dinner. Mei even made five salads every week even though, with Dagger out of the country, there were only four of us at dinner. That fifth salad always went home with me and it seemed to be just one more way she found to support me without making me feel bad. I felt such appreciation for her and Phil and Ethan and I hated that I would never be able to pay them back for all they do for me.

When I got back to my phone, I was stunned to see a reply from Andrei.

Oh, Kat. It's so hard thinking back to that time when I was so busy and stressed and basically trying to survive. I can't figure out how everything happened. I honestly think it's all our uncle's fault, I don't know how, but I believe he somehow orchestrated the whole situation, including disrupting all possible communication between us. But what we as teenagers should or shouldn't have known about his lying and manipulations and weird games at the time, I don't know. I think we were just busy trying to grow up. But I sure don't think we should blame ourselves or each other. Right now I think we need to start over fresh, catch up on our lives, and try to reconnect. I can't wait for you to meet my wife and kids. And we'll have plenty of time, especially after I'm back home, to finally hold Uncle accountable and get some answers. I don't expect in any way that he'll tell the truth, but there has to be a paper trail for all the financial stuff that we can access. My wife is a bookkeeper so she can help us figure that stuff out.

You haven't mentioned how Stefan is doing. Is he still living with Uncle? Graduated from college yet? He's turning twenty-one next month. Mom and Dad's will says that now the three of us can legally sell the house. And that means we can kick Uncle out on his ass. Sounds like that would feel particularly good to you. I'm looking forward to calling him out on all his dishonesty and his all-around criminal jackassery!

Are you safe? You said one of your friends was killed? At the hospital? Is Dagger back home and looking out for you? You better be taking care of yourself.

Tears gathered and then spilled down my face, partially because of the sadness of our lost time together, but also oddly because of the relief of having Andrei back in my life. When our parents died, holding on to Andrei kept me from giving into the abject despair of that situation. Nothing will ever be as hard as that was, but having Andrei by my side again makes any and every problem that might come my way easier to face.

As I got ready to reply I realized that Andrei might not understand why I didn't know what was happening with Stefan. Andrei and I had worked very hard to take care of Stefan, who was only eight years old when our folks died and Uncle moved into our house and took over our lives. Would Andrei understand that Stefan had completely abandoned me, first gradually after I left for those seven years of college, then abruptly and fully the minute that Uncle had turned on me?

That fateful day, when I was nonchalantly getting ready for a nice weekend away with my best friend Jane, my uncle attacked me about my choice to start an internship instead of working at a regular job with a professional salary straight out of school. I had tried to explain my plans for my future, at that time becoming a board certified surgeon, for which I vitally needed the internship step. Of course that plan had changed, but the internship certainly accomplished the even more important task of allowing me to discover that I did not in fact want to be a surgeon. It reminded me of people who say that their prayers weren't answered, when in fact they didn't appreciate that the answer they received was no! My internship turned out to be necessary to discover what path I shouldn't take. I suddenly recognized that my thoughts were starting to scatter away from the email I was supposed to be writing, so I took a break to make a smoothie to keep my brain focused until I had time to cook.

I didn't know what to say to Andrei, and I didn't really have any grasp on how he would react to anything I had to tell him. Would he be mad at how I treated Stefan or at how he treated me or mad at both of us for allowing Uncle to direct our relationship in such unhealthy ways? I decided to reply as dispassionately as I could, answering all his questions, but trying not to talk too much more about my pain. Once again I didn't want his pity, but I sure didn't want him to blame me for abandoning Stefan when it was he who deserted me. Stefan had gleefully torn my precious belongings out of my arms as my uncle loudly abused me all because money wasn't my prime motivator. I hoped Andrei could hear the deep truth that ran through my stream of consciousness ramblings. I reread his email and allowed myself to laugh about his 'all-around criminal jackassery' expression. Maybe the next time a rude client lays into me I'll call Detective Warner and beg him to arrest them for criminal jackassery! With a grin on my face, I started to type.

Andrei, I have to admit that I'm in an odd emotional frame of mind. My friend Melanie was murdered in the hospital, the police investigation is so upsetting and totally out of our control. At the same time we crave the police presence so that they can find out who did this, bring them to justice, and keep all of us safe from the same fate in the meanwhile. I'm now a staff veterinarian with new responsibilities with the interns and they are just the most terrible human beings. Oddly enough they are okay doctors, although lazy and entitled, but just nobody you'd choose to spend significant time with. I miss Dagger, haven't heard from him in many weeks, and it's hard not to feel hopeless that he's ever coming home.

I don't know what to say about Stefan. I have no idea what's going on with him. I haven't spoken to him in a year. And to be completely honest, we didn't have any meaningful conversations for a couple years before that. He was supposed to graduate from Purdue Fort Wayne (It's not IPFW anymore!) this year, but I don't know if he did. At the last minute neither Uncle nor Stefan could make it to my graduation from veterinary school, nor could they help me move out of my apartment like they had promised, so it took me longer than expected to make it back to Fort Wayne. I finally got home for a couple days and expected to reorganize my belongings, spend a mini vacation weekend with Jane, and then head out to the internship I had arranged last minute in Noblesville. There's a much longer conversation about my senior year from hell, due to a lying cheating boyfriend, but I'll save that for some late night in person conversation. Maybe accompanied by some beers.

Uncle was beyond furious that I wasn't going to take some high paying job. He couldn't accept that I chose instead the path of internship and eventual specialization. After hearing my plan, he spent the first day refusing to speak to me and then the second day haranguing me for my irresponsible choice. The third day, when I was leaving the house to drive to Jane's, he absolutely lost his mind. I'll never forget his face, it was contorted with rage and hatred and he actually looked inhuman. You and I probably watched more Sci-Fi movies than we should have in our high school days, but I'd almost swear that there was a repulsive alien or foul devil inside him and the monster was struggling to break through the skin of his face. He screamed obscenities and snatched the car keys out of my hand, claiming the car and everything in it was his because he had bought them with his credit card and threatened to have me arrested for trying to steal them.

Stefan stood there looking like everything Uncle was doing was normal, like all this craziness and venom was right or somehow justified. And when Stefan finally spoke, it wasn't to me at all, it was to Uncle to remind him about my computer and other tech that I had packed to take to Jane's. After he took it all from me, the last words that Stefan spoke were to tell Uncle that I still had an IPod and Uncle demanded I hand it over. And I did. I'm an idiot. I've missed that old music and that ancient iPod more than anything else he took.

I walked away, holding my comforter and pillows and rolling my weekend suitcase behind me as the locksmith drove up. Uncle screamed that he was changing the locks and I was never to set foot in the house again. My own house!

I was completely wiped out, I wasn't sure that I could even write another word. But I quick added an apology for rambling and repeated that I missed him and hit send.

Oh, Kat, I'm sorry you went through all that. What a shit show. As Dad used to say, there's a solution to every problem, and between the two of us I know we can figure out what to do about all of this. It may not be the most elegant of solutions, but we'll make a workable plan. And then we'll tackle him. Maybe by ourselves, maybe surrounded by lawyers and forensic accountants! We'll do what we can to protect Stefan, but he's made some bad choices too.

The personnel we've been waiting for just arrived so I'll be out of touch again, but I promise I'm coming to help you soon. Be safe, Andrei

I didn't even have the energy to cry and felt both worse and better for even having broached the subject of that horrible ordeal of being thrown out of my home. It was my last tangible physical connection to my beloved parents. I believe that living through the trauma of that day created a permanent gaping hole in my heart. But I struggled to force myself off the sofa and called Max to me, determined to take him for a walk and leave these overwhelming feelings behind.

Surprise, I just saw someone we both know.

The short message popped up on my phone and suddenly a fire flared in my heart and hope flooded my chest. Maybe every inference that Dagger made that he was off on some vital secret mission was true and it wasn't some lie to keep me on a string while he was off partying and living the high life. And what kind of a contemptable person was happy that her boyfriend was in danger if it meant he wasn't lying to her?

CHAPTER TWENTY-THREE

It was a relaxed morning, but no one dared comment on it for fear that the 'slow' jinx or the 'quiet' curse would rear its ugly head and wreak havoc on the entire ER. I had paperwork to do, but I was struggling to even get out of my chair and retrieve it all, much less have the energy to complete it. I was happy to be talking to Andrei again and to feel like I had him on my side, but facing the emotions it stirred up sucked the life right out of me. I had worked yesterday's shift like a zombie, and assumed today would be the same. My personal issues were layered on top of Melanie's death, the police investigation with the resultant suspicions of people I cared about, and the absolute criminal jackassery of both the abusive owners and frankly this obnoxious class of interns. I laughed to myself and admitted I was going to overuse that jackassery expression until it stopped giving me a jolt of joy every time it ran across my brain.

I wanted to ask Dr. Drama if the hospital owners had grown tired of worrying about our class of sensitive, empathetic, and perfectionist interns and had actually tried to choose a tougher crew this year. If they did, they way overshot and picked straight out narcissists; these three interns truly didn't care about anyone but themselves, not even each other.

Dr. Blackwell bustled by my desk, juggling an awkward pile of files and lab reports, but slowed after she passed me, backed up and asked, "How you doing Kat?"

"I'm okay," I replied morosely.

She rolled her eyes, sighed, and plopped into the empty chair next to me, and said, "Seriously. What's up?"

I looked at her and tried to put just one of my discordant

thoughts into words. "I don't know. It's like it's just all too much."

She gestured with an open hand around the empty treatment area and quiet ICU and asked, "This is too much?"

I let out a deep breath and admitted, "No. I'm not overwhelmed with work as much as I feel fractured and out of synch. Nothing is how it's supposed to be."

"It happens," she said calmly. "And when it's not busy and we're not distracted by patients that need us, we actually have the time to feel the pain and frustration."

"That makes sense," I said nodding. "Thanks. Lately I've honestly thought I was going a bit crazy."

"Not really something we believe in saying anymore," she corrected with a half-smile.

"Losing touch with reality?" I asked with arched eyebrows.

Giving a soft laugh she said, "Feeling negative emotions when you don't want to?"

"That's really minimizing what we're all going through!" I retorted.

"Your friend died and people are acting like assholes," she replied with a frown. "I'd worry more if you weren't sad and overwhelmed. What rational person would be happy facing those situations? And choosing to feel out of touch with a painful reality? That shows some remarkable strength it seems to me."

I looked at her quizzically. She was still making sense, but somehow it didn't feel as supportive and comforting as I wanted it to. But once again I didn't know how to put any of it into words.

She stared at me for long minutes, maybe she was struggling to verbalize her feelings as much as I was. Finally she said, "It's not the first time that I've faced difficult times, both in my personal life and in my professional life. Fairly early in my career I went through a patch that was difficult enough that I went to a psychologist who helped me a lot. But he also did a bunch of tests including one that they use to determine if some of your problems are because you're in a profession that you aren't well suited to. And I didn't score high on suitability for Veterinary Medicine, but I did score high on other medical service professions like Speech Therapist and Psychologist which was interesting."

I nodded and asked, "Do you feel like you weren't a good fit for veterinary medicine? Are you sorry you became a Veterinarian?"

"Absolutely not," she replied. "I'm honored that I was given a chance to serve the animals and their owners, and I'm proud of what I was able to accomplish. But I had some hard lessons to learn."

"Like?" I asked.

"Like you can't pour tea from an empty pot!" she said with a laugh.

"Huh?" I asked.

"You can't take care of people and pets if you don't take care of yourself," she explained. "It's related to the serenity prayer: 'God grant me the serenity to accept the things I cannot change, the courage to change the things I can, and the wisdom to know the difference.' I probably repeat that to myself at least once a day, twenty times on the really rough days."

I smiled, the concept was very applicable to veterinary medicine. At the very core of practice is the knowledge that our pets are going to grow old and die at a much accelerated rate compared to us and we really aren't going to change that fact. And until animals can find a way to take themselves to veterinarians, basic human nature, both good and bad, will impact the way we do our jobs every single day.

She continued, "I used to repeat the serenity prayer so much that people started thinking I was part of AA. But addiction isn't one of the challenges that I've faced, so I toned down saying it so often. The wisdom to know when to fight is probably the most elusive for me. I've broken my own heart more than once tilting at windmills."

"Yeah," I agreed. "And once I decide to fight I just can't quit, no matter how logical that solution becomes."

"A wise man once told me that I should never say I'm quitting, but say instead that I'm redirecting my energy to a new plan," she said with a warm smile.

"I like it!" I said with my first warm, heartfelt smile of the day.

Dr. Blackwell started piling up her charts and reports and heaved herself out of the chair, "You know what's really funny?"

"What?" I asked.

"A few years ago I was asked to be in Who's Who of America," she waved me off as I tried to say congratulations and continued, "and then through them I was contacted by the people who formulate that suitability test, so that I could represent modern veterinarians. I was asked to take the test again to properly reflect the new dynamics of the veterinary profession, in particular the feminization of the occupation. So if you take the test now, you will be compared to me, and others like me, to see if you are well matched to be a successful veterinarian."

I looked at her in shock and said, "That's amazing!"

She gave me a half hug, juggling her stack awkwardly, and said, "Hop to it! If you finish your charts before me I'll buy you one of your fancy coffees!"

As soon as she left I felt a compulsion to check to see if Andrei had emailed me again, even though I felt guilty for doing it at work. He hadn't replied so I had no choice but to get to work on my records. Initial emergency records were done on the computer so they were completed at release. But I still needed to respond to follow up calls and to review laboratory tests that had been returned from outside labs as well as communicate all that news to owners and their primary care veterinarians. I was actually enjoying the feeling of putting all my ducks in a row until Dr. Harris sat down next to me with his own stack.

He sighed a couple times, side-eyed me three or four times, shifted in his chair multiple times, groaned and rubbed his right shoulder and then poked at a couple of deep scratches on the back of his hand. If he was looking for sympathy from me after his abusive treatment of me, he shouldn't have picked the day after I was forced to confront my deep negative feelings for my abusive uncle. Harris finally got to work on his charts, but his mere presence next to me was very irritating. Made me wonder if some of my dislike and disrespect of him were because of the way that he spoke to people reminded me of my uncle.

I used every last bit of my energy to focus on my remaining two tasks, finished them quickly and waved my hand over my head, calling to Dr. Blackwell, "I'm done!"

"Next coffee run, yours is on me," she said with a grin from across the room.

"Hey," I said with a huff. "That's false advertising! I thought you'd be running out for coffee as soon as I was done!"

"Okay, I can do that," she answered with a grin. "But you know what will happen don't you? The minute I leave, it'll be an ER Armageddon!"

I laughed and replied, "I'm willing to risk it!"

Dr. Blackwell smiled as she walked back over and said, "Do you want anything Dr. Harris? You'll have to chip in since you didn't win a bet."

"I would love some chai," he replied, as he took some bills out of his wallet. "Thank you so much."

I was shocked. Harris had that typical narcissistic, entitled habit of never saying thank you. Or for that matter, he didn't say please, or sorry, or most of all, how can I help you, either. And he never said excuse me when he had to pass you in a tight hallway. He just plowed passed you and you moved aside or got run over.

"Can I ask you a question?" Dr. Harris asked me softly when she had left.

I actually thought about saying no. But I truly didn't want to let his bad behavior change what type of person I was trying to be. I nodded and asked, "What's up?"

"The intern manual explains about schedules and time off," he said, still keeping his voice low. "But what if we have to take time off unexpectedly? Is there a way that can happen without making everybody mad?"

"I'm sure there is," I replied. "Just talk to Molly to arrange it.

It helps her if you can get one of the other interns to cover your shift. It proves you're being proactive."

"Yeah," he agreed reluctantly. "I just really don't want to tell them what's going on. And neither of them will do it without an explanation, I'm sure of that."

"Can you at least tell them the general category of your need?" I asked. As he stared at me rather blankly I added, "You know what I mean: family emergency, medical urgency, mental health crisis, the police want to see you downtown?"

"What?" he exclaimed. "What does that mean?"

"Just teasing," I said. "Stretch and I, and Dr. Drama too, keep getting questioned by the police. Although I guess it sounds better to say we're assisting in their inquiries."

"Oh," he said, then with a slight smile added, "It's medical and they really didn't give me many options for the appointment."

"Somebody will switch with you," I said. After considering that I might be guilty of giving mean-spirited advice, I decided it was vital advice for him to hear, "Be nice to them. People are much more likely to do you a favor if you're humble and ask nicely."

"I can do that," he said quietly, sounding like he had never considered the concept before. What was his problem with dealing with people?

As I turned to face him to ask what medical problem he was facing, the front door chimed in rapid succession and we both turned to watch the monitor. Oh no, Dr. Blackwell's dire prediction of an ER Armageddon as soon as she left the hospital was about to come true! We both popped up out of our chairs and I said, "Let me know if you need help," as I walked out.

CHAPTER TWENTY-FOUR

Another day, another extra-long emergency shift for me. Stretch had the afternoon off to meet with his attorney, Harris was at his mysterious medical appointment, so the hospital staffing was way too thin and they asked me to work a not quite double shift. I had gotten the impression that everyone around me was getting sick of me complaining about being tired and/ or sore so I was trying to act calm and smile as often as I could, but my body was in full betrayal mode. Each hour it seemed like some new body part needed to let me know how abused it felt. It didn't help that every patient required an extreme physical response on my part. I was constantly crouching or lifting or getting slammed into. I'd been working since midnight and now my feet, back, neck, hands and hips were all aching. Each body part also emphasized their discomfort by randomly sending shooting pains as well, just to keep my life interesting.

But my right elbow hurt the worst. A large mixed breed dog had tried to bite my hand and by reflex my arm had snapped back, slamming my elbow hard into the cabinet behind me. And there was absolutely nothing funny about whacking my funny bone with all that force. I loved that I had developed a reflexive jerk to get my hands out of harm's way, but it was a classic spinal reflex, meaning the nerve signal never made it up to my brain. The response rapidly occurred just to and from my spine. The big downside was that there was no opportunity for my brain to figure out that my elbow was going to bang into something hard behind me. It's like stepping barefoot on a Lego and your foot instantly flies up before you even know what happened. Embarrassingly, the same reflex also sometimes happens when an innocent puppy licks at my hand, and without my brain being consulted about if the response is appropriate, my hand can jerk out of the way. Just this week a woman was horrified that I was 'afraid' of her sweet little Snookums. I was so embarrassed at the time, but I sure don't want to curtail that protective reflex. As much as my elbow hurt, I could still do my job; while if my hands get badly mauled, there wouldn't be much I could do to help any patients after that.

Despite my discomfort, I not only managed to treat some adorable kittens with an upper respiratory infection, I managed to fully enjoy it. The eye discharge had glued their eyes shut, and it was urgent that we got that taken care of, but as soon as I cleaned them up and got the first dose of antibiotic ointment in their eyes, they turned into wild play machines and made themselves totally at home in my exam room. I let them entertain me for a couple extra minutes just to recharge my batteries a bit. A tired aching body and painful elbow couldn't compete with the magical power of cavorting kittens.

I walked into the next exam room and it was another young kitten, but it was sick enough it had a whole different attitude, laying listlessly on the table, not even raising its head to check me out when I walked over. It had a rapid heartrate and a bounding pulse, but it wasn't as pale as I thought it was going to be by its attitude, although the mucus membranes were a muddy color which is never good news. I immediately sent the kitten with Tabby to get bloodwork, giving her instructions to push to the front of the line and get the bloodwork stat.

"Tabby took a very detailed history, but I just want to go over a couple things," I said gently. The client looked as tired and stressed as I felt and I wanted to be honest about the seriousness of the kitten's problems without taking away all her hope.

"Sure," she said. "Whatever I can do to help," she replied.

"The kitten had her vaccines and was dewormed two weeks ago, and she's been fine until yesterday?" I asked.

"Yes," she replied. "I'm not sure when she started to feel bad, we're having some problem with our plumbing or the sewers or something and our landlord was there. He said he fixed it, but he didn't, so then he was supposed to come back, and he didn't. Anyway, the point to all that is that the kitten ended up in her carrier for most of the day."

"But no coughing or sneezing or vomiting?" I asked.

"No," she replied thoughtfully. "But I took the baby to my Mom's house for a bath and when I got home it looked like the kitten had spit up a little bit. She seemed quiet, but not like this. I took the baby upstairs to bed and left the kitten downstairs in the carrier. And she was so much worse this morning."

"And you didn't give her anything," I asked intently. "No medicine, nothing over the counter, no milk or anything to eat or drink."

"Absolutely nothing except kitten food and water," she insisted. "I know better, I..."

Tabby interrupted her with a sharp rap and a quickly opened door, and then an exaggerated wave to join her in the hallway. I excused myself and Tabby looked at me with wide eyes and held up a tube of some weird brown colored fluid.

"What's that?" I asked, wondering if she had collected urine or maybe vomit? It didn't look like anything I had ever seen.

"The kitten's blood," she hissed, softly but emphatically. "It's her blood!"

"No!" I hissed back.

"Yes," she insisted.

I froze as my brain did its robotic calculator impression, scrolling through all the information I had stored about unusual looking blood, through all those long years of school and thousands of pages of textbooks. Brown blood. I repeated it to myself a couple times as my feet, seemingly of their own volition, moved me over to a computer station to initiate a search. Brown blood. Wait, chocolate colored blood. I froze again, and tried to recall. Chocolate colored blood: methemoglobinemia. One part of my brain started rehearsing how to explain it to the owner, about how serious it was when the hemoglobin in the red blood cells is changed by a poison and can't carry oxygen anymore. But my hands continued their quest and opened a reference book so I could review all the facts. Tabby watched my face, but she trusted me and my process enough to stand patiently next to me.

She startled a little when I spun by her, darted back into the room, and asked, "Are you absolutely sure, absolutely, that she did not get any acetaminophen?"

"No," she replied. "Nothing."

"Absolutely sure?" I asked again, knowing it might make her angry, but I didn't know what else that could cause this.

"No," she replied emphatically. "I didn't. I wouldn't."

I huffed in weird exasperation and fear and said, "I don't know what else it could be. You sure no baby pain reliever or fever reducer, no Tylenol?"

"I know what acetaminophen is," she said starting to push back. "I gave the kitten nothing, all of our medicine is absolutely kept baby safe and put away."

I rushed back out and grabbed the book again, taking a minute to tell Tabby what tests to run. I brought the reference book back in the room with me and read it in front of the owner. Hidden in the final paragraph I saw the phrase sewer gas and asked, "Did you say you had a sewer gas problem at your house?"

I quickly flipped through the pages for the reference on sewer gas as she answered, "Yes. It smells terrible off and on."

I found the reference in the book, sewer gas could cause the methemoglobinemia too. It would be found down on the lowest levels of the house, on the floor, thus being way more dangerous for the kitten than the people. But the baby! I looked up in shock and asked, "Where's the baby?"

"Back at my Mom's house," she gasped in fear, reading my expression. "My landlord keeps saying its fixed and its safe and it's so very obviously not! I just couldn't have her there."

"Okay, we have to think this through," I said nervously. "Make sure no one goes back to the house. Call your pediatrician and tell them that we suspect the kitten has been poisoned with sewer gas on the same floor area that the baby has been crawling around on. Ask where they want you to go, their office or the ER? Do it now and then I'll give you more instructions."

I gave Tabby her own to-do list for the kitten, including alerting Molly and poison control in case we had to find a source for the antidote, and then turned back to the owner. She was struggling on the phone, stuck on repeating "met, met, methem" but never being able to get the whole word out. I took the phone out of her hand and I emphasized "METHEMAGLOBINEMIA!" and handed the phone right back to her. The minute her doctor's office said that they wanted her to go to the ER, she packed her purse up, doubled checked I had their numbers and announced over her shoulder, "I have to go. My mother's going to meet me with Genevieve at the hospital."

"One more minute," I said desperately. "We're about to cause a huge uproar. Are you absolutely sure the kitten got no medicine, none spilled or dropped?"

"I swear," she said.

"Then I'm going all in that it's sewer gas," I said. "It's going to get tense. I'm not sure who I'm supposed to call so I'm going to call everybody."

"If anyone needs me I'll be at the hospital with my daughter," she said as she opened the door.

I said, "I'll be in touch to catch up on the precise details when we know more. Drive very carefully."

I think I was supposed to call the Board of Public Health, but I wasn't sure where to find their number or if they even had emergency response capabilities. I may have come up with that vital clue about the chocolate colored blood from the massive volumes of facts somehow stored in the recesses of my mind, but I wasn't coming up with any memory about what I'd been taught regarding how to handle this kind of situation. I dialed 911 and threw myself on the mercy of the unlucky dispatcher that happened to answer my call. Her voice sounded vaguely familiar and I hoped she wasn't the same dispatcher that I had embarrassed myself in front of when I found Melanie's body. Although I guess not many people calling 911 are all that calm and composed or thinking particularly logically. I hope we emphasize that fact to our new client service representatives being trained to answer our emergency phones. Nobody's brains work right during trauma!

I wasn't wrong; the response to the crisis did get extremely tense. At the same time it was pretty awesome to see how many people responded to help in the situation. The less than helpful landlord was suddenly the most obliging person on the planet when he heard the baby was in the hospital getting checked out. Happily the baby showed no health problems, her blood was normal and she was eventually allowed to go home. Go home to her Grandmother's house that is, no one was allowed to go back into the death trap house except the professionals who were geared up properly. The kitten passed away very early in the process, and we were all so very sad about it. But her owners had such a wonderful attitude; they had my usual silver lining outlook and managed to see full out blessings. They believed that their precious kitten was an angel sent directly to their family to protect their baby girl. Later on they made us a beautiful angel blanket to use in our comfort room in her honor and I smile every time I see it.

CHAPTER TWENTY-FIVE

I knew I should be doing something productive before I had to drag myself to work, but I didn't have the energy to even contemplate getting off of my comfy spot on the sofa. Max stood in front of me with his tail wagging expectantly, which is usually all it takes to spark movement on my part, but I didn't even care if I disappointed him. I'd never sunk this low before. Of course Max had already been fed and taken out, so it wasn't like I was truly neglecting him. I'm pretty sure if he were hungry or thirsty I would have been able to stand up. But I had definitely shifted both of us to a basic survival mode; there would be no attempt to live our best lives today.

My senior year of veterinary school was miserable and I had successfully survived that series of traumatic events with my basic sense of self intact. At each of the multiple painful events I had been rocked by all sorts of emotions. Sometimes it was all at once, at other times I rotated between the different feelings: rage, shock, frustration, agony, despair, and everything in between. Yet throughout all of that I had been able to hold on to my determination to always do the right thing. And even on the worst days I could focus on pressing forward. I must have said, "Onward and upward!" a thousand times that year. But whatever was going on now was different. I couldn't put a name onto what I was feeling; it was like I was feeling less of everything. I was as unable to feel discouragement and dejection as I was unable to feel anticipation or hope. And yet I couldn't say I was numb. There was no artificial covering up or denial of normal responses; it simply wasn't there at the source deep inside me.

My odd assortment of thoughts and feelings must have been

showing on my face because Max came up demanding attention. He licked at my hands and offered his paw in supplication and in response I rubbed his ears and scratched his back, all the while speaking kindly to him. I realized that sitting and thinking about my odd feelings, or to be more honest my odd lack of any feelings, was not helping me in any way. And having been through hard times I knew what I should do. I needed to eat, not too much or too much sugar or fat, but also not too little. I needed to exercise, again not too much or too little or too obsessed with a single activity. I needed to socialize, be with people, but not in a wild or self-destructive way. But I just didn't want to do any of it. I didn't have the energy to generate my own solutions or boundaries. I wanted someone to do it for me. Or even to me.

After my parents died I had received so little help and support from my uncle that I had somehow lost the ability to trust people enough to ask for help. Maybe even worse, I no longer had the capacity to receive it when it was freely offered to me. My house family wanted nothing more than to help me, but my trauma response made me unable to accept their help, either refusing outright or trying to immediately match it or pay it back. Even now as I was screaming internally that I needed help, I didn't even know what specifically that help would consist of. I thought about the techs being abused by that horrible man while I was shamefully rendered frozen and silent, all because I was concentrating on what I could possibly do to help the dog's medical problems. What the techs really had needed at that time was for me to stop the abuse. They needed someone like Phil to stand up for them and simply tell the abuser to shut up. That could have been me.

Maybe ultimately I only needed someone to stand up for me. Then I thought about the client who rescued me and gave me a safe ride home. And the kitten's owners who honored us for saving their baby even though we couldn't save their pet. And the owners that sent us a thank you card and pictures of their puppy's happy birthday party, long months after we had fought so hard for his life in I.C.U. And my house family who tried to help me while working so hard to hide their support; all so that I could manage to receive that assistance. And Dag who made me feel like he would do anything for me even though he was usually somewhere else fulfilling his own obligations to job and country. And Dr. Drama and Dr. Blackwell, and even Dr. Tolliver in her quiet way, who mentored all of us so faithfully. Day after day they encouraged us to be the best that we could be; at the same time they let us know how much they trusted us and needed our help. People were standing up for me. It was me. It was me that wasn't supporting me.

But I didn't know how to do that. I can't work harder or longer or be any nicer to people. I can't do more. I can't change my family circumstances. I can't make Melanie not be dead. Maybe this weird lack of feelings was me trying to force my emotional work load into a more manageable size. Maybe it was a solution, but it was not how I wanted to live on a permanent basis.

I stood up, shook myself off like a dog, did a couple of Tai Chi stretches and got dressed for work. I packed healthy food for my meals, but dragged out both sweet and salty treats from the back of my cupboard and tucked them in as well. Maybe it wasn't best in the long run to rely on unhealthy snacks, but it is one of the few things I have control over. Once I get to work I can't even control if I get regular bathroom breaks, but I've developed the ability to eat a handful of candy in mere seconds. I apologized to Max for our lack luster morning and left a note for Ethan, telling him that if he had time to do something special for Max it would be great because I had been absolutely worthless to my precious pup so far today.

"Another day, another dollar," Phil said as I walked through the entryway on my way to work.

I almost snapped at him as I was really sick and tired of people accusing us of doing what we do 'just for the money.' If that was our motivation we would be in the human medical field where salaries and benefits are so much higher. Or not be in any of the medical or service professions at all for that matter as they rarely come with super high salaries, just personal satisfaction. But I knew Phil didn't mean anything by his comment, so I serenely replied, "I wish I was just going to work for the paycheck. I'm still weirdly passionate about helping the animals. It really hurts that some of the owners aren't as devoted as we all are."

"I hear you," Phil said. "I managed to stay dedicated to my police profession, but there were times I had to back off so that the shitbirds couldn't shred my soul. It wouldn't be fair to the good people that need my help in emergency situations if I let the bad ones diminish me and my ability to provide that assistance. Same for you."

"Yeah," I agreed, oddly reluctantly. I opened my mouth to repeat my 'onward and upward' mantra, but what I actually said was, "I'm struggling."

"And just remember that toxic people are really confessing when they make weird accusations against you," he said. "If they are accusing you of only caring about the money, it's because THEY only care about the money. Classic."

Then Phil quickly covered the distance between us with a couple gigantic steps and engulfed me in a big hug. I leaned into that hug and clung onto him. He said, "This is just such an adjustment year. You're no longer the rookie, so you're being forced to learn how the real world works."

I stepped back after a final squeeze and said, "One of my favorite professors told me to be the type of veterinarian that you are called to be, and eventually you will attract to yourself pet owners who want that kind of veterinarian. I'm just not sure that's applicable to emergency work. People have little choice because there are so few ERs available."

"Same with police work," Phil said. "So maybe that's the decision you'll have to make. I had to try a couple different jobs within the department to find where I fit best. But you can't let the job you have right now change you to the point you won't be ready to move to that better fit. And different jobs fit better at different stages of your life."

"Thanks Phil," I said with a small, but real, smile and reached for the door. "Onward I go!"

Everyone was busy when I got to the hospital, but after quick rounds, there wasn't actually that much for me to do. I double-checked my paperwork, which shockingly was caught up, and then wandered through the medical and ICU wards to get a better feel for the hospitalized patients. Today, as the second shift emergency doctor, I'd have a major responsibility for their care as the other shifts wrapped up their days and went home. The technicians did a lion's share of the treatments and testing, but there was still a tremendous work load for me, to interpret any test results, add treatments and procedures, and coordinate their care with the different departments' contributions. In the human hospitals, they call the physicians that handle this responsibility hospitalists so I've borrowed that term. So today I'm the hospitalist and my primary responsibility will be taking care of all the patients in the hospital. I'll also be backup for the emergency doctor and see new patients if the numbers get overwhelming, which happens ninety percent of the time on the weekends and holidays.

It's why when we're short staffed and there aren't two veterinarians, emergency and hospitalist, for these busy shifts, it creates an incredible amount of stress because no matter how hard you work or how much caffeine you drink you can't be in two places at once. Well trained technician partners are the only thing that makes the situation even bearable, but when problems strike that makes you short staffed, like the flu epidemic or bad weather, it often affects the techs and the doctors equally. So on those hellacious days you have to do twice the work with half the help. I don't know why I am even thinking about it today. We were fully staffed and there was a lull in cases that needed to be admitted, so things were running rather smoothly. I think the last horror of a short staffed shift that I had suffered through had given me some kind of weird PTSD.

I walked into the far back ward, the same place I keep

accidentally hearing people say terrible things about me, but thank goodness no one was there talking about anyone today. But the first dog to see me did a classic startle bark, increasing in volume and ending in an almost howl of warning that a monster had entered the ward. One by one the other dogs joined the chorus, each with their own pitch and tune, but all expressing their shock that I had entered their space. I'm a snob when it comes to the use of the word cacophony. For me the only two sounds that are harsh and discordant enough are: a kennel full of irate barking dogs and taxicabs honking their horns in a traffic jam in New York City. I feel like most every other collection of sounds fails to meet this high standard. But today's kennel chorus was a full blown cacophony, which is rare in the hospital where most patients aren't feeling well enough to create a fuss, or they have been sedated or are on pain killers. It sure can happen in the boarding kennels where it's all healthy dogs, but the hospital usually has pretty quiet wards.

I spoke calmly, calling them by name, and telling them to settle and lie down. I was starting to have an effect when suddenly a hand grabbed my shoulder and when I screeched in shock it started them all up again. Dr. Drama apologized and gestured for me to follow him out of the ward.

"You need to jump into the paperwork and start sending some of that choir home," he said. "They are feeling way too good to be here."

"What are you doing here?" I asked.

"Emergency back surgery," he replied.

"Dachshund?" I asked.

"Yep," he replied. "Although they caught the problem early because I had done the same surgery on their Beagle a few years ago."

I nodded and thought about asking him how he dealt with working long hours and then being called away from his family for emergency surgeries, but I hesitated. I didn't want to make his time away from his loved ones any harder or longer than it had to be just to counsel me. I smiled and said, "Sorry about stirring up the hounds of the Baskervilles. I was just trying to get a sense of how everyone was doing."

"Glad to see you doing that," he said with a smile. "But let's go back up front and let sleeping dogs lie for now."

"I hear you," I said with a grin. "I've probably told owners a thousand times about how disruptive visiting in the wards would be, but honestly it doesn't usually start a full out barkfest. Too bad I didn't take a video of that to show them what can happen!"

He smiled in response and headed back to the surgery area, as always getting the last word over his shoulder, "Get them out of here."

I don't know why, but today I didn't just go along with him and retorted, "Half of them are surgery cases!"

Dr. Drama whipped around, immediately checking the records closest to him, and replied mildly, "So they are."

CHAPTER TWENTY-SIX

I no more than walked into the treatment area than Dr. Harris sidled up to me and said, "I've got to talk to you."

"What's up?" I asked graciously while I screamed on the inside. I was sure it was going to be some excuse why he couldn't possibly do his fair share of the work today.

His expression was strangely apprehensive as he said, "I have to miss my shift again tomorrow. I saw you were off, can you trade me for the next day?"

I hesitated for a minute. I had to make good decisions for my own mental health, but I didn't actually care which of the two days I had off so I said, "That could work out, but I'd like to know what's going on. Are you okay?"

His eyes shifted down to stare at the floor, and said, "The doctor is concerned and scheduled a workup on my enlarged lymph node."

I should have had a more empathetic reaction, but something about standing in the hospital environment made me transition to my medical investigator persona instead and I asked, "Where?"

He pointed to the lymph node under his right arm and gestured so that I knew it would be okay for me to palpate it. I felt the definitely enlarged node, then reached up and felt to see if there were similarly enlarged lymph nodes nearby in his neck and then checked under his other armpit.

"Which arm did you get your vaccines?" I asked.

"My left," he said regretfully. "Never in the right. I didn't want to work with my dominant arm sore. So it's not post vaccine."

"Any others enlarged?" I asked rapid fire. "Blood work okay? Are they doing a biopsy or a fine needle aspirate tomorrow?'

"No others enlarged," he replied. "Bloodwork good so far. But the doctor mentioned lymphoma. Hodgkin lymphoma."

I wanted to react in horror, but I know I couldn't do that to him no matter how much I felt like it, so I said, "I'm sure he was just mentioning the scariest possibility to make sure you didn't try to skip the test."

"Sure," he agreed with a small smile, but it didn't reach his eyes and he looked petrified.

"Yeah," I said reassuringly. "Gotta check it out, but I'm sure it'll be fine."

"Yeah," he repeated, but didn't add any of the typical comments most of us make at those times, like 'it's probably just an infection' or something along those lines.

His lack of response worried me. He seemed to have given himself totally into major cancer concerns without counterbalancing with other better outcome alternatives. I looked at his hand again and asked, "So how are they ruling out cat scratch fever then?"

"What?" he asked as if the doctor had never discussed the possibility.

"Look at your scratched up right hand," I said. "Perfect history for Bartonellosis and cat scratch fever! We could take pictures of that scratch on your hand and your swollen lymph node for the textbook chapter on Bartonella."

Harris stared at his hand for a long moment, then gave a brilliant grin full of sudden sunshine and said, "Cat scratch fever!"

"It can be nasty if it's not treated, but it's not cancer!!' I insisted.

"Of course not," he agreed. "When I have a break I'll print out some articles so that I can discuss it intelligently with the doctor."

Harris patted my arm companionably and picked up the next patient chart without trying to find one that would suit him better. Neither action was particularly consistent with his personality, but it was pleasant to see.

The rest of the day was pleasant as well. I wish I could say that having a good interaction with Harris, having great responses in all my sick patients, and dealing with much nicer people than usual instantly changed my basic attitude, but it didn't. And I was still struggling to label my weird outlook. I felt dull, both uninterested and uninteresting, yet those words still didn't fit exactly. I was definitely lacking my typical joie de vivre, but it was more than just a blah mood! I felt deflated, like I was a blow up doll where someone had popped open my valve and my important insides were escaping into the atmosphere.

Suddenly my mind flashed to some advice column story about a big family fight regarding what to do with a family member who wanted to bring his girlfriend doll to the family reunion since everyone else was allowed to bring their significant others. I grimaced, then laughed out loud. I was certainly not going to think about myself as any kind of a blow up doll. That was just way too creepy of a visual. Unless of course it was one of those clown bop punching bags that my brothers and I had played with growing up. They were counterweighted so they would bounce back up after you bopped it and we used to have an awful lot of fun with them. Until that inevitable day when that final bop was just too much and there was just no bouncing back from it for that poor clown. Maybe that was my problem, the combination of recent bops was just too much for me and my wounded spirit had no way to bop back.

But I had an unexpected hint to the secret answer to my attitude issues. Laughing about the blow up doll image had given me the first boost of energy that I had felt in days, maybe in weeks. And no I didn't mean that dolls were going to be any part of the solution, but humor might be the magic answer that I was looking for. I had never seen any humor in any animal's suffering and never would. Nor in any owners' life problems that impacted their ability to care for their precious pets. But I always thought everything that happened to me and my compatriots had comedic potential. I suddenly flashed to last year when Amelia got a basin of dirty kennel water dumped on her head and she responded with "living the dream." I had laughed so hard I had to crawl to get the towels to clean up. Where did that reaction disappear to when clients said such vicious and personal things to us? Why weren't such irrelevant and patently untrue things funny in their absolute absurdity? And finally, what in the world did the size of my ass ever have to do with their pet's medical care? And what would these despicable people do, if instead of being devastated or angry I laughed out loud, grabbed my butt with both hands and yelled, "Oh no!" or started singing that I loved big butts?

I could have gone home, but I headed upstairs to use the computer. I was using the phone to access emails and social media way more than I had in the past, but it was so much easier to type at a regular keyboard. But I wouldn't be stuck here hoping for a reply. I could head out as soon as I was done sending an email to Andrei and then check on the phone for any answer at home.

I sat down and then paused with my hands held awkwardly over the keyboard. Andrei was just barely back in my life and while I knew it was way too early, I wanted more than anything to ask him for help. It was more than wanting to vent to someone. It was hoping that he would join me in whatever tough spot I was in and stand shoulder to shoulder with me, figuratively of course since he was overseas. And if he did support me and reaffirm my feelings and my ability to handle the problem, then every time I confronted some challenge I wouldn't have to picture facing it all by myself.

Hello Andrei! I don't really have anything vital to say, just really struggling with my attitude. Remember how we used to talk about the fire that we have burning inside us? That sometimes it's a full out blaze that not only warms us, but warms everyone around us? And how sometimes it's so depleted that we have to bank the fire so it won't go out and leave us and our loved ones cold and suffering? And you and I had to look up what 'banking a fire" even was and the definition didn't exactly fit our analogy and we kept trying to make it work and ended up laughing ourselves sick over the whole thing? I miss having someone with whom I can laugh myself sick over stupid stuff. And even more right now I sorely miss being able to feel that fire inside me.

Hope you are doing well. I try to respect your privacy and safety so I don't ever speculate where you are, but it's hard not to imagine you in the middle of whatever hot spot is in the news. Love you Andrei and I'm praying for you!

I hit send and then sat there for a few minutes, just in case Andrei was sitting right there at his computer and could immediately write back. But he didn't so I decided to head out, but I no more than stood up than Dr. Harris tromped up the stairs and grinned when he saw me.

"I sent my Doc pictures of my hand and some good cat scratch fever references and he wants to do some additional blood work," Harris said happily. "Do you mind still switching days off so that I can be flexible with his new diagnostic plan?"

"No problem," I said graciously. "I know you want to get answers as soon as possible."

"I sure do," he agreed. "Thanks for helping me out."

"No problem," I said sincerely. But I didn't in any way forget the way that he had treated me in the past. If my help made him view me as useful, he would treat me better, and that might make my work days more pleasant. But it wasn't the type of relationship that I wanted to occupy a large part of my life. Yes, of course I want to be useful, and I want to be appreciated for it, but I had been wounded badly being used and abused by despicable people. Since my parents died I had been raised by a man who loved money and used people and I had spent all the psychological energy on that twisted life view that I was going to spend in this lifetime.

CHAPTER TWENTY-SEVEN

I skipped Tai Chi class this morning, the same way I avoided our first puppy get together at Maisy's kennel last night. I had made sure Ethan was available to take Max so my poor pup didn't have to miss out, but I just couldn't face socializing, even with my friends. I felt there was no choice except to pretend I was okay at work, but I didn't want to fake a good mood with people that I had fought so hard to be my authentic self with.

I was scheduled to work the crazy second shift again, but I attempted to console myself with the fact that it was midweek which tended to be less busy than those monstrous weekend and holiday shifts. Plus the clients were much more likely to be sober. And the weather was nice and cool for a summer day, which cut the chances of seeing heatstroke cases on top of all the other emergencies. But I still didn't want to go to work anymore than I wanted to go to my Tai Chi class or a fun puppy party.

I did that robot thing where I dissociated from my feelings and mechanically did all the proper actions to get ready, as always preparing to work a shift that might last hours longer than the schedule would ever reflect. Max was still worn out from last night's get together and I do remember that he was in an adorable mood and didn't resist when I cut short his pre-work walk. Then I found myself parking at the backdoor of the hospital without really remembering any of my prep time or the drive over. But I was happily surprised to see that all the stuff I needed was sitting on the passenger seat next to me.

As I passed by I saw Tessa peeking through the little window in the door to the reception area and heard her say, "Dr. Kat is here! I told you she's always early!"

I dumped my supplies and then headed out front, surprised to see Detective Warner instead of a client waiting for me.

"Hi, Dr. Kat," he said in a friendly tone of voice. "Do you have a couple of minutes to talk?"

"Sure," I answered, after giving a questioning look and receiving a reassuring nod from Tessa. "Let's head to the office upstairs."

"How's everyone doing?" he asked as we walked through the hospital.

"I think we've recovered from the shock," I replied. "But now the pain and grief has settled over all of us."

"That's typical," he said quietly as we entered the office. "And we know how hard it is to wait for us to gather information and for all the tests to come back."

"What can you share?" I asked as calmly as I could manage. I was sick and tired of no one being able to tell me anything. My uncle had weaponized information dissemination, withholding what he knew or what he was planning, just to keep as much of the power in any situation to himself. Usually it was to work everything to his advantage, but sometimes it was part of an elaborate plan to hide lies, concoct misinformation, and most of all to escape the consequences of his unscrupulous behavior. A master manipulator like him absolutely understood that context and timing of information sharing could be used to control people, especially someone under his charge. And sometimes I swear he withheld facts simply hoping to make people look foolish as they reacted without the proper data. This is just one of many wounds my uncle left me with, but I still hated with a deep passion not being told what I needed to know to make good decisions and plans.

I knew Dagger, Andrei, and Detective Warner were all trying to do the right thing, keeping confidentiality, following the law, etc. I did it myself. I had to sit and take it when someone complained about their long wait, when I wanted to share I had been frantically doing CPR in the treatment area until my arms gave out and my back screamed in pain. All of which I had done, even though it looked hopeless, to try against all odds to save the dog who was a young girl's only family because everyone else she loved had died in the same house fire. And yet I couldn't share that explanation due to my own confidentiality issues. But even understanding their reasons, this lack of information from people still hurt me. Did I have a boyfriend or not? Was Andrei back in my life or not? Was there a crazy murderer coming to get us every time we went to the parking lot or not? Did any of these people I called 'friend' care about me beyond the most superficial way or not? Were all these people really doing the right thing, trying to make good moral and legal choices, or were they all covering up lies or trying to manipulate me like my uncle used to do?

Detective Warner was looking at me oddly and I realized that all these thoughts had probably just played across my very expressive face for him to see. I didn't feel like I could share any of it without looking entirely pitiful so I looked at him blankly until he spoke.

"We've had some contact with Jade Peterson," he said. "We've opened an unrelated fraud case and are pursuing other charges, but we can't determine how she could have been involved in Melanie's death. Do you have any idea how Jade could have accessed the equipment or the training center?"

"I really don't know," I replied. "Your theory that the killer forced Melanie to help is the only thing that makes any sense. If someone threatened the rest of us or her patients, she might have gone along with some bizarre plan."

"We also spoke to Ron Reynolds, the man who accosted you in the parking lot," he said. "If he shows up again, immediately tell him to leave. If he doesn't, call us and we can charge him with trespass. But we don't think he had anything to do with Melanie's death."

"Thank you," I said gratefully. Ron, or 'the screamer' as I've nicknamed him, seemed more of a real threat to me than the shadowy murderer.

"I have an odd question," he said with a half-smile, half-frown. "Is there any reason a Doctor would spit on a roll of that self-adherent wrap stuff that you all use? Or put it in their mouth?"

"No," I said hesitantly as I considered possible scenarios. "That wouldn't be sanitary. I suppose someone could accidentally sneeze or cough on a roll of wrap, but then we'd throw it away. We'd never use it on a patient."

Detective Warner nodded thoughtfully and just kept looking at me. He didn't say anything, but I got the distinct impression that he wanted to share something he knew with me. But he stood up and said, "Thank you for your help," and walked away instead.

I had another good shift. As always, there were multiple factors to good days, the same way there were multiple factors to bad days, but today the positive feelings were definitely driven by the comradery of the crew that we had working. It's so much easier doing absolutely everything when you are working with people that you like and respect, that you know without hesitation have your back. Today we were on fire; efficiency and compassion magically melded together instead of fighting against each other. I wish every shift could be just like this one.

And yet, while I laughed and joked and worked hard, deep inside I still knew that something was missing. Somehow I had been traumatized at such a deep level that even multiple good shifts were not going to easily fix my issues. I wondered if it would be way easier to prevent these kinds of problems than it would be to fix it once it was established. Just like with diseases, I could picture the minor effort and small amount of money needed to give a puppy a vaccine to protect against parvo, versus the massive effort and huge amounts of money required to treat that same patient in ICU for a week with full blown Parvovirus disease. I hadn't taken the steps I needed to do to prevent the hopelessness and despair I was feeling, so it would take significant effort and time to combat the results. But that battle would be easier being surrounded by this extraordinary crew of people.

As weird as I felt inside, I was outwardly happy when we made it to evening rounds without any surprises or drama. I was paying close attention to the presenters in rounds since we did have some mystery cases and not only could I learn a lot from what the specialists and my more experienced mentors had to say, I might be the one that knew a vital fact that would crack the case wide open. A couple days ago I had known about a possible drug interaction that no one else knew about which greatly sped up the diagnosis, and thus the treatment, for an adorable Pug.

Dr. Blackwell wiggled into our circle next to me and immediately focused on the patients in the three kennels in front of us. She reached out to grasp my arm and whispered, "Get the chart of the dog in the middle cage."

I found it over on the treatment table, and attempted to read it as I walked it back over to her. She was way too excited about something, so after I handed it to her I stared at the patient trying to see what had caught her eye.

"Hey!" she called out loudly. "We need to start with Ringo. He's got tetanus!"

"What?" Dr. Drama said as he jogged in from surgery. "I've never seen a case."

"Look at his face," she said. "Look at how his ears are pulled together on the top of his head and his lips are curled. Plus he came in with an untreated wound on his leg in a filthy wet bandage."

We clustered around his cage, Stretch pulled up pictures on his iPad and I was distracted for a minute by how envious I was of his tech, but I had to admit Dr. Blackwell called it right. Ringo looked just like the pictures!

Dr. Blackwell picked up the intercom phone and called Molly to the treatment area. I assume she wanted to prep Molly that she may have to find a source of tetanus antitoxin. Then Dr. Blackwell made a general announcement for all doctors and technicians to come to the treatment area as soon as they could.

I turned to her and with raised eyebrows silently asked why, and she immediately replied, "Twenty-five years ago when I was a student at the University, my resident called all of us to the wards and said, 'Look at this dog, it has tetanus. Sear this picture into your memory. In small animal medicine you won't see another case for twenty years and I want you to be able to know what it is at first look. So never forget.' So I want to do the same thing for every doctor in the building!"

I gave her a side hug and whispered, "Thank you!" as I listened to the entire discussion. It was fascinating, and yet so sad because in most canine cases it can be prevented with simple common sense hygiene. People would never put a Band-Aid on their own wound without cleaning it first, why would they put a bandage on a filthy gash without cleaning it on their pet? And then, way worse, leave it on to get wet and filthy and most importantly not seek immediate veterinary care?

Rounds wrapped up as everyone in the hospital continued to file through the area to get a look at the tetanus case. It was like Ringo was as famous a rock star celebrity as his namesake the way we were all so fascinated by him.

Molly dropped all her other responsibilities to reach out to the owners so that treatment could be started as quickly as possible. Part of me was worried that people who would bandage a dirty wound without cleaning it or seeking veterinary care, would never pay for the extensive treatment that a tetanus case would require. But I was happy to be totally wrong. The owners authorized the entire quote and rushed right over to pay the down payment. Cases like Ringo is why I am so drawn to client education. I never want to make people feel bad, but if I can educate them so nothing like this happens again, isn't that my responsibility too? Maybe they truly didn't know the wound had to be washed and the bandage had to be kept clean and dry while they were seeking veterinary care? Next time a dirty wet bandage might cause septicemia or gangrene, conditions that aren't as rare and dramatic as tetanus in the dog, but certainly just as deadly.

I left by the backdoor, half my brain thinking about Ringo and the weird excitement of seeing a disease I had only ever read about, while the other half of my brain was still trying to process the realization that one bad day can have long reaching negative effects on my mood and mental health, while one excellent, successful day doesn't have anywhere near the same level of a positive effect on me. What I didn't do was use any part of my brain to think about my safety or consider my surroundings. I wasn't dumb enough to be looking at my phone, but I was certainly just as lost in my thoughts, not conscious of anything going on around me.

My first awareness that I wasn't alone was when the hand grabbed my arm in the darkness. I did a full startle response, throwing my hands up and awkwardly moving backwards. I screamed, and threw my purse at my attacker and then ineffectually struck out in front of me, flailing more than punching.

"Honey, stop," a familiar voice said. "It's Daniel. You're safe."

I stopped and stared at him. Daniel? Dagger never used his real name, I'm assuming it's a habit because he's undercover so often. I wish I had hugged and kissed him, but I didn't. For long seconds I did nothing until I was finally able to take a deep breath and attempt to speak. But then I stopped and, wrapping my arms tightly around my middle, burst out sobbing instead.

CHAPTER TWENTY-EIGHT

Dagger enveloped me in a deep hug, whispering nonsense into my hair, something along the lines of, "you're okay, it's fine, everything's alright."

We stood there for a little while as I calmed down, but I didn't unwrap my self-comforting arms and grab on to Dag. I simply leaned my wrapped up self against him. I was beyond glad that I was being surprised and not attacked. And I was happy that Dag was back in town. But I still felt somehow isolated, outside the loop of what was happening. And as bad as being lonely is when you're all by yourself, it's a thousand times worse to finally be with your most significant person and feel almost as isolated. It felt like my challenges were mine alone and my absent boyfriend showing up didn't really change any of that. And those recent feelings that I was finally ready to ask my people for help? As safe as I felt physically with Dagger by my side, it did not transfer to feeling safe emotionally, at least not enough to feel like I was able to ask for or expect help of any kind.

He gently held my face, wiping the tears off with his thumbs, and said, "I came back as soon as Andrei told me you were struggling. He wanted to come too, but his crew was still needed."

"I'm glad you're here," I said, but my deep sigh turned into a sob. I wasn't unhappy he was there; I was unhappy that I wasn't flooded with ecstasy at his arrival. I had no confidence he was the sole solution to my problems.

"Did I wait too long?" he asked desperately, as if he could sense what I was feeling. "I didn't want to stay away, but I did think that I could take the chance, that we had time. Was I wrong? Did our moment slip away?'

I may not have understood much of what was going on with me, but I did know this answer. So I quickly answered, "No. Our time hasn't slipped away, but maybe mine has. Maybe I'm simply broken. All I ever wanted was to be a veterinarian and I gave the process absolutely everything I had to make it to this point. Maybe the cost was too high and there's nothing of me left."

"I don't believe that," he said softly. "You're the strongest person I know. Let's go home and you can tell me all about it."

"You're using the name Daniel?" I asked. "Is it just a slip, or is it a hint that things are significantly changing for you?"

"Maybe a little of both," he said with a half-smile. "But if it's a struggle for you to switch back and forth then you better stick with Dagger for a little while longer."

My heart momentarily leapt in my chest and a kernel of hope bloomed inside. Maybe I still cared about all the things I used to, including Dag, but they were simply buried too deep inside for me to be able to access easily. I remember last year Dr. Drama talked about balancing the passion you felt for your profession and the passion you felt for your family and how important it was to acknowledge that being tugged back and forth between them kept you from being overwhelmed by either one. Maybe the trouble and estrangement with my family, along with Dagger being gone, had put me in the position that I lost that precious balance in my life. I had partially realized something was wrong when I decided I needed to pull away from doing only dog related pastimes like weekly dog training classes, and tried to find some unrelated interests like Tai Chi instead. Maybe changing my activities was too little too late, but it pointed to the fact that I could feel myself drowning in that all consuming passion and an unrelenting focus on my patients.

Dagger took my elbow and guided me over to my, actually his, SUV, and then followed me home in a cute little sports car. I think it was the one we'd gone out in last year, but I'm really not very up on kinds of cars. I'm like those people who admit they don't know much about art, but insist they do know what they like. I don't know much about cars, but I do know I really like that little red sports car!

Max was so happy to see Dagger, he unabashedly bounced around the room celebrating the return of his favorite fun person. His hundred pound body reached some pretty unbelievable heights, then landed heavily before he sprang again into another athletic display, jumping on and off the chair and sofa, darting into the bedroom, then flying back to jump up on Dagger. I hoped Ethan was either up late working or playing a video game in the apartment below us and not trying to sleep through the racket of Max's zoomies. I tried to slow Max down, but he was unstoppable. If he had been sad I would say he was inconsolable, but he was overcome with joy instead and I'm not sure what the word for that kind of joyous manifestation would be. Maybe irrepressible? I finally decided to relax and enjoy it. I may not be in an emotional place to feel the same way, but at least I could enjoy it vicariously. Dagger certainly deserved the response. From both of us.

When Max finally settled down, the three of us snuggled on the couch. I hoped Dagger wasn't disappointed that I hadn't thrown myself around the room like Max at his return, because he seemed a little subdued himself.

"Are you okay?" I asked gently.

"I am," he said. "I'm jet lagged and concerned about the state of the world. And a little worried about you."

"I'm okay," I said as honestly as I could. "But I'm struggling and don't understand what's going on with me. Or why, for that matter. Well, except some of the big things like Melanie being murdered."

"Yeah," he said with a wry smile. "I think it would be a much bigger problem if you felt normal after your friend died."

"But it doesn't feel like simple grief or fear," I tried to explain. "It's like the light inside me was turned off."

"Yeah," Dagger repeated softly. "Andrei tried to explain how you both talk about having a fire burning inside, and how that affects everything else in your life. Can you tell me about that? I think a lot of us use a fire analogy to describe emotions, like describing some emotion as being a burning force in our life. But I didn't really understand more specifically what Andrei was trying to describe."

"It's difficult to explain," I said as I tried to clarify. "I think what makes our imagery different is that we think of the fire as interactive, admit that other people's actions can impact your internal fire even if you try very hard to stay self-sufficient."

"That makes sense," he agreed.

"And intention counts," I insisted rather vigorously. Dagger raised his eyebrows questioningly and I continued, "If someone trips and accidentally spills red wine on your favorite white sweater, it feels different than if they, knowing how much you love that sweater, toss the wine all over you with malice aforethought as they say. Either way your evening out might be disrupted and the sweater may be ruined, and you may be sad or even a little mad about that. But the accidental spill? It's not going to affect your core fire; it's a much more superficial reaction that will never impact who you are deep inside. But when someone hurts you on purpose and gets pleasure from causing you pain? That diminishes the flame inside you, but it's even more destructive to their fire, even if they don't acknowledge it."

Dagger nodded, but I could tell he was still pondering the theory so I continued, "Maybe a better example would be if you had only one way to listen to music at your house, like my old iPod. If I knew that my friend was going through a rough time and had no access to music to console herself, and I gave her my iPod, even though I wanted to keep it and use it myself, that sacrifice would deeply affect the fire inside of both of us. She'd be invigorated, her fire would grow and be a source of warmth, because she would so appreciate not only the music, but the fact that I cared so much for her that I would sacrifice something I cared about for her. But my fire would also increase, even more than hers, because giving away, truly sharing something you care about, doesn't deplete the quality or quantity of your fire, it multiples it, adds fuel to the fire so to speak."

"That makes sense," he said thoughtfully. "Like the fire stands for spirit, the same way people talk about inner light."

"Yeah," I said. "I use those words sometimes too. Light, fire, energy, spirit."

"But if I had that exact same iPod and someone snuck into my house and stole it?" I said theatrically. "Completely different response on my part; I'd feel so much loss because it had been taken from me. Even though in both cases I wouldn't have any way to listen to my music. And the thief? They'd have all that wonderful music, but it would never add to their light or fire."

"Coming from combat," Dagger said, "It's more about life and death situations and trying to maintain a warrior mentality. I'd hate it if someone stole from me, but in the grand scheme of things I'd try to keep perspective."

"I can see that." I replied.

"But I agree intention matters," Dagger said. "And that does apply to all kinds of people: liars and cheaters and betrayers. You can see them changing in front of your very eyes."

"I think that's what happened to my uncle," I said. "I don't know what started his downhill slide, but every time he cheated or stole or blamed other people for his mistakes, he was diminished. It really didn't have anything to do with us kids."

Dagger drew me to him and softly kissed my face, high on my cheekbones, low on my jawline, and finally tenderly on my lips and I melted into him. We snuggled close and continued to kiss rather passionately. It was odd because while I was certainly engaged, part of my brain was still judging my physical and emotional response, trying to figure out if I still did or didn't have an internal fire that could be stoked by anything, including physical contact. Sweet touches from the best looking and most intriguing man I'd ever met? If I didn't feel some heat over that, I'd have to admit that my internal fire was lifeless ashes.

He pulled back and asked, "What are you thinking about? I used to be able to practically read your mind, and now I really can't."

"Maybe last year it was my fire you were reading," I replied sadly. "Maybe there's nothing left for you to read now."

"I don't believe that," Dagger insisted. "You're still you, you've just had to switch to survival mode. Now you need to tap into your warrior spirit and fight back."

I sighed and leaned up against him. I wanted to say something profound that would flood us both with hope and excitement for the future, but all I could think of was my new favorite saying that 'I got nothing'. I caught his eye, grinned a little, and admitted, "Sorry. I got nothing!"

He grinned back and said, "I got nothing as well. And I'm so exhausted that I'm afraid I'd fall asleep mid-sentence if I thought of something insightful to share."

"So you're going to be around for a while?" I asked hesitantly.

"I am," he said with a tender smile. "We have plenty of time to reconnect and talk long into the night. Just not tonight."

"Sounds good. Maybe tomorrow," I said with a return smile.

"I could go back to my apartment," he said with a rather shy expression. "Or I could stay with you and we could cuddle all night like we did last year after all the neighborhood excitement."

"You mean when you arrested Maisy's husband and son?" I asked.

"I didn't arrest anyone," he replied with a sly smile.

I huffed with exasperation at the same time I thought about his offer and he played with my hair as he loved to do. Finally he said, "I promise to be a perfect gentleman, but you can't blame me for falling right to sleep."

I relaxed, grinned, and said, "It's a plan," and I took his hand and led him to the bedroom, happily accompanied by the still exuberant Max.

CHAPTER TWENTY-NINE

I woke up snuggled back to back with a still sleeping Dagger. It was a glorious feeling! We had fallen asleep relatively quickly, but we had enough cuddling time to give me that connected feeling again. I reached over and turned off my alarm before it even had a chance to go off so hopefully he could sleep in. But as soon as I shifted my weight, his eyes opened and he gave me a lazy smile.

I smiled back warmly and asked, "You need the SUV today?"

"Nah," he said. "Grandpa told me to keep the car as long as I needed to."

"Nice," I said. "I've really enjoyed using your SUV, it made a huge difference. But financially I certainly can look for a used car any time now, especially if you help me check them out. I still can't afford to pick a lemon."

"Nothing is going to move fast with the SUV," Dagger said. "You can count on keeping it for a couple more months at the least. And if I need a bigger vehicle on a particular day, I'll trade you for Sheila."

"Sheila?" I asked chuckling.

"Yep," he replied with a grin. "And don't give me trouble about that name, take that up with Grandpa."

"If you need the SUV I promise to treat Sheila with great love and respect!" I assured him.

"Can I drive you to work and then go get everybody coffee?" Dagger asked as I got Max ready to go outside. "I want people to remember who I am. Especially since I plan to creep around the place."

"Sure," I said happily. Dag took Max's leash from me, easily sliding into my morning routine, with him naturally helping me to do what needed to get done.

I was almost late to work, but Dag quickly parked Sheila and speed walked in with me to get everyone's orders. Dr. Drama was over the top excited to see Dag. I don't know if it was because he thought having Dag home would make me happy, or if he expected having him around would make the hospital campus safer, or maybe for the sheer drama he hoped Dagger might cause! But he was just barely less effusive in his greeting than Max had been, which was fun and made Dag seem like a bit of a celebrity. Dr. Drama asked Molly to get the coffee order; I think so that he could keep Dag to himself for a few minutes while I checked on the ICU patients.

After Molly finished gathering the orders, Dag and I walked out through the reception area so that I could introduce him to the front office staff. If he did stick around town for a while, I wanted him to have easy access to me at work.

All the clients and pets in the reception area were behaving themselves and I had mixed feelings about that. I certainly wasn't wishing bad behavior for the shift just so that Dag would believe me about how tense everyone was getting and how determined they seemed to be to taking it out on all of us. And yet I wanted him to view me as strong and resilient, courageously facing these formidable challenges, not see me as some hypersensitive wimp making stuff up.

After the introductions, we were almost to the front door when the man checking out started to berate the receptionist about his bill. I turned, ready to do battle on the receptionist's behalf, but Dag beat me to it and forcefully told him, "Shut your filthy dog mouth."

The man looked at him in shock, but Dag leaned towards him and fixed his laser stare deep into his eyes and continued, "I know for a fact client service representatives aren't the ones that set prices around here and more importantly you signed a quote. You had notice. Wasting their time trying to get out of your obligations, which won't work by the way, only raises the prices for all of us, because they have to pay someone to stand there and listen to you complain."

The man looked both sheepish and offended as he silently handed Tess his credit card, looking everywhere but at Dag. We turned back to the front door and as he passed a large Malamute, Dag spoke to him in a pleasant voice, "I wasn't talking to you," and then turned to me and explained, "I didn't want him to think I was saying he had a filthy dog mouth."

It was such a surprise I started laughing and couldn't stop until we got to his car. I leaned in and kissed him, which was the whole reason I walked him out to the parking lot since I'd probably be busy when he got back. It was a much more connected kiss than we had last night and I was really glad he was back.

I reluctantly let him go on his way, and continued to chuckle about him apologizing to the dog until I reached the front door. Mrs. Carson, the woman whose dog Rose had been shot with a pellet gun in her jugular vein, was entering at the same time. I sometimes struggle to remember which patient belonged with which owner, but that pellet episode had been so dramatic that I would never forget!

I held the door for her and asked, "Hi, Mrs. Carson. How's Rose doing?"

"Great!" she said. "You'd never know anything happened to her. Thanks again for taking great care of her."

"You're so welcome!" I replied happily. "She's such a good girl!"

"She is!" she agreed. "I did discover what happened. The neighbor's oldest boy was playing around with a pellet gun in his backyard and had no idea how far that pellet could travel. And certainly had no clue that he could have killed little Rosie."

"Well, I'm glad you found out what happened," I said. "And I'm glad no one was trying to hurt her."

"Yes," she agreed. "Me too. My neighbors were great. The pellet gun is now gone and the boy has been helping me do chores every Saturday in restitution. I've actually enjoyed getting to know him, and he's really good with Rose. I think he's trying to make it up to her as well."

"That's great to hear," I said.

"How are you all doing here after your colleague's death?" she asked kindly.

"It's been tough," I said honestly. I know she is a prosecutor so it wasn't going to shock her if I admitted to my feelings. "Sad and scary."

She dropped her voice and said, "I talked to some people and it sounds like some crazy stuff happened."

"Yeah," I agreed without adding any details. "What's going on with people?"

Amelia waved at me so I excused myself from Mrs. Carson, saying, "Sorry, it looks like they need me. Good to see you. Give Rose a nice treat from me."

Amelia wanted to warn me that Detective Warner was going to stop by, but she had no more shared the information then he walked through the door. He exchanged friendly greetings with Mrs. Carsen on his way over to me.

"A couple quick questions?" he asked.

"What's up?" I asked somewhat nervously. "As in should we go up to the office upstairs or can we speak down here?"

"Let's go upstairs," he replied, with a small smile that made me think that maybe his questions were private, but not bad news.

We sat down in the doctors' office and Detective Warner repeated some of his previous questions about the IV apparatus. Then he asked again about reasons for someone putting the wrap in their mouth. Once again I gave him my best bewildered face and wracked my brain for an answer. A better question was why he kept asking about it.

I didn't want to say "I got nothing," since I had been saying that way too much recently and he might consider it unhelpful and rude. As the time stretched out, he reluctantly added, "We found DNA from saliva all over the wrap."

"Oh," I said. "That explains a lot. Is there any chance it was used wrap? Dogs chew at anything we put on them, so we often put an extra layer of wrap over all sorts of important stuff to protect it."

Detective Warner's face fell as he replied, "It was Melanie's DNA. Why would she do that?"

My bottom lip started to quiver as I asked, "To try to escape?"

He tilted his head and said, "It was all over the wrap of the right arm, not the left arm where the IV was."

"Maybe she thought she could chew through the right one quicker and then use her dominant hand to pull the IV out?" I offered the first thing that popped into my head as an explanation, as the image of her desperately chewing the wrap to save her life as the drugs flowed into her body broke my heart. The tears welled up, then spilled down my face, and I really didn't care. Dogs, and sometimes cats, chewing out IVs is the bane of every veterinarian's life; it wouldn't be any kind of a stretch to think of it as a solution to save yourself in an emergency situation.

Detective Warner gently said, "The wrap didn't look chewed on at all."

"Was the blue medicine in the IV our euthanasia solution?" I asked and he nodded. I continued, "Then she might have fallen asleep before she could do much of anything. Our euthanasia solution is a barbiturate, so patients literally go to sleep, i.e. under anesthesia, before they stop breathing and their heart stops beating."

"That might explain it," he said thoughtfully. "It looked more like she had held the wrap in her mouth which is weird."

I made a funny sound, like a sigh with a hitch in the middle of it, as I tried not to cry any more. He patted me awkwardly on the forearm and suggested that we head back downstairs.

Dag was passing out drinks when we got to the treatment area and at first sight he smiled at me and pointed at a huge cup on my desk. But then his entire attitude changed as he took note of my expression and my red eyes. He strode so aggressively up on Detective Warner that the detective's body language rapidly turned defensive. I wanted to defuse the situation, and to do that my first inclination was to introduce them, but I didn't even know what name to use for Dag so I hesitated. But something passed between them; they exchanged odd looks of recognition and hesitation, and Dag abruptly stopped, turned to me and asked, "You okay?"

"I'm fine," I replied. "It's hard talking about Melanie. But I do want to help."

Detective Warner thanked me and walked to the door. Dag smiled at me again, and hurried after him, calling out to him, "I'll walk you out."

I would have loved to be a fly on the wall for that conversation, but my focus was suddenly all about the self-adherent wrap and how easy or hard it would be to chew. I took out a partial roll, turned my back so no one could see what I was doing, and pulled at it with my teeth. I could pull it off the roll, but I couldn't easily chew it apart.

I ran outside to see if I could catch Detective Warner and found him with Dag huddled together close to Dag's car. They were talking animatedly, but stopped speaking when I approached. I handed the detective a fresh roll of wrap and said, "I couldn't chew it, but I could grab it with my teeth and relatively easily pull it off the roll."

"Interesting," both men said together, and the detective added, "Thank you."

They looked at me pleasantly, but without saying another word. So I smiled and said, "Good bye," and trotted back inside. Maybe Dag was getting some inside information and later he'd be able to give me some hints about what was going on in the investigation?

CHAPTER THIRTY

I had another good shift. Off and on I was irritated by Dr. Harris, but now he seemed to be receptive to my gentle corrections. I found him complaining about a client who was having a hard time accepting how serious her dog's back problem was, but after a scowl and a simple head shake on my part, he shut up and switched up his attitude. And later when he was sending her home and was getting push back on putting her precious dog on cage rest, he asked me for help and I went into the room to speak with her.

"Mrs. Green," I started, "I'm Dr. Kat, one of the emergency doctors," but then I recognized her as I was speaking and added, "Is Rolo in trouble again?"

"Oh, Dr. Kat, thank goodness!" she said. "There's no way I can keep Rolo in a cage, he'll never tolerate it."

I started to explain, but she continued, "Tell him," pointing at Dr. Harris, "Tell him there's no way Rolo could tolerate it."

"I would, except Dr. Harris is absolutely right," I said gently. "We're doing everything we can to help Rolo. But nothing will help as much as your diligent work to protect him and his precious nerves from further trauma from this bulging disc."

"Disc?" she asked, as if it was the first time she had heard the word.

Dr. Harris shook the client education sheet in his hand on which he had drawn an arrow to the place on the spine the radiologist had seen the disc problem, which proved he had discussed it already. But I was proud that he didn't show any frustration when he told her again, "The disc is bulging and pushing on Rolo's nerves. If it presses any harder he can become paralyzed and need emergency surgery."

Mrs. Green turned horrified eyes in my direction and asked, "What can we do? I don't understand. I would never, ever hit or kick him."

"Think of discs as jelly donuts," I started as Dr. Harris gave me a disbelieving look. "They have an inner layer and an outer layer, just like that donut, and sometimes the jelly just leaks out on its own. But more than anything we have to prevent that jelly from shooting out under pressure and rocketing into the nerves in the spinal cord."

"How do we do that?" she asked anxiously.

I held my fists out in front of me, with a donut sized space between them, then I banged them together. Then I brought my fingers out like a mini explosion and then mimicked everything going limp and I admitted, "My demonstration would have been more dramatic if I had an actual donut to pop jelly all over everywhere."

Mrs. Green was staring at my hands as if she was seeing the imaginary donut disc and asked, surprisingly logically, "How do we keep the jelly inside?"

"Keep him quiet," I explained, "No up and down off things," using my fists again to show the vertebrae stacking up to put pressure on the donut disc, and "No running," then mimicked running and the vertebrae pulsing back and forth and squashing the disc. "The cage is the safest place for Rolo."

"I see that now," she said sadly. "He's not going to like it."

"Tell him he'd like surgery or being stuck in the hospital even less," I said as I left the room.

Later Dr. Harris actually thanked me for the help, but then admitted he didn't think my way of handling it would work for him and that he wouldn't feel right not using more scientific words and explanations.

"You and I are quite different people," I said. "We'll never explain things the exact same way, but it doesn't mean either one of us is wrong. If you really like one of my explanations, but don't feel comfortable using it, you can tell them a story about me. You can't make fun of me, not because it would hurt my feelings, but the owner wouldn't understand if you were agreeing or disagreeing with the advice."

"I don't get it," he said quietly.

"For example," I explained. "When people ask Dr. Blackwell about giving their dogs bones, she says, 'I have lots of good scientific proof why you should not give your dog bones. And I'm happy to go over those facts with you. But one of my earliest mentors used to tell people, 'Sure, give your dog bones. Bones keep veterinarians in business. Bones break important teeth, they get stuck going in and coming out, and cause all sorts of trouble in between. Then it takes lots of work and money to get your precious pet back to being healthy. And I need a new car!' And people would pay way more attention to him than they would to me and my earnest explanations.' So while Dr. Blackwell didn't feel comfortable saying it the way her mentor did, she could tell it as a story about him and get the same point across."

"I could say that I'm not as dramatic as Dr. Kat, but tell your story and agree that I don't want that jelly donut to shoot jelly into my patient's spinal cord!" Dr. Harris said with a smile.

"Exactly!" I said with an even wider grin. "I want to give explanations to people using language and examples that they feel comfortable with, but it's difficult sometimes. If I strictly speak only medicalese, they may miss all sorts of important information lost in the medical language. So I try to be adjustable. I've tried to use car analogies with people sometimes, but then I have to admit I don't really know anything about car mechanics."

Dr. Harris laughed softly and admitted, "I won't be using car analogies either. But then why use medical explanations with clients at all then?"

"Because they are way more precise," I replied. "And by using both you educate them step by step. Have you ever spoken to a medical parent about their special needs child? They have learned an incredible amount through each crisis, and definitely know more things about their child than some random doctor does, even though they have learned it all the hard way."

"And you think our owners operate at that level?" he asked.

"Some of them, in some circumstances, yes they do! And we have to listen to them," I replied. "Sometimes I remind them that we have to operate as a partnership, that they know their pet better, but we know the medicine better."

"I'll have to think about that," he said honestly.

"How are you feeling?" I asked. "You seem better."

"I've only been on the doxycycline a couple days," he said as we headed back to the treatment area. "But I swear I'm feeling much better already. I'd bet that no one is ever this happy to have cat scratch fever unless they thought they had cancer first!"

Dr. Drama walked up to us and, with his classic expansive hand motions, gathered all of us for rounds. Then Dag came through the treatment door with an animated expression, pointed back over his shoulder and said, "Walking through your reception area was like navigating a mine field."

"What happened?" I asked anxiously.

"Some guy was running his mouth, trying to plant shit seeds," he explained. "I wanted to shut him down before he filled the room full of shit weeds so I just said 'no reason to be so spicy, everyone's trying to help you,' and he started to step up on me, but I gave him the look and he backed right down. But then this huge dog on the other side of the room, without any kind of a warning, started to piss out his ass, and that owner was horrified and she just kept repeating, 'oh, oh, oh,' getting louder and louder and I didn't have the foggiest idea what to do to help so I thought I better report the action."

I love Dagger's creative vernacular, but this time I really didn't follow what he was trying to tell us. At the same time I was amazed because that was the longest run-on sentence I had ever heard him speak in public. Dagger is usually a big fan of short, succinct accounts. Dr. Drama went on his typical high alert posture, looking all around, but appeared to be as confused as I was over what Dag had just said. Trevor, on the other hand, seemed to get the basics and ran for the bucket of disinfectant and the mop, and then jogged up front with them.

Dr. Drama came to some kind of consensus about what the most important problem was and asked, "Piss out his ass? What does that even mean?"

"Like you eat a bunch of local food and when you hit the head it sounds like it's a horse taking a piss because it's coming out pure liquid under pressure?" Dag explained.

Dr. Drama threw his head back and roared with laughter. "Piss out your ass! That's the funniest thing I've ever heard! We have patients piss out their ass all the time!"

Dag took a small bow and Dr. Drama asked, "And shit seeds?"

"Those little disrespectful seeds of discord that some people love to sow," he said. "Best to deal with them before they grow into shit weeds, which around here could lead to a full out shit storm."

Dr. Drama laughingly shook his head in agreement and said, "Of course they do. Can't let someone fill the reception area chock full of shit weeds. Bad for the patients and the other clients."

He told us to go ahead and start rounds without him and headed to the front. I assume he went to annihilate any seeds that were trying to sprout. He returned a short time later and called me over.

"Mrs. Green is up front with a present for you," he said with a smile. "Go ahead and get it now and you can share them at rounds."

"Okay," I said and exchanged a quick look with Dag. He was totally relaxed and seemed to truly understand there was no leaving on time in my world. Although I didn't know exactly what he did, it seemed like there might be even less predictability in his world.

Mrs. Green was holding two huge boxes of donuts and said, "The bottom box is a good mix, but the top box is all jelly donuts!"

I laughed out loud and asked, "Enough of them that I can

waste one squashing it in front of the new interns?"

"Absolutely!" she said, then asked, "May I sneak in and watch?"

"Just for a minute," I answered tentatively. "We're pretty empty, but there are still privacy issues, so sneak back out before rounds start up again."

"I promise," she said, waving off my offer to help carry the big boxes.

I grabbed a jelly donut as Mrs. Green hung back and as I approached the group I said, "In honor of Dr. Harris's disc case, I give you this demonstration," as I gently tossed the donut up in front of me, as perfect of a set as I ever made in volleyball. Then in the equally most perfectly timed hit of my career, I smashed my fists together and caught the donut perfectly. Jelly shot out under force and hit a low hanging light above me. Half of the bright red jelly deflected off the lamp and onto me, covering my face and smock. The rest fell to the floor beside me. It was glorious!

I looked up at my colleagues and they seemed to be playing a game of statues because no one made a move. They just stared at me all making that classic surprised emoji face. I turned and checked that Mrs. Green had snuck back out and then I started laughing as I grabbed a roll of paper towels and spray cleaner. Dag joined in on my hilarity and grabbed a wad of paper towels to help with my cleanup as well. Once Dr. Drama started laughing the entire group joined in as we wiped up all the evidence of my donut crime.

My little demonstration led to a good debate about the different ways we could communicate with our owners. Rounds broke up as the discussion deteriorated into complaints about attempting to explain anything the least bit complicated to owners that come in drunk or under the influence of drugs or in the midst of mental health crises. I felt stressed about the impossibility of devising a simple plan to communicate with so many people that had such wide variations in education and experience, much less those seriously impaired by drugs or alcohol or personal problems. Each person is different in their ability and their level of interest. My own father was very intelligent and compassionate, but really had no interest in anything remotely medical or gross. To please him you'd have to discuss the medical details as little as possible. As I walked away to find Dag and go home it was all I could think about, but I tried to switch my focus to the family and friends side of my life instead of my work life. And I had an important question to immediately decide: did I take a quick shower and rudely go to the much anticipated house dinner with sopping wet hair or did I try to cover up evidence of my full day at the hospital with baby wipes and my smell good spray?

CHAPTER THIRTY-ONE

It felt so incredibly good for all of us, including Dag, to be gathered around Phil's beautiful mahogany dining room table. And the food provided was perfection. Mei outdid herself with a gorgeous green salad topped with fresh raspberries from her garden. Phil chose to serve his classic spaghetti and home grown, homemade marinara sauce main course, which was lavishly topped with meatballs because they're Dag's favorite. My contribution was the fresh broccoli that I had prepped yesterday and Ethan had popped into the steamer for me today. We didn't expect Dag to bring anything, but sometime today between getting coffee and driving me to and from work he had made it to Panera for our favorite sourdough bread. He even remembered to set the butter out so it was soft and easy to spread, an absolute luxury in my life. Ethan was in charge of dessert, but it wasn't on the table so I didn't know if it was going to be something in tune with our new strict rules to fit Phil's restrictions or if Dag's return was enough of a reason to splurge on one of Ethan's masterpiece cakes or cookie bars?

Phil and I are normally the biggest talkers, while Ethan and Dag are typically more moderate and their participation can really depend on the topic up for discussion. And Mei usually says the least, but her wise comments are most often my favorite because they cut to the heart of the matter that we're discussing. But today we all seemed starved for conversation and contributed pretty equally. We were mostly being polite, but sometimes someone, usually me, spoke over someone else, because we were so excited to be back together.

Everyone had a funny story to tell. I started with the dog that bounced a ball out his butt in reception, but then moved to poor Rolo, not using his name of course, who was so enamored of his blanket that he got it stuck on his poor penis.

"His red rocket, you mean," Phil corrected me, and then retold that story from last year to refresh everyone's memory. I jumped back in and told the story about the rude guy who brought me a human crab louse to identify. That story set us free and everyone laughed so hard and so long that finishing dinner took way longer than it usually did. Each of my comrades repeated, "You sir have crabs," at least once. Dag must have said it five or six times, each time laughing a bit louder, finally his face was completely scrunched up and I swear he had tears in his eyes from laughing so hard.

We moved on to stories from Phil about the crazy things he caught people doing while he was on patrol on the night shift. Ethan was a little wild eyed, but laughed as much as any of us. His stories, as usual, were all about his family who said the most unreasonable things to him. They were unaccepting of his differences and totally envious of his success, but always tried to put him down in ways that only proved how completely ignorant they were. Their horrible comments were only hilarious because they were so far off the mark. Once again I told Ethan that they only proved that they didn't have an ounce of self-awareness or a single clue about how extraordinary he was. Dag told a couple funny stories, but they seemed to lack some details to be truly relatable. It reminded me of some of my curtailed storytelling attempts when I realize halfway through that the ending is really sad or really gross and try to change my story on the fly. It made me a little sad to think he felt he had to do the same thing, even with us.

Mei's story seemed the funniest because, while she is the sweetest, kindest person who has the softest heart for people, her sense of humor is oriented to slapstick physical humor. Nothing is funnier to her than a good slip and fall. She told the story about seeing a series of students wiping out on a patch of wet grass right next to a 'stay off the grass' sign. I'm not sure the story was that funny, but watching quiet Mei be so tickled was sidesplitting.

At one point I was complaining about someone causing a fuss for no good reason up front, and I wanted to sound funny instead of whiney, so I said, "It was straight out criminal jackassery!"

Phil sputtered out his last sip of tea and then laughed out loud. Dag grinned, but immediately countered with, "I don't think that his complaining about the wait time while standing in front of a blood trail across the lobby, even though his word choices were creative, actually reaches the standard of criminal jackassery. It's more like plain old dipshittery."

Phil got a serious look on his face and insisted, "I disagree. I think it at least qualifies as first degree dipshittery, and there should be some kind of a consequence."

"First degree?" Dag asked. "I'm straight out of combat. I'm having trouble feeling your outrage."

They laughed together fairly riotously and we all joined in. I was happy to have another expression to amuse myself with the next time someone was wasting our time grumbling about their self-involved minutia instead of trying to work with us to help their pet.

By the time Ethan brought out his angel food cake and berries dessert, we had all calmed down and hit a mellow spot. I don't want to oversimplify the problems that we are facing in the veterinary profession, and really in all the other service oriented professions that are struggling. However I was now convinced that flat out laughing at all the entitled manipulators, posing as people seeking help, was part of the answer to surviving their attacks.

Totally relaxed from the great food and the excellent comradery, we regrouped in the living room. I snuggled up close to Dag on the couch and he draped his arm on the cushion behind me. We were all quiet, and more than anything I felt relaxed and comfortable. But then I really couldn't think of any normal, everyday topics of conversation. Surprisingly it was Dag who started by asking, "How is everyone doing? I mean honestly, is everyone hanging in there through all the craziness?"

We exchanged glances thoughtfully and Mei spoke gently, "I'm doing well and having a good year at work. But I'm concerned about the general unhappiness of people. I've never seen so many crabby people just walking to class or shopping at the grocery store."

"You mean it's not only at our hospital?" I asked.

"No," Mei and Ethan said together and then both chuckled. Mei continued, "My friend, who's a therapist, says there are increasing problems with anxiety and depression in the general population."

Dag smiled wryly and said, "That seems odd to me coming from an area of the world where everyday life is a thousand times harder."

Mei thoughtfully said, "That must be a difficult adjustment."

I asked, "Does your friend have a theory as to why?"

"She says she is struggling with having circular thinking about the issue: that dealing with the trauma of everyone else's bad behavior seems to be causing many people's negative reactions and toxic behavior," she replied. "But we need to know what is causing and feeding the cycle. It's like people are displacing their feelings on to everyone around them. We need to find the cause and find healthier ways to deal with those feelings."

I started laughing inappropriately, shaking my head, and admitted, "Anytime someone talks about displacement behavior I see a cat being yelled at for something, like being on a forbidden counter, who immediately turns and starts vigorously cleaning themselves. It's a very funny visual if you translate it to human behavior."

Everyone's faces went from confusion to humor as they pictured what I was saying. Mei laughed as she said, "I meant running or practicing jujitsu or volunteering to help others."

That changed the topic to the newly renovated training

building and, after sharing all the details about the final remodel, Mei asked Dag, "So any chance we can start having martial arts classes now that you're home?"

"Sure," he answered. "I'm not sure what my plans are, and I'll definitely need to be doing some traveling, but between the two of us we should be able to reliably cover classes."

"Good," Mei said simply. I wasn't sure if she was just pleased about the classes or if she was as glad as I was that he'd be mostly staying home.

"From now on my life is going to be centered right here," he said, pointing down at the living room floor and tightening his grip around my shoulders. A deep warmth spread through my chest and I smiled first at my friends and then up into Dag's face.

He smiled back at me and asked, "Don't you have an early day tomorrow?"

"I do," I said regretfully. "These rotating hours are killing me."

"Good thing you're young," Phil said as Dag stood up and gave me his hand to pull me up out of the super soft sofa.

"At least an early start time means I should easily make the six p.m. Tai Chi class," I said exchanging a look with Mei.

Phil packed up the leftovers for me and I started to make a joke about how much less there was now that Dag was there, but I held back. I wasn't confident that he'd know I was teasing and that I'd truly rather eat nothing all week if it meant having him here with me. I had lost that easy connected feeling, where we each would assume that the other was saying something positive or at worst teasing. Last year if one of us didn't get a joke or felt a bit attacked in some way, we would have reacted with confusion not anger, and then easily challenged the other to explain. I didn't feel the same comfort level now.

Dag walked me upstairs and immediately offered to take Max out for a nice walk and playtime in his yard while I got ready for bed. I hesitated because I felt like I should go with them. I didn't want to waste any of our precious time together, to skip any chance to be connected. But I was exhausted and I hadn't done anything to get ready for my next shift. Lots of people go to work and have plenty of time to figure out where they want to eat their leisurely lunch, what kind of coffee to get on their multiple breaks, or a thousand other daily life details, but I don't have that luxury. No one at our hospital does. We have to come prepared for almost anything and hit the door ready to roll.

Just as I sighed in indecision, Dag kind of slid over to me, hugged me close, and said, "We have plenty of time to take it slow. Plenty of time."

"Okay," I said and he kissed me softly. Tears sprang to my eyes, and surprisingly it felt good. The tears were sad and hopeful at the same time and way better than that blank robotic feeling.

"What the heck?" Dag said, awkwardly attempting to brush something white clinging to his pants leg.

"What's that?" I asked as I reached down to help. As I grabbed a couple of the tiny white beads I began to laugh and continued, "I'm still finding microbeads from that pillow that Max destroyed. I promise I've vacuumed a hundred times!"

Dag laughed, shook his head as he called Max to him to go outside, and said, "We'll take a nice long walk and I expect you to be in bed when we get back."

I thought about giving him some deeply profound reply of gratitude, but then simply said, "Thank you."

CHAPTER THIRTY-TWO

I stopped for a minute, took a deep breath, and tried to remember what I was doing and where I was going. I could distinctly recall that I was rushing up front, but then Tabby had asked me a couple questions about the ICU cases, after which Tessa had asked me a couple of questions about the paperwork for one of my big cases that was finally going home. Now I couldn't remember where I was rushing off to. This was embarrassing.

Tessa looked back at me quizzically and asked, "Isn't Detective Warner waiting for you?"

"Yes!" I said with a bright smile. No wonder she was one of my favorites. She might distract me with just as many questions as anyone else, but she was kind enough to put me back on track after she did.

I was used to the detective's interrogation routine now and automatically showed him to the upstairs office without asking.

"I have a couple things to tell you, but I won't be able to answer many of your questions," he said with a tentative smile.

"Okay," I agreed reluctantly. Being left out by the detective wouldn't bother me so much if I didn't know that I could be so much more help if I only had more facts.

"We found only Melanie's DNA on the tape," he said softly.

"How can that be?" I asked incredulously.

He shrugged his shoulders and looked at me pointedly like he thought I knew the answer. I shrugged my shoulders back at him and glared a little, but the tears gathering in my eyes refuted my slightly feisty reaction. I finally said, "She didn't do this to herself."

"She didn't?" he asked.

"You saw her!" I retorted sharply. "Who would do that to themselves? And how could they do it?"

"Everyone told us that she was very unhappy," he replied. "The most common thing people said was that she felt her situation was completely hopeless."

I took a couple deep breaths as guilt flooded through me. I knew she had been struggling, but it hadn't seemed that bad to me. And by that I mean her situation didn't seem that desperate and her reaction didn't seem to be that full of despair. She couldn't have killed herself. That last shift we had worked together, when she hadn't been able to face Jade, she had done a good job on my cases. How could she do that if she were so full of misery and hopelessness that she was hours away from giving up?

"She left a note on her desk at home," he said. "And there was evidence that she had been drinking."

"A suicide note?" I asked and my head started to spin. No, the room was starting to spin and I abruptly sat on the floor so that if I passed out I wouldn't have so far to fall. Dark patches started appearing wherever I looked, so I stretched out flat to get my head down onto the floor. I concentrated on taking deep breaths and my vision cleared, but I felt terrible.

"Are you okay?" he asked, grabbing at his left shoulder area, forcefully enough to make me concerned about him having a heart attack, but then he took out his phone. I realized he had been grabbing for a nonexistent radio like Phil does sometimes in a crisis when he flashes back to his patrol days.

"Stop," I said. "I'm okay, just dizzy. Can you go get me a pop? There's a machine just around the corner. I'll pay you back."

I sat up while he was gone so if I got sick it wouldn't be so humiliating, but thankfully everything stayed where it was supposed to. He brought me a Pepsi, which is my absolute favorite, so that was a plus. I took a couple quick gulps and let the sugar support flood through me.

"What did the note say?" I asked softly.

"If you find me dead, Jade Peterson killed me," he replied hesitantly, as if he was afraid I was going to get faint again.

"And why wouldn't that make you think it was murder," I asked. "And that Jade is responsible?"

"Turns out Jade has a good alibi," he said.

"Which was?" I asked curtly.

"Can't talk about it," he replied with a half-smile. "But law enforcement was involved. Sometimes criminals get an alibi for one crime because they were caught committing a different crime."

"Oh," I said morosely. None of it made any sense. Somebody had to have taped Melanie to that chair. She couldn't have done it to herself.

Tessa knocked on the door, eased it open, and while staring at me on the floor, asked, "Mr. Dag would like to speak to both of you. May I send him up?"

I looked up at Detective Warner and he nodded so I said, "Sure," as I carefully stood up and took a few more sips of the Pepsi.

We could hear Dag bound up the stairs, then his steps slowed down as he approached the door and he glided into the room. He was silent as he intently took in the scene, including me holding on to the back of the chair for support. Then he handed me a cup of coffee, looking at the pop can in my hand suspiciously. I almost never allow myself that pleasure since while I adore the sugar spike I detest the bottoming out when my sugar unfailingly drops. He turned to shake the detective's hand and asked, "What's up?" including both of us in the question.

I knew I'd tell Dag everything, but I sure wasn't going to do it in front of Detective Warner after he'd told me not to say anything to anybody. Dag and I quietly waited for Detective Warner to speak and he finally said, "The investigation is progressing and we're concerned Melanie's death may have been self-inflicted."

"I don't believe it," I insisted firmly, yet my expression had to be revealing my doubt and concern. The two men calmly stared at me until I couldn't take the pressure anymore so I added, "But let's see if I can tape myself into the same setup she might have used, all by myself. That would at least give us an idea if it was possible."

The three of us collected the needed equipment and went back over to the training facility for the privacy. I taped the catheter and IV set up onto my arm. I wasn't going to stick myself for the experiment, but I was confident that I could have placed a catheter one-handed if I had been determined to. Then I easily, with one hand, wound the tape around my arm and included the arm of the chair. But at that point I couldn't tape down my right arm so I had to unwrap my left arm and preplace the tape on the right arm of the chair. Then, after rewrapping my left arm, I was able to pull the tape with my teeth to finish wrapping my right arm.

I sniffled a little bit then said, "Melanie would have had to practice first. Not that I in any way think that she did this. I really don't. But she would have had to have the IV and injection port completely set up and ready to go, start it, then finish the tape wrapping in a relatively short time. There could be no starting over like I did."

"I can see that," Detective Warner said thoughtfully. "We found some wrap and other supplies in her trash at home."

"There could be lots of reasons for that," I said. "You wouldn't believe all the stuff I pull out of my pockets when I get home from a busy shift. Jade must have done this."

"You didn't think so before," Detective Warner said gently.

"If the choice is between Melanie, a sweet, compassionate person who just wanted to help animals, and Jade, a selfish, lying, cheating criminal who hurts animals for attention and money," I said vehemently, "then I choose that Jade did this terrible thing."

"From what I understand, suicide is often simply about stopping unbearable pain," Dag said softly. "People can feel like the quality of their life simply isn't worth living."

I thought about his statement then reluctantly said, "At

least once a day, sometimes three or four times on a bad day, veterinarians have deep discussions about acceptable quality of life while making life and death decisions for beloved pets. Maybe I could see her getting fixated on that concept in her depression."

"We're waiting for the coroner to make his final ruling," Detective Warner said sympathetically. "I'll call Dr. Vincent when we get a ruling."

Dag said "Thank you," and shook the detective's hand and when he turned towards me I stuck out my hand as well. It dawned on me I might not be seeing him again. It was an odd feeling, like when I euthanize a pet on emergency and I've never met the owners before. In that moment in time, we have this incredible deep bond, but then we walk away from each other, maybe forever. The detectives had been so essential during this terrible trauma, but for the first time I realized they wouldn't stay in our lives.

"Thank you so much for your help." Detective Warner said. "I'm glad we're getting some answers for her friends and family even if we may never understand everything Melanie was going through or every decision she made."

After we walked Detective Warner to the front door, Dag and I made plans that he would come back to get me in about an hour and we could get a quick bite to eat before Tai Chi class. I scurried back to join rounds and then settled in to finish up my paperwork. Thoughts of Melanie swirled around my brain and threatened to take over, but I kept forcing them to the back of my mind. She couldn't have killed herself. Could she?

But for once all my cases wrapped up smoothly and I was ready to go when Dag returned. I was even relatively confident that I smelled socially acceptable. Someone had brought in a bottle of especially great smelling soap for the locker room sink so that helped me feel presentable. Whenever I need to do that antianxiety exercise of concentrating on my different senses, and I'm supposed to find five things to smell, I always rush to sniff that bottle of soap! That and doggy Frito feet and sweet puppy breath if they are available, but most pleasant smells are not that easily accessible in an emergency hospital setting. For a while I was carrying a little bag of cloves in my purse to assure I could count on at least one thing to be as nonhospital smelling as possible. These silly random thoughts had me grinning when I climbed into the car with Dag.

He smiled at me and asked, "What's so funny?"

"Stupid stuff," I replied. "You know I can lose myself in various deep thoughts, but today I'm trying really hard to keep everything superficial. Which leads to oddity, but not sadness."

"I always deeply admire your ability to see silver linings in all the dark storms we face," Dag said with a gentle look on his face.

I looked at him questioningly as I thought back on my reactions in the past weeks and said, "Maybe that's what I've been missing lately. You're right, that is my normal reaction and recently I haven't had my typical resilient bounce back after something goes wrong. I remember my brother and I used to call it being 'coped out.' Like we had used up our coping reserve and there was nothing left when we needed it."

"Like being burned out," Dag said.

"They also talk a lot about compassion fatigue in the medical fields," I said. "But this seems to be more because of the sheer amount of personal and professional stress we're all facing, maybe not so much about a lack of balance between our personal and professional lives."

"Yeah," Dag said nodding. "The people writing articles don't seem to acknowledge that hard times and tragedies sometimes can cluster together and simply be overwhelming. Like plain old math, it basically adds up."

"Like perfect storms of emotional crises," I agreed. "I was asking myself why we don't outright laugh in the faces of these aggressive jerks that cuss us out. I think it may be because we're overwhelmed."

"That's why we need to rely on our friends for help when that happens," Dag said. "Their support can supplement your low supply of resilience and ability to cope. Sometime later you can do it for them."

"I agree in theory," I said smiling up at him. "But in this situation most of my friends are work friends and they are all in the same condition. We all lost Melanie and we're all hurt and confused, and honestly feeling guilty we didn't stop it somehow."

He hugged me tight and pleaded with me, "Please let me help. I care about you so much and would do anything for you. I know I haven't been here, but I'm here now."

I looked directly at him and said, "I can admit I want help. And I can even admit that I need help. What I'm not sure is if I can accept anyone's help. It's been pointed out to me that my fierce independence may be a trauma response, but I don't know what to do with that knowledge."

"I don't either," Dag said somewhat sadly. "But I want you to know that I won't let you down. Give me a chance to prove it to you."

CHAPTER THIRTY-THREE

It was going to be one of those days. I'd only been in rounds for a couple of minutes when I was called out to see a critical emergency. Dr. Drama was in one of his fabulously animated moods so I regretted missing his show. Empathetic me may soak up other people's pain, but I can get equally pumped up by someone's energy and positivity. I jogged up front and as soon as I saw the little dog, all extraneous thoughts bolted from my mind. The tiny Miniature Pinscher (Min Pin) had big scared eyes that were begging me for help and her color was that pale lavender color that was heading toward blue. And she was struggling to breathe. The owner looked at me with the same frightened, suffering eyes, but I held my hand up to stop her from speaking and instead forced my stethoscope in my ears and started listening to the dog's chest, carefully avoiding the surprisingly small areas of visible trauma on both sides of her chest from the dog attack. After that quick listen, now my eyes were equally horrified and I gave the owner the absolutely briefest explanation possible before I picked up the dog and then ran her to the back.

Dr. Drama was still performing for the group gathered in front of the ICU, but he and Stretch immediately left rounds. With a hand on my back, he guided me into the surgery area as the surgery techs reformed around us.

"Big dog, little dog," I reported quickly. "No paperwork yet, but I got verbal permission for emergency treatment. Do you want me to assist Tabby with the forms or help back here?"

"Go get our forms signed," Dr. Drama said with an odd smile. "We're heading to surgery stat. My first cruciate surgery canceled, so for once the timing works in my favor." He repeated, "Go," again and gave me a little push. You'd think that would have made me mad, but it really didn't bother me. We literally push and guide and direct each other; I often lean on or over my colleagues to find the correct position to get my job done on reluctant patients.

I hustled back into the room and Tabatha already had most of the paperwork done, but she seemed relieved to see me and said, "Mrs. Knoll has some questions…"

I interrupted and said, "And I'd be happy to answer them. Itsy-Bitsy is being cared for by Dr. Vincent, our board certified surgeon, so I have some time to talk while Tabatha gets these forms to him."

Mrs. Knoll started crying and I continued, "Itsy-Bitsy is doing okay. She's on oxygen and the technicians are already getting her IV started. Then they'll give her pain medication through that IV so it'll work very quickly."

"It was terrible," she said between sobs. "Bitsy and I were on my porch and the new neighbor's dog came from nowhere. He wasn't on a leash and the owner was nowhere to be seen. And that monster just grabbed her. She didn't do anything. She didn't bark or anything and it happened so fast that I didn't do anything. And then he shook her. And shook her. Like she was a dog toy. Oh God, it was so horrible. He's huge. Then I picked up a pot that was out there and I hit him on the top of his head. Just brought it down onto his head as hard as I could. And he dropped her and ran off. I picked her up and just ran to the car. My husband finally heard something and ran outside in his underwear and I told him to go get dressed and meet me here, but I wasn't waiting for him. And I drove her here as fast as I could. I think I slid through a red light."

I patted her shoulder with tears in my eyes and said, "You did so good."

"I've never hit a living being, human or animal, in my whole life," she said sobbing.

"You did what you had to," I reassured her. "These attacks

can happen so fast. No time to think, only react."

"But why is Bitsy doing so badly?" she asked. "There wasn't that much blood and just a few small holes on her sides."

"We aren't making a weird joke when we refer to this kind of incident as a big dog-little dog attack," I explained. "Because what you see on the outside is nothing compared to what is going on inside. That shaking can do some terrible damage which is why we sometimes have to rush them directly into surgery. It's totally different than what happens in more equally sized dogs, either two small dogs or two large dogs. Those dog bites can still cause significant damage, but it's different."

Mrs. Knoll sobbed quietly, but pitifully, each soft cry full of anguish. Finally she physically relaxed down onto the exam room bench as if she knew her active part in this tragedy was over.

"Mrs. Knoll," I said, "do you have any questions at this time?"

As she started to speak, loud male voices rang out from the waiting room, and she raised wide eyes to me and said, "I think that's my husband and the neighbor."

I stepped out into the waiting room just as the two men came close enough together to bump chests and I called out, "Mr. Knoll, let me take you to your wife," but when both men ignored me I raised my voice, "MR. KNOLL! Come with me now."

"Start giving those people," he said pointing at our client care specialists over his shoulder as he came towards me, continuing to scream at the neighbor, "your information and credit card. You'll be paying every penny of this bill."

I decided I'd wait a few minutes for him to calm down before I explained to Mr. Knoll that he and his wife had to be the ones that would guarantee payment with us. The neighbor might be morally responsible and eventually civilly liable to pay the bill, but only the legal owner could make a treatment and payment contract with us. Mr. Knoll grabbed his wife and held her tight and I was so happy to see how kind and supportive they were being with each other. We see a lot of displacement aggression in the waiting room and exam rooms among family members.

Their displacement always reminds me of an indoor cat that is so enraged by the sight of an outdoor cat passing by the window that they viciously attack their house mate quietly sitting on a chair minding their own business.

"I'm going to check on Bitsy and then I'll come back and see if you have any more questions," I said, concentrating on keeping my voice and gestures calm.

Mrs. Knoll nodded as she continued to pat her husband's back. I think she was suffering from what she had to see and do, while he was suffering because he hadn't been there to see or do anything. I made my way to surgery where Dr. Drama and Stretch were gathered around the view screen studying Bitsy's radiographic images.

"We're going to surgery right now," Dr. Drama said. "She'll need a chest tube and repair of the chest wall, and maybe the removal of a lung lobe if I can't stop the bleeding."

"I'll update the owners if you want," I said. "But first the owner of the dog that did this is up front and I think I need to get him to leave before he has another confrontation with Mr. Knoll."

"Stretch can stay with Bitsy and I'll briefly speak with the Knolls then," Dr. Drama said thoughtfully. "And you move the other gentleman out of here. No good can come of him hanging around."

"I'll speak to him briefly in one of the consultation rooms and then escort him out," I said. "And I'll follow the rules."

Dr. Drama grinned as he snapped his wide open mouth shut; he had obviously been about to warn me about what I could and couldn't say. I shouldn't talk about Bitsy's specific medical condition or care, but it didn't mean I had to ignore his own dog's behavior. Poor Melanie had been caught in that dilemma when Jade falsely accused her of all sorts of misconduct on social media and she couldn't defend herself without breaking patient confidentiality. Maybe that is the way I could honor Melanie. I could discover a way to fight the liars attacking veterinarians with impunity on all kinds of social media. Isn't that slander or defamation or something? I bet there was a legal way we could go after them. Maybe we could help Melanie's family sue Jade to stop her reign of terror on innocent animals and veterinary staff. I realized that I was starting to accept that Melanie had hurt herself, although I would blame Jade until the end of time for her part in shredding Melanie's vulnerable soul.

As I approached the owner of the attacking dog, he spun on his heel, threw his hands up in frustration and shouted, "What the fuck are you telling them? That dog was barely bleeding. "

"Barely bleeding on the outside," I retorted without thinking. "Your dog shook her like she was a ragdoll. Luckily it didn't break her neck. In dog attacks like this Dr. Vincent often has to use all his surgical skill to repair the muscles that hold the chest together because they've been crushed into hamburger."

"You're just trying to run the bill up because he's a Rottweiler," he snapped.

"I had no clue what kind of dog he was," I said.

"Like I believe that," he said shaking his head in disgust. "Looking for a big payday."

"Looking to try to save the poor dog's life after it was attacked by an off leash dog on her own porch," I countered quickly.

"Fucking bitch," he spat back.

"Fucking idiot," I retorted just as quickly.

"Heeeeey," Dr. Drama said as he came out of the room, and he was zeroed in on me, not the jerk yelling at me. "You," he said gesturing at me, "Meet me in treatment. And you," he said glaring at the attacker's owner, "get out of my hospital. You don't have a patient here."

I lowered my voice and snapped at the idiot as I turned to leave, "You have to go NOW. The police can contact you at your home for the bite report. And if you don't go now after being asked to leave, they can charge you with trespass."

He spun away from me and forcefully strode to the front door. As it slid open, he turned back and repeated, "You're a fucking bitch. And you'd better watch out."

225

A big blonde man dressed in an olive t-shirt and black cargo pants was standing just inside the door, and he seemed to simultaneously survey the room, glance at me, and quicker than I could even follow his hands, he reached out and grabbed the man by the throat and said, "You're the one that needs to watch out."

The blonde man turned and marched the man out of the hospital without releasing his grip on his neck. The Rottweiler's owner had to rise up on his tiptoes to keep the pressure bearable, and my heart began to pound with a sudden familiarity. "My sister doesn't need me to handle any little conflicts for her. She is more than capable of dealing with the likes of you. But know this, she will never fight alone if I'm anywhere in her vicinity."

"She's just blaming my dog because he's a Rottweiler," he whined.

"I'm blaming YOU because YOU didn't socialize, train, or properly restrain your dog," I shouted forcefully. "It isn't the dog's fault. It's YOUR fault."

Andrei propelled the man stumbling across the parking lot and bellowed, "Get out of here and don't come back."

As soon as the owner made it to his car I wrapped my arms around Andrei and said, "I'm so incredibly happy to see you. Come inside with me, but I'll have to go face the music with Dr. Drama before we can catch up. I shouldn't have been exchanging expletives with that loser in reception."

Andrei shrugged his shoulders, grinned, and said, "Seemed like a pretty proportional response to me. Maybe a little spicy, but he deserved it. People blatantly in the wrong always go on the most vicious attacks. If you let them distract you with their venom, they will steamroll right over you and then doing the right thing will become impossible."

"Yeah," I said ruefully. "But Dr. Drama just gave us a long lecture about de-escalation techniques and never once mentioned calling someone a fucking idiot as an approved method to accomplish that."

Andrei nodded and agreed, "That's a good point."

Andrei and I went to the surgical prep area, and I quickly told Dr. Drama, "I am so sorry. I was thinking about Melanie and kind of lost my mind. I'll totally take my punishment, but first may I introduce my brother Andrei?"

Dr. Drama pulled his mask up, stepped over to the surgical prep sink, and started to vigorously scrub his hands. He looked at Andrei and said, "Very nice to meet you. Thanks for your help."

"So nice to meet you," Andrei said. "Kat has told us so many wonderful things about you and your hospital."

"Thank you," Dr. Drama said and huffed out a bit of frustration. "A little hard to keep my righteous indignation going now. But I do want to be able to concentrate on this surgery and not worry about fisticuffs in the reception area."

Andrei grinned and promised, "I'll make them take it outside."

Dr. Drama frowned and started to say something, as conflicting emotions played across his face, and he finally said, "As long as it doesn't disturb me. And despite what I've said in the past, we need to absolutely enforce a no swearing rule on the clients AND the doctors to keep an atmosphere of civility around here!"

CHAPTER THIRTY-FOUR

I didn't know what to do. Obviously I wanted to spend time with Andrei, but my puppy group had made me promise to attend our little get-together at Mr. Emerson's house tonight. In fact they had scheduled it specifically at this time to make sure I could make it. I had been looking forward to seeing everyone, human and canine, and was so happy that my missing emotions had started to reappear. But this was Andrei. I hadn't seen him in way too long. My chest actually ached thinking about missing the tiniest bit of time with him.

I looked into his eyes and smiled. There was no choice. I had to disappoint my friends. But as I started to speak, Andrei asked, "What? I know I was a surprise so don't worry; I'll be in town a couple days. I knew you might have plans."

I couldn't believe he could still tune in so well to my thoughts and feelings and said, "No, I just couldn't. They'll have to understand."

"Actually Dagger and I have an errand to run," Andrei said. "And then we could get together afterwards?"

"It's just a neighborhood gathering of my puppy class friends," I explained. "When you're done you could come over and meet them?"

"That sounds like fun," he said with a wide Andrei grin. I had missed him so much. Tears welled up, but when I felt my chin start to quiver I shook my head to stop it.

Dagger honked from the parking lot from his little red sports car and Andrei waved back then gestured a couple more times which I think meant he'd be there in a minute. I gave him an enthusiastic hug, told him that Dagger knew where I'd be when they were done, and sent him off with a wide grin of my own.

I went back inside to get Max, I was still bringing him to work for my protection. Or maybe it was only for my comfort? But I was stopped cold by the expression on Dr. Drama's face as he walked toward me.

"What?" I asked desperately. "I thought Itsy-Bitsy came through surgery with flying colors?"

"She's fine. But we're meeting upstairs in my office," he said soberly.

"We who?" I asked with a slight quiver to my voice. "Why?"

Dr. Drama took my elbow and guided me out of the treatment area as Dr. Tolliver and Dr. Blackwell joined us in the hallway. Doctors Lane, the father an emergency vet and his daughter our cardiologist, walked with us. While I hadn't worked much with them this year, their close and honest way of relating to each other set a great example for the rest of us. Dr. Stretch was waiting for us in the office and a couple other on duty doctors squeezed in just as he closed the door.

Dr. Drama immediately said, "I just heard from Detective Warner and Detective Strickland. I have devastating news. Melanie's death has been ruled a suicide."

I gasped and asked, "Are they sure? I don't think..."

Dr. Drama held up his hand and said, "Stop," but he had a kind expression on his face and a sad tone to his voice and continued, "I asked the exact same thing. It turns out she sent a letter explaining everything to one of her vet school mentors. The detectives didn't share the letter with me, but they did say that she apologized for choosing to do it at our hospital, but she needed to be with us on her last day. She said we had treated her better than her family ever had. But she couldn't stay here with us because everything hurt too much."

I absolutely lost it. I cried out and loudly sobbed out my pain and loss and frustration. My friends and colleagues immediately mobbed me like we were in some kind of weird rugby scrum. I quieted down in their embrace, but I wasn't the only one with tears streaming down their face. We stayed clustered together for long minutes, then slowly disengaged, while still keeping contact with each other. I had a hand on Stretch and Dr. Blackwell, and Drs. Lane were hugging each other with one arm and reaching out to us with their other arms. Dr. Drama continued to hold onto his wife, Dr. Tolliver, and his best friend, Dr. Blackwell, as he spoke, promising to let us know about funeral arrangements and assuring us we'd do some kind of memorial just for the hospital team as well. He also asked us all to help support the staff through this period of mourning. No one else spoke, but we patted each other and exchanged looks of stunned commiseration. When Dr. Drama opened the door, an eerie sound carried up from downstairs, a heartfelt howl of despair and misery that echoed in the hallway and more than one of us grabbed our chests in response.

I hustled ahead of the group saying, "I think that's Max. He must have heard me."

Stretch followed close behind me in case I somehow needed help, but Max settled down the minute he saw me. Stretch and I talked for a few minutes, then after giving me a big hug, he hurried off to call Taren. I obviously didn't want to go to my puppy party any more, but I felt trapped since Dagger and Andrei were meeting me there. Yes, I could call them, but I didn't think I could hold myself together on a call and didn't want to cause any kind of a fuss in case they were somewhere official. I leashed Max up, gave a huge sigh, and told myself that I can do this. I'm used to doing a heartbreaking euthanasia in one room and then walking into the next room to treat an adorable puppy with a bleeding toenail. I wouldn't need to dump this pain on my friends. Even if they tease me for being late. I can compartmentalize this like I do so many other things. I can definitely do this.

Max and I walked slowly to Mr. Emerson's house to give me time to chill out. But then Max picked up where we were heading and started cavorting beside me. He loved all his puppy class friends but Mr. Emerson's Chip was probably his favorite. I decided I wasn't suppressing my feelings as much as

I was choosing to live in this exact moment in time, the most important life lesson most of us can learn from our dogs.

I released Max into the fenced in backyard to join his comrades and he happily sprang into the writhing mass of dogs. I was going to politely go around to the front door, but Mr. Emerson's voice rang out, "We're in back on the patio. Join us!"

"What do you want to drink?" Mr. Emerson asked as I approached.

"I'll take one of your world famous lemonades," I replied happily. "What are we talking about?"

"Well," Trevor said hesitantly, "we're breaking our new rule about not talking primarily about the dogs, but we're all trying to decide when to neuter them with all this new information out about neuter age and the statistics on cancer."

"Yeah," I added. "There's enough early information to make us all worry, but not enough completed studies to make the decision easy."

"What are you going to do?" Trevor asked.

"I'm aiming at waiting until Max is two like that one study recommended," I replied. "But I'll change my mind immediately if he develops behavior issues. How about you?"

"I already scheduled Licorice for surgery in a couple weeks," Trevor replied. "I also own his mother and they are starting to have issues already. Plus that one study said the two year rule didn't apply to Labradors."

"Yeah," I said. "Every year that passes we'll know so much more, but all of us are stuck having to make a decision now. How about Roman? Are you planning on breeding him?"

Maisy, with a sad smile, said, "I really want to. He has some of the best genetic testing and early orthopedic evaluation results I've ever seen. But my life is beyond chaotic, and I just don't have the money right now to continue to do it right. And I refuse to do it wrong. I've worked too hard to improve the Doberman breed, I'm not going to cut corners now. People see what a puppy costs and think breeding dogs must be this huge money maker. It's not! I felt extraordinarily lucky the years I broke even! I always chose to do what was right for the individual dog and the future of the breed and that doesn't lead to huge profits."

"But your careful breeding and genetic testing is the absolute ultimate in preventative medicine," I insisted proudly. "Think of all the misery you've prevented! On the other hand, corrupt breeders are charging exorbitant money for rare colors, but their dogs can't breathe or walk and are prone to cancer. They keep veterinarians in business, but it's sure not what we want to be doing. We can't make a poorly bred individual normal, no matter how much money someone spends, and sometimes we can't even control the poor pet's suffering. It's so depressing."

"And then everyone wants to blame all breeders for the actions of the rotten ones," Maisy said sadly.

"That's true," I agreed. "Although that's also true in lots of professions including my own."

"I'm definitely taking a year off from planning any litters," Maisy said. "I'm simplifying my life in every way I can right now. Which sadly means I'm slowly placing some of my dogs with other reputable kennels. But Roman is staying with me! So we'll see what the future holds."

"How about Chip?" I asked.

"I don't know what to do," Mr. Emerson said. "I guess I'll copy you Kat. Aim at two years, but be ready to make a new plan if behavior problems pop up."

Maisy smiled and ran her fingers through her much more modern loose hairstyle, in contrast to last year's 1950's inspired lacquered flip. Which unconsciously called attention to all the other changes she'd made since her divorce, like her jeans and cute top. She said, "I'm trying to become a more independent woman. I want to make good decisions on my own, but most of my plans have to follow that same pattern. Do the best with what facts and resources I have, but then be ready to give up if it's not working."

I chuckled with her and said, "Dagger is a big believer in not saying give up and not using the quit word. Everyone focuses on 'staying the course' and 'never quitting' and is so proud of that attitude, but if conditions change and you stick to the original plan, you're setting yourself up for failure."

"So what does he say instead?" Trevor asked.

"He says something like it's time to make a new plan," I replied thoughtfully.

"Or I say it's time to pivot!" Dagger said with laughter in his voice as he and Andrei entered the backyard.

"Pivot? I like it!" Trevor said as everyone stood up and surrounded the two men.

I introduced Andrei to my friends, which was a shock to everyone since I had never shared with them that my brother was back in my life. The dogs came running over, fascinated by new people, and it was pandemonium for a few minutes as they all were demanding their fair share of the attention. Part of me wanted to tell them the sad news about Melanie, but I decided not to. I wanted to stay in this joyful moment of friendship and family and happy dogs. Andrei was fielding questions as fast as my friends could ask them with a smile on his face, but he gave off an odd energy as if he wasn't totally comfortable.

Dagger was smiling at the group as well, seemingly enjoying it, but looked around like he couldn't quite settle in. Then he took a deep breath, slipped his arm around me, and drew me close. I caught Mr. Emerson checking Dagger out with a slightly stern fatherly expression on his face and I grinned at him when I caught his eye. He nodded like he approved and jumped back into the conversation. I didn't have a way to describe all the odd feelings I had been having lately, but I could feel them slowly slipping away as I concentrated on my connections to these special people. After the quizzing faded away, the conversation evened out and bounced around in a more balanced way.

Mr. Emerson felt bad that we were accidentally leaving Ethan out of this special social time, since he didn't always attend when I was available to bring Max, so the group decided to invite all my house mates to join us. Bonus, they rushed right over and brought all sorts of snacks including Ethan's famous cookie bars fresh out of the oven. We slowly settled around Mr. Emerson's fire pit and stayed talking way later than we usually did at one of these puppy get-togethers. Mr. Emerson brought out all the fixings for S'mores and, with a smile and an indulgent tone, said "My wife Madeline, I called her Maddy, had her own way of doing S'mores and I still do them that exact same way even though she's been gone for a while now."

He stirred up the coals, laid down aluminum foil around the fire on the brick ledge, and arranged graham crackers with squares of chocolate on the foil to melt. Then he passed out marshmallows and roasting sticks to each of us. We sent the dogs away from the fire when they came sniffing around, but they had played so hard already they flopped down in a ring around us without complaint.

I snuggled up to Dagger and exchanged a grin with Andrei and tried to pick the best spot to roast my marshmallows. Everyone else was very polite. Trevor even roasted a couple of marshmallows for Mr. Emerson so he didn't have to crouch down with his bad hip. But Andrei and I reverted back to our childhood habits and turned the roasting experience into much more of a contact sport, jostling each other out of position whenever one of us found a particularly fine coal. Dagger joined in with our shenanigans and laughter spread through the group and jokes abounded. Trevor showed us how to open up Oreos and stick roasted marshmallows and chocolate inside them, informing us that the treat was called S'moreos and Trevor and I laughed like maniacs.

Right after that, I was telling some story and mentioned that my favorite technician was Tabby. Dagger got the funniest look on his face, then struggling to speak because he was laughing so hard asked, "Tabby? And she is paired up with you most of the time? Tabby and Kat? Seriously?"

We got the joke one at a time and then we all were laughing and shaking our heads. I was laughing more at the fact that I had never figured that out before that we were Tabby Kat! And I would never be able to unhear that!

Outwardly our group didn't look like we had that much

in common, ages from seventeen to mid-seventies with very diverse fashion styles, but there were such strong connections between us. Looking at the circle of friends gathered around the fire filled me with strong feelings of love and attachment and belonging that I actually felt like something deep inside me was being renewed and something empty was being filled. I was definitely a pack animal, like a wolf in a pack or a lioness in a pride. Relationships were my joy and my strength. I had to find a way to prioritize my various pack relationships to be my best self.

I leaned into Dagger as that internal light, my spiritual fire, sparked and then ignited and its profound heat flared deep inside me. Dagger looked at me in surprise, as if somehow he could feel it, but I still had no words to describe what was happening. And while I could imagine how much he would appreciate basking in the warmth that might now emanate from me, it was a small fraction compared to what it felt like to be me and to look forward to being energized and comforted by my own internal blaze. It was light and heat and hope personified and now all my gaps and empty spaces were brimming full. Sadly that spirit can be stolen from you just like your belongings or money can be taken. And if you let that happen you'll never have anything to share with anyone else. And it really is true, you can't pour tea from an empty pot.

Dagger and I locked eyes for a long minute, then I looked around at our friends and simply basked in the warm feelings. It turned out to be another one of the best nights of my life, even though deep inside I held the grief of Melanie's loss in my heart the entire time.

CHAPTER THIRTY-FIVE

I practically skipped through the newly planted gardens in the former badlands on my way home. My work day had gone well, not only drama free, but exceptionally straight and normal, as Dagger always says, and I was looking forward to relaxing at our family dinner. I expected to be tired because of the late night last night, but I felt energized instead. On the walk home from that wonderful night at Mr. Emerson's house we had decided to invite the puppy people: Mr. Emerson, Trevor and Maisy, to a future house family dinner to thank them for the wonderful evening we had all just enjoyed. But tonight was only for the house family so that they could get to know Andrei. I hoped it would be as warm and comforting for me as last night had been, but I had the feeling the conversation would take a more serious turn since I needed to tell them about Melanie.

As I was leaving work I walked out through reception to give them my pile of completed records and stopped to say good night to Dr. Drama. Then one of his recent surgery case's owners walked in, spotted him, and bellowed, "You're my fucking hero!" as he enveloped Dr. Drama in a huge bear hug. Everyone in the waiting room was grinning at the heartfelt sentiment and it gave us all such a rush of joy. I can only imagine how it must have made Dr. Drama feel. As he walked by me afterwards he smiled and whispered, "I guess it's okay to allow for some swearing after all, but only in the heat of the moment!"

Andrei was staying at Dagger's apartment since it was a two bedroom and set up for guests. But it meant I hadn't gotten to discuss anything with Dagger last night that wasn't fit for public consumption. I was off for two days in a row starting tomorrow, so I would get some significant time with Andrei before he left. Maybe Dagger and I could grab a little alone time tonight after dinner?

I rushed into my kitchen and decided that I had time to make a fancier vegetable dish than I usually did. I was pretty proud when I popped my parmesan roasted zucchini, green beans, and cauliflower recipe into the oven and certainly hoped that Andrei liked it. It was odd to feel incredibly close to him and yet have no idea about his normal every day likes or dislikes, for example what was his favorite food now or was he trying to eat vegetarian or keto or ? At least everything I had been able to decipher led me to believe he and Dagger were fresh from a war zone which made me think my cooking skills had to do well in comparison to that.

I took extra time with my appearance as my vegetables baked, of course trying to impress Dagger more than Andrei. Growing up Andrei had never complimented my efforts with makeup or hairstyle; he only complained about the time I took in the bathroom getting ready. I even dabbed on a little bit of perfume, something I didn't usually do since it would be unkind to the dogs and cats that I cared for. Sometimes I had been trapped in a small exam room with a woman who had so overindulged with her perfume spritzer that it made me nauseous. Then I'd feel extra sad and distressed for her poor dog with his nose up to ten thousand times more sensitive than mine.

I still don't own a serving dish so, whistling for Max and using my thrift store potholders, I carried the entire baking sheet downstairs to Phil's apartment as soon as the vegetables were done. Ethan met me in the hallway carrying a couple of pecan pies and said, "I originally made the cookie bars for tonight, but I'm glad I brought them to Mr. Emerson's house."

"Everyone enjoyed them!" I said with a smile. "But thanks for making something special tonight for Andrei. I really appreciate it."

"You're welcome," he said softly. "And I'm glad Dagger is

home."

"Me too," I agreed.

Luckily Phil threw open the door, since we both had our hands full, and took the baking sheet and potholders from me and headed to his kitchen. Dagger, Andrei, and Mei were standing in the living room chatting, and while they all looked pleased to see us, Dagger seemed extra happy. I really regretted my original subdued greetings when he arrived home and wished I could go back and do a Max worthy response instead. Speaking of which, Max started to wag his tail in that whole body way that forecasts some kind of cavorting explosion of love and excitement, and I decided I was not going to be outdone by my dog once again. I grabbed his collar and ordered him to sit, then bounded over to Dagger and launched myself up into his arms and wrapped my legs around him. He laughed, hugged me tight, and twirled me around multiple times and, while it sounds odd, my brother and all our friends clapped for us enthusiastically. But it wasn't as weird or awkward as it sounds! Then I kissed him and said, "I'm glad you're home."

When he finally put me down, we moved into the dining room and took our seats. Phil served an impressive chicken parmesan with spaghetti, Dagger produced his cheesy garlic bread, Mei brought a Caesar salad, and of course there were my parmesan roasted vegetables. It made for a rather themed dinner. Phil personalized his usual grace for the occasion, mentioning us all by name, and Andrei looked at me with affection when he chimed in with his Amen at the end. And, unusual for such a chatty bunch, we were relatively quiet until our plates were clean.

"That was excellent!" Andrei exclaimed, tilting his chair back and adjusting his belt buckle to give himself more room. "My wife is such a good cook that I'm spoiled, but that is right up there with one of her welcome home feasts."

Phil grinned and said, "Thank you! But you probably shouldn't tell her that! Sorry your family homecoming was postponed due to her Mom's surgery, but we're so glad you were able to come visit us."

"I'm very anxious to see my family," he said seriously. "But I think I was meant to be here now."

"My first sight of my brother in almost ten years was of his hands around the neck of some guy threatening me," I said excitedly. "I call that good timing."

"What?" Phil said as he partially rose out of his chair. "What was that about?"

I reached over and patted his hand, "Some dumb guy trying to deflect attention from how much he messed up and got his neighbor's dog hurt."

Everyone at the table looked at me with worried eyes. Phil, Andrei, and Dagger were predominantly mad-concerned, while Mei and Ethan were mainly sad-concerned, but they were all emotional on my behalf. I really didn't want to explain, since I already felt some kind of closure with what had happened. Bitsy was recovering and we had already filed official reports on the situation. I was trying to concentrate on the fact that I could only control my own behavior in any situation, and that I couldn't control other people's reactions and the bad consequences they might face because of their choices. I felt like I needed to tell them about Melanie, but I paused to figure out how to say it. Their expressions deepened as they read my body language. The mad got madder and the sad got sadder, so I knew I had to get it out before they decided to form a posse, mount up, and ride out to chase down the despicable villain that threatened me.

"I'm sorry," I said quietly. "I don't mean to worry you. That guy is handled; I'm not worried about him. But I have some bad news to share. The coroner has ruled that Melanie's death was suicide. And I'm very sad, and certainly feel like I somehow should have done more, that I failed her, but I honestly don't know what I could have done differently."

Expressions around me changed, still an odd mixture of sad and mad, but less action oriented and more contemplative. We discussed it for a while. All of us had lost a friend to suicide in the past few years and there was an element of disbelief and horror in the fact that not one of us had been spared.

Dagger turned to me and said, "I read a recent study on suicide…"

I smiled a small smile and interrupted, "You do know the magic words to get my attention, don't you?"

Dagger smiled back and continued, "And the main difference in thought process between those that died by suicide and those that didn't, was those that did it believed that the pain they felt was unbearable and that it absolutely would be worse tomorrow. I've decided to focus on the fact that there are solutions to most problems and that I believe deep in my soul that tomorrow always has the possibility to be better. And that's what I needed to be telling people that are suffering. But ultimately their choices are their own."

I shrugged my shoulders and struggled to reply, but finally said, "I may never understand why she did it, what caused her despair. But I'm absolutely done with letting people abuse me or the people that work with me when we are just trying to help. And it's time that there are consequences to their bad behavior. Will that help save some lives? I don't know, but I have to believe it will."

The sad discussion continued for a bit, but when Ethan served up his pecan pie piled high with whipped cream, we moved on to talking about plans and hopes and dreams. I'm not sure we'll be able to accomplish everything we put on our wish lists, but I'm positive I'll make it to North Carolina to spend time with Andrei and his family sometime very soon. And never again will I be scheduled off work and have nowhere to go!

I wasn't the only one yawning when I finally stood up and said my good nights. My house family friends weren't always huge huggers except during crises, but I really felt called to tonight and no one seemed to mind. I started with Phil as I thanked him profusely for the wonderful dinner for Andrei and for always watching out for me, then I engulfed Mei who I thanked for being my friend and for bringing Tai Chi into my life, and finally hugged Ethan and thanked him for taking such great care of me and Max. I really was incredibly lucky to have them in my life.

Andrei, Dagger and I walked out together with Max, but as I headed over to the stairs Andrei said, "Do you guys have a few minutes? I'm exhausted, but I feel like we need to have a brief war council about what we're going to do about Uncle and Stefan."

Dagger and I exchanged looks, then I nodded and said, "Sure, let's head up to my apartment and talk."

Andrei said, "I just want to come up with a bare bones plan, then I'll head over to Dag's apartment and hit the rack."

"I'm sorry Andrei," I said. "I should have realized you'd still be jet lagged."

"It's fine," he said with a smile. "I'm glad I got to know your house family. It seems like they take good care of you."

"They do!" I agreed enthusiastically.

When we entered my apartment, Andrei made a beeline for my turquoise chair, enfolded himself into it, and asked, "Did you buy this because it was Mom's favorite color?"

I chuckled and replied, "I didn't buy any of my furniture. Everything I have is due to the kindness of my house family, speaking of being taken care of! But maybe the color is why I love it so much!"

Andrei looked at Dagger and me with a puzzled expression and then asked, "You can't afford it? But you had the trust fund and now you're a doctor?"

"I paid for seven years of college," I reminded him. "Most of my colleagues have more than a hundred and fifty thousand dollars in loans they have to pay off. I feel pretty lucky that I only have to skimp on my furniture purchases."

"Do you think Uncle stole from your trust?" Andrei asked thoughtfully.

I shrugged my shoulders and said, "I don't know if he outright stole anything until he stole my computer and car last year. But I'm sure he worked every financial angle only for his own benefit."

"Well then I recommend the first thing you two do is hire a lawyer and a forensic accountant. They can find out exactly what's been going on and get access to all the paperwork," Dagger said emphatically. "We'll need that information when we sell the house anyway."

"Money to pay for professional help is an issue," I said sadly and Andrei nodded.

"I'll get you the family discount," Dagger said smiling. "I have cousins who are absolute beasts at white collar crime. And it sounds like Andrei's wife can help us make sense of the numbers."

"Sounds good," Andrei and I said together.

"That's the easy part," Dagger said. "The harder part is what do we do then? When they are caught, people like your uncle never apologize or try to make things right. They just double down and play the victim. Kat, are you looking for a dramatic showdown like you had with your creepy ex-boyfriend at my Grandpa's charity event last year?"

Andrei demanded to hear that whole story, which Dagger quickly related, ending with when I threatened to scratch Justin's eyes out and then screamed that I was going to let Dagger come after him. Dagger and I finished the story by simultaneously yelling "IN THE MIDDLE OF THE NIGHT" just like I did last year. Max got up and barked at the door, totally confused about what was going on, but wanting to give his support somehow.

We laughed companionably together, but then I answered seriously, "I don't need nor do I want a dramatic showdown. I want to give Stefan, on his own and away from Uncle's influence, an honest chance to repair our relationship. I want him to hear the truth, review his own behavior in the light of the truth, and decide if he wants to have an open and honest relationship with either one of us. I'm done with Uncle. He hurt me when I was a vulnerable child and he hurt me when I was a successful adult. That's his problem. I'm done."

"I couldn't have said it better," Andrei said. "But if he forces a showdown on us, in court or in some social situation, I'm absolutely fine with a dramatic confrontation. Honestly I'd prefer it, but I won't go looking for it if you don't want that."

Dagger nodded as if he too would prefer a confrontation, his face looking like the more dramatic the better for him, but added calmly, "I'll call my cousins and talk to some experts at work, and let you know what they advise."

I agreed, but I was still considering what I wanted to do. I didn't want a confrontation. I'd fought hard to be a totally different person than Uncle. He certainly deserved the worst treatment I could imagine, but I didn't want to be anything like him. On the other hand, I was absolutely done with being lied to and stolen from. And I was done with appeasement behavior; it never worked to change his behavior and oddly made me feel complicit. I was done with backing down from his toddler tantrums and I'd never again allow him to cheat me unchallenged.

There was much more to discuss, but we had the initial plan we needed for now so I said, "We have a place to start, and we're all agreed? And we do this together, right?"

The men nodded vigorously and I felt like we should do some kind of sports related cheer or something, but I simply said, "Making the plan is the hardest part. Andrei you should get some sleep. Do you want to use my secret door to Dagger's apartment?"

"Nah," he replied, "I have to get something from my car."

I gave him a big hug and told him how much it meant that he had come to see me. After we assured each other that we would spend the entire day together tomorrow, I sent him on his way.

Dagger asked as he relocked my front door, "How about you? Have enough energy to talk some more?"

"Sure," I said as I gave Max a treat and told him to settle.

"I've been thinking," he said as he slipped his arms around me and drew me close, and I immediately said, "That can't be good."

Dagger laughed and said, "No, this time I think it's good."

"You're not leaving again, are you?" I asked nervously.

"No," he said reassuringly. "But I will eventually need to do some traveling and I've been thinking about how we can make that easier on both of us."

I tilted my head and looked up into his eyes as I tried to figure out what he was going to suggest. The only thing that would make it easier would be if he could tell me what he was doing and where he was going and when he'd be coming back. I didn't mean to be suspicious, but I had family that lied and cheated and stole from me. And an ex-boyfriend who was even worse. I just needed to have a firm idea of the reality of the situation. Having Andrei treat him as an honored colleague made me feel less vulnerable, but I didn't want to make another mistake. It really wasn't Daniel that I didn't trust, it was me. I had trusted liars in the past; who's to say I wasn't doing that again?

My doubt must have played across my face because he sighed and said, "I'm sorry this is so hard Kat, but what has been happening in the world does actually affect what I'm asked to do. And I really don't have a lot of control of it."

"I do understand that Daniel," I said. "When I read news stories I always worry that you are caught up in whatever is happening."

"Maybe I was," he said. "But what I've been thinking about is that we'd both get more support if we bring you on board."

"I may not know what exactly you do, but I don't think a veterinarian would fit in. I can't imagine them even letting me join up?" I asked hesitantly.

"Join up?" he asked incredulously. "What? No, I didn't mean that."

"What?" I asked awkwardly. What was he talking about?

"Wait," he said, looking rather adoringly into my eyes, but also looking like he was trying not to laugh. "Let me start over. I'm in love with you Kat. I think I have been since our first house dinner. I love you as a person, but more importantly I'm so in love with you as a man who loves a woman, so much that I can hardly stand being away from you. But I love you so intensely and deeply that I only want what's best for you. I have this crazy job that takes me away and sends me into danger. But despite all that, I honestly believe that I'm what's best for you. Even with everything that my job involves."

Tears welled up and ran down my face, but deep inside I knew he was speaking his truth. And I knew without a doubt how I felt, so I said, "I love you too Daniel. The same way. With all the complications. I adore you, I'm devoted to you, I want you, I need you," and I smiled through my tears and continued, "but I don't know what you mean about being brought on board."

"I think we should get married," he said as he covered my face in soft kisses. "That would let us do all the official things with my job and then you'd formally be part of that work family and receive all the support that entails. But we'd have to keep it low key out in the world for a couple years until my assignment changes. We could tell the house family. Maybe Andrei if you want. Maybe a couple people from my family like my grandfather and sister."

I probably should have asked a thousand different questions, but the only thing I asked was, "When?"

"Soon," he said, getting a thin black leather wallet out of his back pocket.

"Okay," I replied, looking at the wallet.

"Do you want to see where I work?" he asked with a grin.

"Yes!" I exclaimed. He flipped it open and I said, "That's incredibly cool!"

"So we're secretly engaged?" he asked.

"Yep," I said.

"Want a pretty non-engagement looking engagement ring?" he asked.

"Yep," I answered and fell into his arms. And no matter what I might have thought on previous occasions, tonight was in fact going to be the best night of my life.

Made in United States
Troutdale, OR
04/06/2024

18993364R00148